I stepped towards th
upon a side table drew back the cu
my astonishment I saw before me the slim, pale body of Mlle Femelle, spread like a starfish upon the sheets. Her body resembled rather that of a person in a medieval painting than anything else – for the middle part was long and lean, her waist willowy, the deep, dark knot of her navel marking its centre. Her breasts were small and round, marked at the centre by little brown roundels; the only remarkable thing (though no news to me) being the cleft which lay between her thighs, where rather than the bush which normally disguises the passage to heaven, the lips themselves were laid open to view – the candle-light darkening them to a smudged brown – between which a darker aperture seemed to cry out for a caress more intimate than that which my attentive fingers had already afforded . . .

Also available from Headline

Eros in Springtime

Anonymous

HEADLINE

First published in 1993
by HEADLINE BOOK PUBLISHING LTD

10 9 8 7 6 5 4 3 2 1

ISBN 0 7472 4287 9

Typeset by
Letterpart Limited, Reigate, Surrey

Printed and bound in Great Britain by
HarperCollins Manufacturing, Glasgow

HEADLINE BOOK PUBLISHING LTD
A Member of the Hodder Headline PLC Group
Headline House
79 Great Titchfield Street
London W1P 7FN

For the convenience of the reader
we here record a note of
IMPORTANT PEOPLE APPEARING IN THE NARRATIVE
in the order of their appearance

Andrew Archer Esq., M.P., our hero.
Mrs Sophia Nelham, our heroine.
Anthony Treweers, a steward.
Miss Purity Puckey, an unfortunate maid.
Jake Puckey, a low person.
Cain Trevanion, a well-meaning labourer.
Mlle Elaine Femelle, a young woman.
Madame Charlotte le Semblant, an old friend.
M. Michel Lebaissant, a social student.
Mr Charles Graham, a balloonist.
Mrs Graham, his wife.
Jack Fortescue Esq., a squire.
A number of young people.
A May King.
A May Queen.
Mrs Tregunter, a madam.
John Dawson Esq., a professor of dancing and fencing.
Jem, a country lad.
Molly, his friend.
Colin Ford, a mere youngster.
Mrs Betsy Bunting, a trollop.

Roger Glasson, or The Ferret, her accomplice.
The Rev. Michael Ford, a Rector.
Davy Rundall, a youth.
Sam Fox, his friend.
Jeremy Bright, a preventive officer.
Mrs Lavinia Job, a lady of parts.
Captain Josiah Barnett, a smuggler.
His Honour Mr Justice Stele.
Richd. Bodinnick Esq., M.P.
Towser, a catamite.
Ned Keen, another.
A trooper (later revealed as Bob St Clare, Esq.).
His sister (later revealed as Miss Ellen Treleaven).

Chapter One

The Adventures of Andy

I had for some time intended to revisit the Cornish constituency that I represented as its Member of Parliament; but, in common with other Members, had found that those ladies and gentlemen, my electors, were able to get on with their lives with perfect diligence and amiability without my spending more time upon them than the very occasional petition demanded – which usually was concerned with agricultural wages or demands for litigation against highwaymen (whose activities, though abated in the more civilised parts of the country, flourished – like incest – where the roads were bad).

Nevertheless, as a show of interest I had set aside a month or so in the spring of the year of '30, intending to spend some time at Vycken, my friend Sir Franklin Franklyn's house near the county town of Bodmin (which he allowed me to use as my own); and my friend Mrs Sophie Nelham – who, as constant readers will know, invariably joins me in these volumes of mutual memoirs – signified her intention of joining me merely for the pleasure of the journey. Although she had visited the West

Country on a couple of occasions, she knew it but indifferently, and had an appetite to know it better, admiring the wildness of its landscapes, the mildness of its climate, and the amiability of its inhabitants.

We were packed and ready to set off from London when a message from Frank (who as usual was at Alcovary, his estate near Cambridge) brought the sad news that a vicious fire had destroyed the greater part of the house – but begged that, rather than cancel our visit, we should at his expense take a property in the vicinity and oversee the rebuilding of the house, which he had determined immediately to set in hand.

We could not, of course, deny him – nor indeed did we wish to do so. And so it was that, having jolted over worsening roads from Bristol to the West and crossed the River Tamar at Plymouth upon the remarkable floating bridge which now joined the counties of Devon and Cornwall, our carriage turned at last into the drive of Vycken House as the trees began to take on the gentle green that bespoke the full blossoming of spring. We were greeted not by the sight of that handsome Elizabethan manor, but mere tumbled walls, gaping holes where doors and windows once hung, and a pile of blackened rubble – though upon the lawns under canvas were piles of furniture happily saved from the fire by the exertions of the steward, Mr Treweers, who now met us with exclamations partly of pleasure at our arrival and partly at sorrow for the sight we saw: 'Wisht! wisht! – 'tes wishter than wisht!' he exclaimed, using local terminology which, if it was as strange to us as Arabic, could at least be interpreted by the accents of the speech, which in this case intimated his horror at the late disaster.

A message had been sent to the good man, in advance of our arrival, inviting him to search out a convenient house for us somewhere in the neighbourhood. This, he promised us, he had done; but for the coming night kindly forsook his own bed on our behalf. This kindly action might have been less than welcome at another time, for the bed was both surrounded and to some extent buried by more of Frank's rescued property – and moreover would have been uncomfortably restricted in size for one tenant, let alone for two; but we were exhausted by our journey, and slept like wooden blocks until the following morning, when after a generous breakfast of barley bread, pilchards and cream (which might seem an eccentric enough meal to those unfamiliar with Cornish victuals but, I assure you, one extremely welcome) we were escorted the next morning to the village of Penruddock Monachorum, on the edge of Bodmin Moor.

This was a place of no more than two dozen houses, and those (while perfectly respectable) far from handsome – though pretty enough, their whitewashed walls built of carelessly piled stones (up which various species of wild flowers were invariably trained to climb) and their roofs either thatched or made of piled turves. At the centre of the village was a church so small as almost to seem a toy – opposite it, a public house – and that, it seemed, was all; we wondered which of those tiny tenements Treweers had in mind for us.

None, as it happened; for we drove right through the village, and at the last cottage turned off along a short drive between high-growing shrubs, and turning a sharp corner found ourselves before a small house of quite another character: here was a low garden wall, with a gate of pleasant ironwork, whence a path strode – between borders which in a week or so would be gay with sweet-williams and other blooms – to a substantial porch, built like the rest of the house of substantial moorland granite.

Standing aside, Treweers waved us forward. Even Sophie had to bend her head in order to step through the low front door, then down two steps which led safely into a front passage which gave into a little parlour (known as the 'hale'), furnished with a decent table and chairs, and no doubt warmed in winter by a fine open hearth with a mantelpiece on which stood a copper kettle, a pair of china dogs, two tall brass candlesticks and a strange instrument which my friend assured me was an Italian iron for ironing old ladies' caps!

The house was, we were told, that of a recently deceased farmer, and on Frank's advice Treweers had bought it at auction for our use – and subsequently as a place which could be used for the convenience of whoever might require it.

The upstairs accommodation was perfectly acceptable – two small bedrooms with reasonably capacious double beds in each, and tin baths for our ablutions. Not precisely what either of us was used to in our house in Regent's Park in the newly developed West End of London; but perfectly adequate and even comfortable to those whose lives had by no means always been lived in that luxury to which we had lately become accustomed.

No servants were in attendance, but we could manage on our own until we engaged some – which Treweers opined would be perfectly easy, either in Penruddock itself or in Bodmin, only a few miles away.

He then took his leave; and we spent the day unpacking our belongings from the luggage coach which had now arrived, and making the small house as perfectly in accord with our wishes as could be contrived. After this we found ourselves again somewhat tired, and having taken a walk through the village – where we met not a single soul, though from distant scuffling, the ill-controlled growling of invisible dogs, and the twitching of shutters we believed that we were indeed being observed – we repaired to our beds, and again slept soundly.

I woke at dawn, the first rays of a fine spring sun pouring through the window and falling upon my pillow. Looking out I found the finest of mornings, and, though my watch showed only half an hour after five, put on my clothes, determining upon a walk before breakfast.

Opening the gate as noiselessly as possible in order not to disturb my friend (who was a remarkably light sleeper), I turned down the little drive – and just before emerging into the lane which passed for the main road into the village, seemed to hear something between a sigh and a groan –

though so light that for a moment, until it came a second time, I thought I might have imagined it.

That I had not done so, however, became apparent upon my looking into the hedge – for there, protruding from beneath a hydrangea bush, I saw what was unquestionably a naked female foot, which stirred uneasily as my eye fell upon it. I bent and placed my hand on its sole, which was cold as any stone – and on my lifting a branch, I found that the body to which it was attached was that of a slight women – nay, even a girl – who appeared to be clothed only in the lightest of dresses, and seemed to be asleep; on my shaking her by the shoulder, she merely stirred slightly, and refused to be awakened.

Not for an instant pausing, I caught her up in my arms – she weighed so little that I almost overbalanced in the action – and made for the house. The dress she wore was not only thin, but soaking wet from the night mists and the morning dew, and through it I could feel that her flesh had the awful damp chill more usually associated with a corpse – though her breast rose and fell, and from her lips escaped the slight whisper of repeated breaths.

Kicking the gate open, I made for the door, and found it simple to support the young person merely by throwing her across my shoulder while I opened it. I placed her upon the table while I reached for a flask of spirits which I always kept near me, and let a few drops fall between her lips; she coughed a little at this, but made no movement, and though placing my hand upon her breast I could feel the slight beating of a living heart, again I was struck by the fearful cold of her body.

We had made no fire, for the spring of '30 (as those who remember it will recall) was uncommonly warm – save that at night the temperature was by no means sufficient to make sleeping in a hedgerow a comfortable experience, as this poor creature had found.

There was only one thing for it. Picking her up once more, and throwing her again across my shoulder, I mounted the stairs, entered my bedroom, and placing her upon the bed divested myself of my clothing before removing her dress (which was so damp that I was forced positively to tear it from her body), and climbing into bed beside her folded her in my arms. It was a method which I had learned, in my travels, was used on board ship to recover those chilled by falling overboard, and though I had never encountered circumstances in which I had been called upon to employ it, my memory happily recalled it to me in this emergency.

I am a warm-blooded man (as my constant readers will attest), but even so was for a few moments struck to the marrow by the coldness of the flesh which was stretched along my own: cheeks, shoulders, breasts, belly, thighs – all were as marble in winter. I threw my leg across the young girl's body so that my thigh lay across her belly, and placing my right hand upon one bosom contrived to lay the inside of my forearm across the other, while I stopped her mouth with a kiss less amorous than intent upon breathing warm air between her lips.

In a remarkably short time – perhaps as little as five minutes – while my own body had certainly lost some warmth, I could feel a flow of blood returning to hers; and on lifting aside the bedclothes (which I had piled on top of us) could see that the dead white of her flesh now had a sort of pallid glow, which at her breast (when I lifted my hand) became almost pink. At the same time I felt her body stir, and on my lifting my thigh from her belly (for the inside of it had become, truth to tell, too cold for my comfort) she half turned upon her side and thrust one of her legs between my own, trapping my left hand – which had lain at my side – in just that quarter of her body where a seducer might have wished to place it: that is, about the chief attribute of her femininity – where its presence seemed yet again to act as a warmer, for lips which at the first instance seemed cold soon began to glow.

I could not, now the immediate danger of her decease (which I had positively feared) was over, but find my position an embarrassing one. Conceive of it, gentlemen; imagine it if you can, ladies! Here was I, a relatively young man (for at thirty years my blood still ran as warmly as when I was in my teens) who had been without female company for some few nights, nakedly abed with a young female of not more, as I judged, than seventeen years; whose limbs were handsome, whose face was open and attractive, and who while now breathing regularly (as I could tell from the rise and fall of those bosoms which I now saw to be remarkably well shaped) was in no state to resist any advances I cared to make – and the proximity of whose person, in particular of that thigh which lay between my own, and against which my riding-muscle had perforce been stimulated into a readiness for action, had prepared me not only physically but emotionally for amorous conduct!

Yet could I possibly take advantage of such a situation? What gentleman would find such conduct defensible? Reluctantly, I began to disentangle my limbs from hers, and, getting to my knees at her side, was about to step from the bed when her eyes opened, the first thing she saw on regaining her senses being the masculine generative apparatus in a perfectly upright stance!

Her gasp, if one of initial apprehension was also not entirely devoid of admiration, if I read aright the flush which now made her cheeks as ruddy as those of a young girl in full health.

'My dear, do not be alarmed!' I said, hastily reaching for my breeches; and, in order to relieve myself of that embarrassment consequent upon a certain difficulty in drawing them on, turned my back upon the girl, who when I once more was able to observe her had – to my disappointment, I must admit – drawn a sheet over her person.

She seemed remarkably assured; and accepted without any hesitation my declaration of goodwill – partly, no doubt, because she recalled all too clearly the chill of the night which had fallen as she had tried to compose herself to sleep beneath the shrubs of our drive.

I now felt that any lingering doubts should be dispelled by the presence of another female, and, making my way to my friend's room, woke her and, persuading her to dress (for like myself she had not succumbed to the ridiculous habit of clothing herself for slumber), asked her to accompany me to my room – where she was all sympathy upon hearing my explanation of the circumstances which had resulted in my bed being occupied by a strange and perfectly unclothed young female.

I must here pause to point out that she did not for a moment doubt my explanation of the facts: we had no secrets from each other, and she had too often discovered me abed with some doxy and heard the story of my adventures not to accept my assurance that nothing untoward had passed between me and young Purity Puckey (which she discovered was our visitor's name).

Her enquiries and my own were now answered with complete frankness, so grateful was Purity for my action – which she recognised had probably saved her from an untoward end. This, she said, would have been accountable entirely to the actions of her father – who, throwing her out of doors the previous night, had constructed her predicament, there being no person in the village who would take the risk of getting upon his bad side, so powerful a man was he.

On our enquiring further, we discovered that he had promised his daughter in marriage to a neighbour's son. This – as it seemed to me – was by no means an unusual practice among the labouring classes; but Miss Puckey had taken against the young gentleman who, unpromisingly christened Cain, was (if her description of him was to be trusted) of a disposition not too far removed from that of our ancestor of the same name, being violent in manner and lacking even in those few niceties which might be expected in the inhabitant of so remote a region.

But Mr Jake Puckey was, it seemed, determined on the match, since the young man's father was possessed of a parcel of land to which he was partial, and of which he hoped to assure himself by way of dowry through his daughter's marriage.

Upon his daughter naturally demurring, and even to his face rejecting the gentleman's proposal of marriage – made at her father's prompting – the latter had first attempted to persuade her, and on her proving adamant he had thrown her from his door, instructing her never to darken the threshold again!

Purity became so indignant in retailing this story that quite forgetting herself she sat up in bed, her pert little breasts now as rosy as nature intended, their nipples small and brown as hazelnuts. The sight was one which keenly reminded me of the recent experience of clasping her in my arms, and provoked a sharp rising of my spirits – my discomfort I dare say unnoticed by the girl, but provoking a gleam of amused understanding from Sophie.

Sophie perfectly sympathised with the girl's story, for she herself had been forced into a similar marriage by her own father – the record of which can be found in our very first book of memoirs,

Eros in the Country, put out by our publishers some years since. Happily, the late Mr Nelham lived only so long as to make himself unpleasant to the extent that Sophie was entirely unable to mourn his premature decease; and his name was now all she retained of him save a memory which, as I have said, engaged all her tender feelings on Purity's behalf.

Purity was now in despair, and a tear even escaped from her eyes (which upon observation I found to be delightful and deeply brown). However, I had little doubt of my ability to save the situation – for I knew something of these little local tyrants; and pausing only to know of Purity in which of the village cotts her father dwelt, encouraged her to accompany my friend to her bedroom, where she could bathe herself, and where Sophie would doubtless be able to provide a simple gown for her. This she did, with a little curtsy towards me upon rising – in the middle of which she suddenly realised that she was entirely without clothing, and, protecting herself as fully as she could with the gestures of two remarkably small hands, made good her escape.

'No violence, I beg, Andy!' said my friend, receiving a nod from me as she left.

I now recovered from my trunk a suit of clothes which I had brought with me to serve on any occasion of my having to attend a formal dinner – which sometimes it was my duty to do, on my constituents wishing to entertain me – and dressing myself in it, hung my pistol at my belt, and made my way into the village, and to Mr Puckey's cottage, where, having thundered upon the door, I stepped in immediately.

Whether the house would have appeared any less mean had Puckey's wife been alive (she had died when Purity was ten or eleven years of age) I cannot say; the daughter has doubtless done her best to maintain some standard of cleanliness – but could do little to alleviate the slovenly condition of the place.

Two rooms were divided simply by a wooden partition, which did not reach the roof; and between the ill-fitting door and the open chimney raged a draught, resistance to which had at least so hardened the constitution of the unfortunate Purity to such an extent that sleeping in the open air had failed to kill her!

Two windows about two feet square let in a little light through glass of the most wretched description, full of eyes and knots, and here and there a pane missing, the holes stuffed by rags. The floor consisted of trodden-down earth, and upon it no doubt Purity used to sit, for there was only one chair, now occupied by Mr Puckey – a large and muscular man in appearance somewhat resembling that gorilla or large monkey recently brought from the Africas and placed upon display in a hall in Piccadilly.

As he rose to his feet, I stepped back from the door, thus allowing the daylight to illuminate my figure more clearly than could have been achieved in the gloom of the cottage. I could see that Mr Puckey was somewhat intimidated by my appearance – and I followed up my advantage by enquiring whether I was in the presence of Jake Puckey, Esquire, of the hamlet of Penruddock Monachorum in the Parish of Bodmin.

After a moment (he no doubt found a pause necessary in order to translate the enquiry, couched in language very different from that to which he was used), I continued.

'May I present myself?' I said. 'Andrew Archer, member of Parliament for the constituency of Lostwithiel, in this county. You wish to examine my credentials?' I pulled a document from my pocket (which, had he been able to read and had he taken the trouble to peruse, he would have found to be a list of the laundry my servants had been instructed to forward from London).

He shook his head; and I went on to explain that I had been summoned in order to look into the matter of Miss Purity Puckey, whose body had been found in a hedge nearby that very morning, and who at this moment lay between life and death. Was he aware that a father found guilty of failing to provide proper accommodation for his daughter could be arraigned as a murderer, should harm come to her?

At this he began to shake; and on my remarking upon the coming assizes at Bodmin, after which three hangings were already scheduled for early in May – but that no doubt the hangman could be persuaded to accomplish four – he was ready to make any excuse or perform any act to save himself.

In fact it was but a matter of ten minutes before I was in possession of a paper – hastily scribbled by myself and upon which he made his mark – guaranteeing to free Purity both from the advances of her unwanted suitor, and from his own governance, and appointing me as the maiden's guardian (a position I assumed merely in order to ensure that my protection was legally proper lest later her father should attempt some sort of accusation against me).

Leaving Mr Puckey in a state of collapse, I returned to the house; there found Purity busying herself in the kitchen; and assured her not only of her freedom – but (after some discussion with Sophie) of a place in our household for the time we were at Penruddock, and after that at Vycken, as a general housemaid at the rate of twelve shillings a week and her keep – which at a time when farm labourers were able to achieve only ten shillings a week, from which they must pay for their food, was a more than adequate reward.

That Purity was more than adequately grateful we had no doubt from the willingness with which she had already learned and performed small tasks about the house such as making tea, folding clothes, and general cleaning; and we were able to assure ourselves that we had a bargain.

Her gratitude I took for granted, and did not think of requiring any sign of it other than those verbal thanks which were readily outlaid; so that it was all the more pleasant a surprise to find it taking a more corporeal form that evening. My surprise was even greater for the fact that she had previously . . . But I will leave the episode I was about to describe to my friend's chapter, which immediately follows – merely remarking that I had not long retired to bed when a soft knock came at the door, which then opened to reveal the girl, who had left the corner we had prepared for her in the kitchen and had come (as she put it) to show that she was not usually as cold as she had been that morning. And before I was able to respond either with a yea or a nay (the former being, I must confess, the more likely) she was bare as a bodkin and, drawing back the bedclothes, had laid herself once more against my body, her flesh this time giving out the normal glow of enthusiastic womanhood.

It did, I must confess, for a moment occur to me to wonder whether I should accept the offer; I had not enquired her age, and, though it was clearly such that her father had believed her ready for marriage, she must be almost young enough to be my daughter – and surely innocent of those actions performed between lovers . . .?

I was soon, however, disabused of the latter speculation at least, for, raising herself, she bowed her head, and – her long black hair falling all about my middle parts – took between her lips with the utmost eagerness a machine which was as ready for action as it had been some hours previously, and began to toy with it in the most inspiriting manner, while at the same time manipulating my cods in such a familiar way that she could not be a tyro.

I did not enquire the source of her experience; but recalling my own childhood – for I grew up in a cottage not so different from that she had inhabited, and in poverty almost as great – assumed that if she had not been relieved of her virginity at an early age by a brother or cousin, some country swain must have taken that office as soon as she was ready for the act, and not without teaching her some of the niceties of the game. That she enjoyed the game was clear, for her wriggling and writhing, her kissing and toying, the charming manner in which she threw her arms and legs about me, and finally the enticing gleam in her eye as, rising from the bed, she leaned forward, her folded arms upon a chair, and presented me with the firmest and most inviting bottom, below which an irresistible target was ready to be hit, were all signals of a relish which completely relieved me of any feeling of guilt at being abed with so young a gamester.

I fear that our pleasure was rather noisier than I credited, for in the midst of it the door opened and Sophie appeared – having feared (as she later confessed) that the sounds she heard advertised some nightmare from which I should be awakened, or after which I might need comfort. At any other time I would have welcomed – as so often has been the case – the appearance of my beloved friend, herself in a state of nature and happy to accommodate any wish of mine; but on this occasion my physical powers were otherwise accommodated, and the sight which met her eyes was of my buttocks clenching and unclenching as I plumbed to her depths a charming female no less eager in her response – a picture (she said) that needed neither explanatory caption nor further elaboration.

In fine, Miss Purity proved an admirable and useful addition to the household in every way – for apart from the fact that she was always ready for a romp (though not impertinent enough to demand my continual attention) her manner was friendly without being familiar, and the polite services she provided were entirely satisfactory both to my friend and to myself.

Chapter Two

Sophie's Story

The unfortunate accident that reduced my brother Frank's handsome Cornish house to a pile of blackened wreckage was indeed a sad one, for, although I had once before fleetingly visited it, I had been looking forward to a leisurely holiday centred upon those graceful rooms and that charming park Andy had so often and graphically described.

However, what cannot be cured must be endured – to quote a motto none the less infuriating for being practical, and while the first night's accommodation offered by Frank's steward, Mr Treweers (formerly his butler) was sufficiently uncomfortable to be less than ingratiating, the little cottage which he had provided for us in a small village not too far from the house was cosy enough. We settled into it with immediate pleasure, and I was able to enjoy a night's slumber which was the first thorough rest I had had since leaving Regent's Park.

I was awakened next morning by Andy shaking my shoulder, and was not as astonished as some ladies might have been to find an unclothed young female in his room and bed, for Sir Andrew has never been slow to take advantage of any circumstance which permits him familiarity with a beautiful member of the female sex. In this case, however, the story Miss Purity Puckey had to tell was a sufficiently moving one to gain my immediate sympathy and friendship, my memories of my own father's insistence on my marrying the late Mr Nelham being inexpungable from my memory.

As for Andy, I was perfectly prepared to believe that his rescue of the young woman from her predicament was (at least in the first instance) motivated entirely by humane instincts, though I was incapable of supposing that the method he had adopted to warm her had not also warmed him – and indeed on Miss Purity so far forgetting herself (in the excitement of her narrative) as to sit up in bed, revealing a pair of springy young breasts which could compete for charm with any in antique marble, I descried a light in his eyes which ensured the young person of his amorous intentions sooner rather than later.

However, his intentions were perfectly honourable as to the matter of rescuing her from an unwanted suitor, and while I took the liberty of advising him to refrain from undue violence in his argument with Mr Puckey it was with my approval that he set off, shortly afterwards, dressed to impress and ready to enforce his views.

Meanwhile, first providing her with one of my less elaborate gowns, I encouraged the young person to start a fire and boil water, and thereafter took her to my room (where a tin tub was set for my convenience) and encouraged her to bathe herself, which she did with evident pleasure – her normal means of cleansing her body being to wipe it with a damp rag, as she informed me. Her delight in using soap and warm water was only matched by her enthusiasm, for (as she told me) she wished to better herself, and was perfectly aware that employment by the gentry depended at least to some extent on personal cleanliness.

My own view was that she could find such employment without difficulty, and I wagered that it would be available in the close vicinity of our home – indeed, had Andy been able to watch the scene as Miss Purity passed the soapy cloth over her breasts and belly and about a pair of thighs and buttocks as firm and round as any gentleman could desire, he would doubtless have employed her on the spot, in one capacity or another.

However, I must press on with my narrative, which now takes a more interesting turn, for in the course of our conversation – and Miss's eagerness to talk convinced me that she had been kept short of female company – she confessed that her antipathy to young Mr Cain was based not so much on his person (which she confessed with a blush was not altogether unprepossessing) as on his attitude to her, which he had expressed by adopting the view that the moment the marriage was suggested he was free to treat her with as little ceremony as a bull treats a cow: in fact, upon her father signifying his enthusiastic approval of the match, the suitor had waited only until the pair were alone to thrust her (without the least persuasion or preparation) up against a wall and, lifting her skirts with one hand, to take in another a piece of equipment which . . .

At this stage the girl's eyes expressed at the same time horror and admiration (the latter, if I am to be pressed, seeming predominate).

What did she do? I enquired – at which she confessed to some violent work with a piece of farming equipment, which had left Cain with a sore head, and had for the moment dissuaded him from amorous activity.

It had been his importunity (I was now convinced) which had set the young woman against him: while she had never read a romance, her wish was clearly to be persuaded rather than bullied, to be wooed rather than raped.

It seemed to me that all things being equal she was perhaps being too hasty in rejecting the young man: for though her father was evidently a heavy-handed bully, to whom it was proper that Andy should teach a lesson, she could obviously aspire no higher than the son of a farmer, possessed of some land, of his health, and of an evident wish to marry her.

I was curious to see the gentleman, and attiring myself not in the height of fashion but so modestly as to appear not unfamiliar with the life of the countryside, I announced my intention of taking a walk, inviting Miss Purity in the meantime, if she would, to occupy her time in tidying away those of our belongings which were still not in place about the house.

During our conversation, she had explained that

her suitor's task, of a morning, was to see to his herd of cows in fields to the north of the hamlet by which our cottage was placed; and it was therefore to the north that I took my way – the village, where even now I supposed that Andy was occupying himself in spirited argument with her father, being in the opposite direction.

Emerging in a while from a high-hedged lane, what was my surprise to find myself the witness of a number of bales of hay flying unaided through the air and over the hedge between one field and the next. On coming into a clearer view of the field from which the hay-bales were flying, I saw that they were propelled by the brawny arms of a young gentleman built upon the proportions of a brick privy, with muscles bulging upon his arms and chest (which was uncovered) and which could be clearly seen to strain against the cloth of the legs of the pair of breeches which he wore upon his lower person.

There could be no doubt both from his general appearance and from the particularity of his wearing a somewhat unkempt black beard (not common among the youth of Cornwall) that this was Master Cain. He heaved another two bales of hay into the neighbouring field, from the pile in front of him, then stopped to wipe the back of his hand across his forehead – for he was a muck of sweat in the warmth of the midday sun, which was uncommonly hot for the time of the year.

I stepped back for a moment, for I was not sure that I wished to introduce myself; but his eye had been caught by some incident elsewhere, and he was now keenly observing some activity which from my viewpoint I could not discern. As he watched, his interest seemed to grow even keener, and in a moment he dropped his hand to his belly, loosened the belt of his breeches, and even began (as I thought, for he had his back to me) to be stimulating that area of his person where amorous feelings are concentrated. Stepping forward, I was able to see what interested him: which was merely the copulation of a bull and a cow – something he must surely have observed many times before, and which might have been thought to be for that reason uninteresting – though certainly the bull was a sturdy fellow, whose ploughing must be at once efficient and to a degree pleasure-giving (though from the cow's placidity one could not be sure of it).

From his avid attention, I supposed that the young man's amorous feelings were high and to an extent unsatisfied, for, his eyes fixed on the scene, he was now most vigorously tossing at his muscle and doubtless thus counterfeiting the emotions felt by the bull upon which his attention was fixed. I cannot deny that the scene had its comic aspect, for from my vantage point his breeches were half-fallen, revealing the cleft of his arse, about which they hung with a sort of dejected untidiness which could not but provoke a laugh – which I was insufficiently efficient in suppressing.

Cain immediately swung round, revealing himself to be (as I had suspected) in that state in which most gentlemen are reluctant to reveal themselves to unknown ladies. However, he was not in the least embarrassed – and indeed in a single movement thrust his breeches completely to the ground, and stepping half out of them took a sufficient number of steps towards me (trailing the breeches behind him, in one leg of which a foot was still entangled) to be within arms' length.

I stood my ground, not being willing to give way to any man; but could not resist glancing almost with apprehension at the remarkable prick which he displayed in all that state of perpendicularity redolent of lust – for the first sight of it could not but impress even so experienced a female as myself; not even among the black men of Africa, a number of whom I count among my friends as well as my lovers, had I seen such a remarkable machine – for not only was it of an admirable length, but it was of the thickness of my wrist, and swelled at the tip to a bulb which seemed almost the size of my clenched fist.

Seeing my eyes fall upon this device, the fellow took it for granted that the sight pleased me (it may be that my eyes indeed betrayed that instinctive admiration which was mixed with alarm), and having paused only for the twentieth part of a second – as it seemed – took another step forward, seized me by the arms and threw me to the ground (fortunately the grass in that part of the field was thick, and the dew had dried from it). The next moment he had thrust my gown about my waist and was parting my thighs with a roughness born of extreme avidity, and had penetrated my person with his gigantic instrument.

I am aware that those ladies whose eyes fall

upon this page – and indeed those gentlemen who (the nature of the sexes being as it is) are perhaps even more likely to peruse it – will regard the preceding paragraphs as very likely the product of exaggeration. The author (it may be believed) either indulges herself in wishful thinking, wishes to thrill her female readers and make jealous those of the other sex, or simply suffers from a delusion. Such words as 'remarkable' and 'gigantic' (when applied to the male appendage) are commonly found in those lubricious inventions set down by those who make a living by inventing stories of amorous adventure in which every gentleman is magnificently endowed and every female is at all times eager to test him.

In this case, however, I do not exaggerate – and must confess that the experience was in the first instance not a pleasant one; I was, it will be remembered, completely unready for amorous play, my parts therefore entirely unlubricated by desire. Even had they been so, and had the gentleman been sufficiently careful to proceed with a considerate care, the entry into my most tender part of a device which might best be likened to a miniature tree trunk would have been uncomfortable; as it was, it was painful to a degree which provoked (I must confess) a scream; of which Cain took no notice, for by now he was rutting with all the determination of the bull across the field, which had now completed his action and retired, leaving the cow placidly chewing the cud with a disinterest which I confess to envying.

Happily (in one sense) the young man had

thrust into me no more than four or five times when, like the bull, he reached his apogee; and removing himself from between my thighs, almost as swiftly as he had placed himself there, fell upon his side, panting. The happiness of which I speak was the product of the relief I could not but feel through being relieved of a weight, a pressure and a vigour applied too violently to be pleasant; on the other hand, I could not but be roused by the proximity of so remarkable an animal, whose simple power and vigour could not but be inspiriting.

In short, I could appreciate both the repulsion felt by Miss Puckey and the attraction which was married to it, and saw the latter more clearly upon taking a few moments to observe the figure at my side (which for a moment was still, the youth lying upon his back with his eyes closed, his breast still rising and falling with the effort of his recent activity).

His figure was not one which I would put forward as ideal – my own taste being for the more slender, even effete kind of youth, both because of the greater mobility and scope for amorous experiment offered by a physique not overweighed by too great a solidity, and because it seems invariably the case (and I can give no reason for what seems to me to be a fact) that gentlemen formed with limbs and body proportionate rather than overweeningly muscular or large are in general more considerate lovers than those who from reasons of self-esteem or of labour are endowed with swelling shoulders and thighs.

However, having made that point, I must

confess not only that others than myself would find Cain's person attractive, but that it was by no means devoid of attraction to me, especially when in a reposeful and therefore unthreatening attitude, as was now the case: although his shoulders and chest were certainly deep and broad, his thighs thick and heavily muscled, his belly somewhat swollen, and the whole covered with a positive overcoat of black hair, which lay even upon his forearms and the backs of his enormous hands – all these features were in proportion, and even the swelling muscles no more evident than one might expect of a man of equivalent power who was used to daily exercise.

Then, of course, there was the feature most immediately to be noticed by a lady, and now positively offered to view by Cain's thighs being laid together; his cods and cock being thus raised and presented (as it were) to the onlooker, much as though they were served up upon a plate. As a result of his recent enjoyment the chief feature had now shrunken to an amenable degree, and the whole ensemble could be seen to be entirely of human proportions. While there was certainly nothing for any man to be ashamed of in the proportions of his relaxed prick, it was only when the compulsive flow of thick and amorous blood had prepared him for congress that all eyebrows must be raised.

As I looked, the gentleman opened his eyes; and, with a modesty which was the more endearing for being unexpected, immediately covered the equipment of which I have spoken with his hands.

'I trust, sir,' I said, reclining upon one elbow and observing the still panting youth, 'that your satisfaction is complete?'

His surprise on hearing my tones was considerable, and he had the grace to blush at the realisation that he had raped a lady rather than merely pleasuring a country girl.

'Because,' I went on, 'my own is far from so.'

He looked entirely blank.

'Are you not aware, sir, of the necessity to ensure the satisfaction of your mistress in sportive play, as well as your own?'

He was silent – indeed, dumb.

'I see you are not,' I went on. 'Yet how can you hope to win so fine a young lady as Miss Puckey if you fall upon her in the same unceremonious manner in which you have just fucked me?'

My use of the informal verb startled him no less than my town accent.

'I dunna understand 'ee,' he remarked after a moment.

I bent forward, and, taking his wrist and lifting his hand from his lap, laid a finger upon his cock.

'This,' I said, 'is a thing with which you can give enormous pleasure to any lady; but it must be used with care, rather than as a battering ram, or applied as you see the bull applying his phallus to the cow!'

His face betrayed the fact that he had no idea of my meaning.

'You may not be aware,' I continued, 'that we ladies are capable of enjoying the same pleasure as you gentlemen, during the congress of the sexes . . .'

His face was blank; clearly the language I used might as well be Lithuanian, for all the sense he could make of it.

I therefore determined to be plainer.

'Women enjoy the game as much as men,' I said. His expression showed at once that he both comprehended and disbelieved me.

'The difference is this,' I continued. 'While you young men can discharge your gun in a matter of half a minute, with us the process must be a slower one; and it therefore behoves a lover who wishes to captivate his mistress, to address her with greater care and a more provoking leisure . . .'

But by his expression I had lost him again.

'In other words,' I said, 'take your time. You will not win Purity by the sort of attack which you have just made upon me. That is, if you wish to win her.'

A bright red flush spread over his face.

'I take it you do,' I said, whereupon he lowered his eyes and nodded. I began after all to like this young man, and to feel that he might not be entirely unregenerate.

'Perhaps I might give you a practical lesson,' I went on, first enquiring whether we were likely to be disturbed, at which he explained that he frequently spent the entire day in that place without seeing another human being.

I therefore began by informing him that should he feel, upon preparing to court his young lady, that the pressure upon his manhood was too great to be controlled, he should relieve that pressure with the aid of Mrs Palm and her five fingers. On his looking confused at this, I took his hand and closing it about the stem of his prick – which had by now once more raised its head somewhat at a conversation so unexpectedly lubricious – and began to move it up and down; whereat he immediately took my meaning, but blushed and turned away in such a confusion that I feared I had been too free. However, I explained that my experience of gentlemen was such that I was entirely aware of those practises which were of assistance to them when no female was available to assuage the lust of a growing lad – and even remarked (in order to relieve his confusion to a greater degree) that forms of self-satisfaction were also employed by young females, and laid my finger upon my own person in that position which will be familiar to those of my female readers who honesty will compel to recognise the truth of my words.

This action indeed seemed to relieve him of embarrassment while at the same time further raising his spirits, for his prick now began to assume that phenomenal size which had at first impressed me. Indeed, he leaned over and began to fumble with the neck of my gown (which he had failed either to remove or allow me the time to remove during our recent engagement, and which therefore still covered the upper part of my body).

Striking his hand aside – for I had no wish for the garment to be entirely destroyed by his importunity – I raised it over my head, and was rewarded by an admiring look which proved that while Purity might be a decade my junior, she was not so superior in handsomeness as to make it impossible for her lover to admire me. Indeed, stretching out a hand, he now with a sort of clumsy gentleness placed a finger upon my nipple and began to agitate it – at which it swiftly hardened, a fact that seemed to surprise him, and therefore persuaded me that any coupling he had previously had must have been quick, confused and probably in darkness, for his eyes grew big as I allowed him to play about my body (which I must confess, without wishing to boast, though no longer that of a maiden is not of entirely unhandsome proportions).

I even encouraged him at that play, directing his fingers with my own, and by exaggerating that delight which was concomitant with his attention to those zones where pleasure lies, taught him the beginnings of a lesson in conveying such pleasure.

I now placed my hand at the back of his neck, and pressing his head downward brought it to my breast – when, with an instinct that may have been born in the cradle but was now applied in an entirely adult manner, he applied his lips first to one nipple and then to the other. The sensation this provoked was of course by no means new to me, though the tickling of his beard if anything increased and sharpened it, while the instinctive gentleness with which he nibbled added to a distinct pleasure – which I rewarded by taking my own hand to his thighs, and laying it upon a cock now once more as sturdy as it was large, first stroking and encircling it, then tumbling a pair of cods in proportion to the column they supported.

This, I can believe by his reaction, was the first time that any human hand but his own had found its way to that part of his body; and his movements became so delighted and so energetic that I feared the worst, and removed the source of his pleasure – but at his protest laid my finger upon my lips, and pressed him to the ground.

His disappointment at this was almost comic: he thought he had been rejected, for he clearly had no notion of congress except in the way of falling upon the woman. Nor did any other refinement occur to him, and on my briefly saluting his prick with my lips (merely to reassure him that my interest had not been withdrawn) displayed an expression at once so astonished and delighted as to force me to laugh – at which in a moment he joined me, a circumstance which gave me renewed hope that here was, beneath the country manners, a man capable of sensitivity and understanding, however unsophisticated his situation.

I now threw my leg across him, and drawing my lower lips apart (again, astonishment flew across his features at so bold an action from a young woman!) brought them into contact with his staff, and (this time with less discomfort, for both his sword and my scabbard were now lubricated with viscous fluid) with difficulty but not without delight drew its head within the fleshy portals and, by slowing sinking downward, permitted it to penetrate my vitals until that golden zone which has been so admired by lovers more sophisticated than this met those black wires which lay about the base of his machine. The obelisk thrust so deeply into my person as to seem likely to penetrate my breast, and was at first distinctly uncomfortable – but once the passage was complete, the pleasure given by so massive a presence outweighed the discomfort to such an extent as to make the operation entirely agreeable.

Cain was clearly astonished at the attitude I had adopted, and at the motion which I now undertook – of moving gently up and down, permitting his instrument first to vanish within the tunnel it so confidently filled, and then to reappear, glistening and adamant; in pausing just as it was about to slip altogether from its groove, I was able to administer to its most sensitive tip just that soft touch of the lips which gives gentlemen the most inspiriting pleasure; and only two or three motions of my body brought him almost to the point of an explosion – at which I immediately ceased, and, on his attempting to buck upwards with his hips in order to continue to provoke the ardour I had instigated, placed my hands firmly upon his shoulders – an action which could by no means have restrained him had he insisted on continuing, but which when accompanied by a grave expression persuaded him to lie still while I explained that just the emotion he at present felt was – or could be – experienced by the female who administered it.

Would he wish to deprive a partner of such pleasure? I asked (accompanying my words by a little wriggling motion of my arse which stirred him strangely). He agreed that he would not. And could he imagine that any female to whom such an emotion was properly conveyed, could possibly refuse him anything? He thought for a moment, and then shook his head.

Then (I said) could I contrive a meeting between himself and Miss Purity, would he take the lesson I had taught, and apply it as gently as he could contrive? – and at this stage began once more the smooth and easy motion which for the moment I had ceased.

He was now quite unable to answer me except by an expressive rolling of the eyes and a noise approximating to assent, for once more his spirits were roused, and as I slowly accelerated the motion, now accompanying it by the application of a finger and thumb to each of the nipples of his broad chest (which were as considerable in size as those of many a maiden, though set upon platforms less round than muscular and flat) his emotion became uncontrollable, and he began involuntarily to thrust his hips upward to meet my downward stroke, until (I must confess) I seemed once again likely to be split by so tremendous an engine so energetically applied.

I am not, as I have perhaps already intimated, one of those ladies who looks for size above anything else in a gentleman's parts; especially when that gentleman is as unlearned in the arts of love – nay, as ignorant! – as Mr Cain; but must confess that the simple battering of which I was now in receipt is, once in a while, inspiring; and on his (in no long time) giving a final thrust and by the paroxysm which seized his loins expressing the culmination of his pleasure, I must confess that my own was considerable (heightened by the fact that at that final moment he seized my hips in his callused hands and held me aloft as he made his final lunge).

I confess to a degree of exhaustion, and was for a while content to fall forward and recline upon that broad breast the hairs of which were now spongy with perspiration, and which rose and fell with such deeply drawn breaths as to threaten to throw me even from so secure a platform.

The young man recovered soon enough – sooner, I may say, than I (the difference in years between us being of a decade); and I was pleased to note that I had taught him his manners at least to such an extent that rather than merely thrusting me from him, he assisted me to a recumbent position upon the grass, and – if in a mumbled and none too expressive a manner – thanked me not only for the pleasure I had assisted him in, but for my advice; for (he said) his admiration for Miss Purity was such that even her rejection of him – which had followed, he admitted, upon his thrusting her up against the wall of his father's house one night, when he would have had her but for her dextrous use of a short spade upon which her hand had fallen – had only made his enthusiasm for her the greater.

I now took the liberty of advising him to present himself to her that night at our cottage at eight o'clock, when I hoped to guarantee that she would at least hear his offers; and donning my gown (which he politely assisted in drawing over my head) returned to the house, where I found Miss Purity finishing the cleaning of my room.

I had little difficulty in persuading her to keep the rendezvous I had arranged; I had talked to Cain (I explained) and believed that his courtship of her would now be gentler and more respectful. I hoped (I said) that she would not reject his suit out of hand, merely because his actions were not precisely those of a gentleman. He had, after all, certain qualities . . .? She looked for a moment confused, but then blushed with a mixture of pleasure and (I believed) anticipation.

It was at this point that Andy returned from his interview with her father, with the news that she would no longer have to take his views into account when choosing a husband. She blushed and was silent at this; and it was left to me to explain to him that it might be that he had had his trouble for nothing (except that no lesson taught to an importunate and vicious parent could be wasted).

My friend was by no means so ill natured as to be displeased by my news, and completed the girl's pleasure by suggesting that she might care to remain with us as a maid of all work, offering her a sum somewhat larger (I must confess) than I would have proposed. The girl's pleasure at this was almost as great as her anticipation of the meeting I had arranged with her putative lover.

How, asked Andy (when we were alone) had I proceeded?

I had (I said) interviewed the young gentleman

in question, had persuaded him to reconsider the manner of his courting, and . . .

Andy's lips, at this, parted in a smile to which the adjective 'knowing' could certainly be applied; our lifelong friendship being as close as it is, it was impossible for me to disguise from him the nature of the interview I had had with the young man in question. He would make a good husband? he enquired.

He had the chief attributes necessary to the task, I replied, and I believed could be counted upon, should he act on my advice, to use them with dexterity and taste.

'So you have taught him his manners!' he said – to which I replied that we must wait and see; which we did. At eight o'clock we were seated in my room, at the back of the house, the window of which overlooked the garden, when a knock upon the back door brought Purity to meet her lover.

The latter's words (through shyness no less than mumbling) were unclear; but there followed a pause, after which came a clearly audible sigh from Purity, another silence, and then a gasp which could have been either of pleasure or of pain.

On our putting our heads out of the window, the sound proved to be indeed an expression of pleasure (though no doubt with an element of the latter), for, below us upon a patch of grass which lay between the path and the vegetable garden, Miss Purity lay upon her back, her petticoats thrown up, while between her legs lay the estimable Cain, his breeches about his knees, and a pair of buttocks large and firm enough to be those of a young heifer at work at a considered and measured pace uncharacteristic of country copulatives, and just such as to give maximum pleasure to the lady – whose eyes, meeting my own, could only through their rolling express what I took to be acknowledgement and thanks.

Closing the window, we could not but laugh, and Andy congratulated me first with a kiss and then a caress, clearly warmed by the sight we had glimpsed. Alas, while he had started the day aroused to erotic emotion by his kindly embraces of the frozen maid, and his feelings were still unrelieved, I must confess that my passage with so hardworking a lover as Cain had made my parts somewhat sore and distressed, and I made my excuses – which Andy, though clearly with some regret, respected, and so retired.

I took myself to bed, and for a while slept – but was awakened by a sound from the neighbouring room which (I confess) aroused my curiosity as much as my apprehension; for Andy was not given to nightmares – nor were the sounds he made entirely unfamiliar to ears which had certainly heard them before, and at rather closer quarters.

On opening his door I was not altogether surprised to see his delightfully familiar, smooth, tight arse at work between a pair of slim thighs which could only be those of our new maid, no doubt expressing her thanks for his kindness. I suspected, however, that while she had been aroused by her lover's new tenderness, young Cain was as yet inexpert in bringing her to a complete culmination. If any man could do so, my friend was that man, however; and even as the thought crossed my mind, and a little shriek from the young woman acknowledged his skill, he ceased his ploughing and withdrawing himself from the classic position wriggled downward until he could compliment with his lips first the young lady's breasts, then her belly, then . . .

Andy (I reflected as I closed the door behind me) was welcoming Miss Purity with all that warmth and kindness he always showed to servants – and had clearly found us one who would be useful in every chamber of the house, and whose gratitude would ensure that every aspect of her work would give, at least himself, entire satisfaction.

Chapter Three

The Adventures of Andy

We settled into a country routine with more ease than I would have imagined possible. I have of course from time to time lived a life away from the city; but it has usually been the case that this has been a matter of moving from town to town, village to village; I have very rarely stayed in a particular rural setting for more than a few days – and would have thought myself likely to be overcome by boredom in very short order.

Yet this was not the case. The pressure upon my time was not great – the supervision of the clearance of the ruins at Vycken, and a call or two upon my Parliamentary supporters in the constituency occupied only a little time, and in the interim I found it possible to fall without difficulty into a contemplative vein, spending much of my time in the garden of our little house at Penruddock, looking through the latest books – which I had my bookseller dispatch to me from Piccadilly upon a regular basis. So, I much enjoyed a novel from northern America, entitled *The Last of the Mohicans* by a Mr Fennimore Cooper, and even struggled through a remarkable work from France by

M. Stendhal, *Le Rouge et le Noir* – though no doubt missing some of the subtleties of an extraordinary work through my indifferent knowledge of the language. In addition, I endeavoured to take an interest in local matters, being by right of my possession of a Parliamentary seat an *ex officio* member of the local Bench of Magistrates (of which I shall have more to say at a later date), and diligently reading that admirable local newspaper *The West Briton*, which reported the adventures of the inhabitants of the whole county.

Our household was still a small one: Purity, indifferently reconciled to her father, lived in the house, occupying a little closet on the ground floor, once a scullery and now set up as a pleasant little bedroom. There, she entertained her lover, Cain – a gentleman whose demands upon her were matched only by the pleasure she took in fulfilling them (as was advertised by the sounds of satisfaction – articulated by them both – which were to be heard from her room at night, upon a regular basis). Though I rarely have reason to regret any of the actions of my friend Sophie, it must be noted that the rapprochement she had contrived between our maid and her man had the effect of depriving me of that young lady's amorous company, apart from the single grateful act which followed their reconciliation. Though I have no doubt that if I had applied to her, she would have felt it proper (in recognition of my kindness) to oblige me with a place in her bed, the difficulty this would have caused with Mr Cain (not only on her account, but perhaps on mine) seemed to make the game not worth the candle.

And so Sophie and I settled down almost like an old married couple, enjoying each other's company from time to time in the manner of companions each of whom knew best how to please the other.

We were sitting one day in the garden in the morning sun over a dish of chocolate and a plate of newly baked bread, when Sophie exclaimed that the county showed signs of joining the twentieth century. Handing me the newspaper she indicated a column in which I read of the establishment upon the coast, in the town of Fowey (at the seaside not too far from our present domicile) of a set of sea-water baths whose appointments provided, the advertisement pronounced, 'everything useful and convenient for the accommodation of ladies and gentlemen bathing', and went on to boast that the house (established by a Mr Jennings)

> 'consists of two excellent warm baths, a cold bath, a pump room and a handsome spacious waiting room over the baths, which commands a delightful view of the coast. This establishment has been erected at the cost of upwards of six hundred pounds, and is now in complete repair and good condition.'

Well (I remarked), would it not be pleasant to test the efficacy of the healthful recreation offered by such an establishment? We had after all been complaining that the waters around the coast had not yet been warmed by the sun to an extent which made bathing in them likely to be pleasurable;

warm sea baths were another matter, and my past experience of them was one which persuaded me that they had a beneficial effect upon one's system. Moreover, the place where the baths were established was one in which a friend of mine was resident – Madame Charlotte le Semblant (who with her husband Maurice was introduced to our readers in the volume entitled *Eros in High Places*, first published in the year of '91); it would be pleasant to have the opportunity of renewing our acquaintance.

We therefore decided on an excursion, ordered up the gig – which I drove myself – for that very afternoon, and set off towards the coast. The sun was remarkably warm for the time of the year, the roads free of those tedious heavy carts which so often impede the progress of smarter vehicles, and we covered the seventeen miles or so without undue haste in not more than two hours and a half, taking rooms at the Ship Hotel (that admirable hostelry in Lostwithiel Street which was once the town house of the Rashleigh family, and a part of which forms the south toll gate into the town).

The assiduous landlord, surprisingly recognising me from the representation published in the prints upon my arrival in the county, paid us the compliment of personally attending upon us. He served us up an excellent supper, and proved extremely knowledgeable about the neighbourhood, assuring me of the popularity there of M. and Madame le Semblant (though Monsieur was, he believed, at present travelling upon the Continent).

We occupied ourselves during the remainder of the evening in strolling about the place amid the fashionable people – who for the most part consisted of little local beauties, pert and pretty enough to take the gaze (and I believe that a few of the local men were fortunate enough to catch the attention of my companion, ever open to the appeal of a bright eye).

It was on the following morning at the decent hour of eleven o'clock that we made our way to Mr Jennings' establishment, and found it to be as admirable as the advertisement which spoke so well of it. We were shown first to the waiting room, neatly furnished, where a surprisingly excellent jug of coffee was prepared for us, which we drank as we looked over the harbour below, the innumerable small boats juggling for places about the hulls of larger vessels being provisioned for voyages to many destinations about Europe and further afield – for although no longer a port of the importance it had attained during the years of the great Elizabeth, Fowey was still a place of some account in maritime business.

A decent young body next came to escort us to the baths, first having assured herself that we wished to try the heated waters before any possibility of immersing ourselves in the cold ones. Though the advertisement seemed to speak of two rooms, in fact there was but one large space, flooded to a depth of perhaps three feet, so that when one sat upon the comfortable benches about the sides of the room the water (heated to a pleasant but not enervating degree by furnaces somewhere below) reached almost to one's shoulders.

I had supposed the accommodation to comprise a chamber for gentlemen and another for females; however though, as I have said, but one room was available, the decencies were preserved by the erection of a partition placed across the room, rising from the surface of the water almost to the roof. This barrier however was likely to arouse rather than dampen the amorous spirits of any normally spirited young gentleman, for while the persons of those females partaking of the waters in the next compartment were for the most part concealed, a portion of their lower limbs could be seen below the water, somewhat waveringly conveyed to the eyes by rays of light diffused by the refraction of the light passing through the aqueous barrier.

Sitting at first far from the barrier (I found myself alone in my half of the chamber), I quite clearly saw the calves and feet of Sophie as she descended the steps into the water beyond it. Upon her sitting down next to the partition, the lines of her lower body became visible – which made me wonder how it came about that the local ladies (ever more prudish, in my experience, than those from Town) acceded to such a display. But perhaps Mr Jennings took a more liberal view of the tastes of the local populace than a visitor might be inclined to?

At all events, I must confess that the warmth of the waters, which always produces in me a delightful torpor, had had something of a rousing effect upon my amorous proclivities; it had been several days since my last connection with my dear friend, and the circumstances now prompted me to move myself to a seat next to the barrier which alone separated me from her, and without hesitation I stretched out my hand and placed it upon the upper surface of her thigh.

As I assumed would be the case, she made no motion to reject my advance (though I fancied I heard a momentary drawing in of breath which signified surprise at the ease with which communication between the sexes was possible in so relatively public a place); and on my moving my hand slightly so that it fell upon the inside of her thigh, she even shifted her position in order that my fingers might more easily reach that bower which lay between them – when with a shock of surprise and delight I found it to be entirely depilated, its lips as bare and smooth as if the property of a young child: yet so warmly receptive of the digit I slipped between them that they must belong to a woman who fully knew of the pleasure to be given and received by the receptacle of which they formed only the portals. This was not Sophie, who would no more have thought of shaving pussy than of shaving her head!

It would have been extremely impolite of me to show surprise, much less rejection, by removing my hand – and I was certainly disinclined to be anything other than acquiescent when I felt the hand of the unknown fair, slipped beneath the barrier, fall upon my own knee. Since she had (through my being somewhat taller) a difficulty in reaching further than my thigh, I moved from my seat and knelt with my face towards the barrier, the better to enable her to coddle my prick, which in no time had reached a state of rigidity which my invisible acquaintance evidently found inspiriting, from the enthusiastic manner in which she stroked and admired it.

My eyes had momentarily been closed – for, to be frank, the room in which I sat was not so charming as to recommend itself as a setting for amorous play. However, the insinuating movements of that anonymous female hand persuaded me to open my eyes and glance downward. As I looked, the dainty fingers were withdrawn from the barrel of my riding muscle, and began to stroke my inner thighs; as they moved upward to my belly, I saw not only how slim and sensitive they were, but a wrist dainty and poised – and, upon a forefinger, a gold ring with a little knot of sapphires upon it.

My constant readers will know me too well to suppose that I repined at the sight of so dainty a hand, clearly belonging to no country wench, but a woman of quality. On the contrary, a peculiar spice was added to the situation, and I did not for a moment consider withdrawing myself from it – indeed, renewing the assiduity with which I was complimenting the unknown fair. That she had any objection to this could not be thought, for she had now spread her lower limbs wide to my complimenting hands, both of which were occupied about them – and so welcome did she make my gestures that I was encouraged to place three, nay four fingers within those portals where I would far rather have placed that staff at which she now clutched with almost a frenzy, one of her hands about its base, and the other moving upon its length with a violence which would have been uncomfortable had my spirits not now been raised to such a height that any wildness would have been welcome.

I need not perhaps go further than to say that within a few moments an explosion of emotion took place so palpable that the concealed lady could have been in no doubt of it, no less from the convulsion which tightened my cods than to the violence with which a ring of muscle closed about that forefinger which, with a boldness which seemed to indicate an unusual degree of sophistication, she had inserted in an aperture which, while susceptible of the utmost degree of feeling, is often neglected by all but the most considerate of mistresses.

I had only to persist in my own toying with my invisible companion's nether region for a moment longer, when she closed her thighs together, almost painfully, upon my hand, and an imperfectly stifled shriek of pleasure signalled a similar paroxysm.

We stayed for a moment in those positions which we had adopted: I felt a pang, I must confess, that it was not possible to take the lady in my arms and administer a more tender caress, in acknowledgement of the pleasure she had afforded me; and from the warm withdrawing caress she gave to my already shrunken cock as she removed her hand, she may have felt the same regret.

I must confess that I hurried from the room and dressed myself with remarkable speed, hoping to encounter my unknown companion before she left the premises, and persuade her perhaps to an assignation more comfortable; but it was not to be – not only because there was no sign of her, but because as I stepped into the pump room I saw the reason why Sophie had not herself descended into the baths: for she was sitting over a glass of the health-giving liquid with none other than Charlotte le Semblant!

'My dear,' the latter was saying as I walked in, 'my dear, you *must* have him! He's positively *effroyable*! Not, you understand, of tremendous size – but . . .'

However, at that interesting point she became aware of my presence, and, turning, rose and saluted me with an enthusiastic kiss upon the lips. She was, as far as could be seen – and her gown was not so full as entirely to disguise the lines of her figure – no less enticing than she had been when I first saw her, bound to a tree in a clearing in a wood (for reasons not unconnected with highway robbery) – an occasion on which her figure had been more open to the view than now, my first sight of her revealing a pair of breasts so luscious that the failure of the highwayman to rape as well as rob her gave me serious doubts as to his manhood.

'My dear Archer!' she cried, '*quel plaisir*!' (She had evidently caught from her husband the eccentricity of exclaiming in the French language, no doubt less from affectation than from habit.

'Charlotte!' I replied. 'And how is Maurice?'

'He is at the moment upon the Continent,' she said, 'conducting business. But he is well; and you are as handsome as ever, and no doubt as vigorous!'

I am not sure that I did not blush at so obvious a tribute, which clearly complimented me upon activity more personal than (for example) gardening or carpentry!

'But I was just insisting that you and dear Sophie dine with me and spend the night. I have a friend, Michel Lebaissant, as a house guest: he is a young man at present studying the social habits of the English, and is always interested to make new acquaintances. I am sure that he will be pleased to converse with you both – and in particular, my dear, with you . . .' (Her last remark being addressed to Sophie, whose disinterested attitude was a little too obviously contrived.)

'I have no doubt of it – any more than that (if I rightly understand the words I overheard) Sophie will be especially interested to converse with him,' I remarked.

Not one whit discomfited, Charlotte smiled broadly.

'That is certainly the case,' she said. 'She may expect a most interesting exchange of confidences. But while she and Michel are discussing the weather, the state of relations between our countries, or whatever other topic occurs to them, I am quite sure that you and I will find equal pleasure in renewing our friendship.'

There was little doubt in my mind as to the nature of the pleasure to which she alluded; our friendship had been keen, even before she had met M. le Semblant – indeed, she was the only woman to whom I had ever made an offer of marriage (though only a moment after making it, I must confess to a certain relief when she rejected it!). Her husband had been generous in acknowledging our friendship, and by no means objecting to it, or (after their marriage) to its occasional renewal, when circumstances permitted. Even though at present somewhat drained by the unexpected entertainment I had recently enjoyed, I could not but warm to the suggestion that I might shortly once more enjoy the person of a lady whose charms still engaged an affectionate corner of my heart.

I had no hesitation then, in company with Sophie, in accepting her kind invitation – at which Charlotte showed delight, rose to her feet, and drew us towards the door – only to be met there by a young lady who looked somewhat confusedly at the party.

'My dear Elaine,' said Charlotte, 'I trust you enjoyed your *baignade*.'

'*Certainement, madame*,' said the young lady.

'Allow me to present Mademoiselle Elaine Femelle, a cousin of Maurice,' said Charlotte, at which the girl – whose years could surely not add up to more than seventeen? – made a pretty curtsy, and, raising her right hand to her chin, displayed to me a gold ring with a little knot of sapphires sparkling at its centre.

Her dark eyes, as they met mine, were wonderfully deep and clear – and happily without the slightest trace of embarrassment; she evidently had no notion that I was the gentleman whose fingers had recently penetrated her secret treasure – though yet again, I would not have believed so young a person (even of French origin) could have emerged from so recent and strange an encounter and, without more time than ten minutes to quieten her emotions, could appear so cool! I must moreover confess that it was almost alarmingly arousing to be in the presence of a young lady of the utmost self-possession and poise, dressed in the most elegant habillements of fashion, and to recollect the naked – more than naked – mound which but recently had nuzzled the palm of my hand. My eyes, I fear, fixed themselves upon the young person with even more avidity than they would normally engage in observing even so attractive a female; nor can I suppose that Charlotte and Sophie were unaware of my interest – they were too closely cognizant of my amorous predilections to overlook it; though I fancy Mlle Femelle did not recognise my interest, at least to the extent of its keenness.

Charlotte's carriage was waiting nearby, and we took our seats in it – Sophie and Charlotte upon one bench, and myself and Mlle Femelle opposite them; the confines of the vehicle were sufficiently snug to make it impossible for my thigh not to be laid along that of the lady on my left – nor could I control a slight trembling which disturbed my poise; for I must now admit that I found her presence extremely disturbing – no less so because a woman whose person I had frequently and warmly enjoyed sat opposite me, and clearly expected to invite me to enjoy her company not only at supper, but later in the evening.

The air was sufficiently cool to enable me to keep my emotions under control as we travelled along the road out of the town, with the harbour waters sparkling below us; and, after a mile and a half, turned into a drive which led to the le Semblants' house – a sixteenth-century building consisting of three wings set about a square courtyard, and a castellated wall with a loggia of seven bays upon the ground floor supported by fat, heavy Tuscan columns.

We were ushered into a fine hall with linen-fold panelling and prettily patterned ceiling beams, and shown briefly over a house which was none the less welcoming for being of the most generous and handsome proportions.

'Perhaps you will not object to sharing a room?' Charlotte exclaimed, showing us into a nicely furnished bedroom upon the first floor, in which a large four-poster took pride of place. 'I think it unlikely that you will spend much time here,' she added, with a complaisant glance which included both me and Sophie. 'Nor do I suppose that you will be in need of any night clothes: not that I recall either of you being much concerned about such matters . . .'

I looked around to see if Mlle Femelle was being made familiar in this way with our personal habits; but she had not accompanied us – and I took the opportunity of enquiring as to her origin.

Charlotte, smiling (I fancied) somewhat knowingly at my interest, supplied the information that her cousin was spending a while with her until, six months hence, she was to be married to a French aristocrat who had settled in the East Indies.

'She is an agreeable child, is she not?' she remarked, 'and an enthusiast for life, as you and I are, my dear Andy; indeed, I believe that her one regret at spending time here is that we are to some extent devoid of fashionable company – so I look to you to entertain her to the best of your ability.'

She then turned to Sophie and directed her eyes out of the window, with, 'There is M. Lebaissant, see, crossing the lawn! He has offered his services to my friend Elaine upon several occasions, but perhaps he rather too closely resembles the gentlemen with whom she is normally familiar to be a temptation. It is, however,' (with a meaningful look at Sophie) 'I assure you, her loss!'

The young man in question was certainly elegant, and though with a distinctly Frenchified air – that is, with more natural grace in his movements, and a somewhat more feminine poise than most English men of his age (which I took to be twenty years or so) – looked pleasant enough. He proved this when we were introduced, downstairs – joined once more by Mlle Femelle, who had now changed from her simple grey gown to a similarly simple white one, which if anything showed off to an even greater degree the lines of her sweetly slim body.

The evening was spent in dining, drinking and desultory conversation. Charlotte had little to relate except the pleasures of concupiscence, of which she spoke with a frankness that recalled the old days of familiarity – but it seemed a little strange in the presence of M. Lebaissant and Mlle Femelle. They nevertheless showed neither surprise nor offence at overhearing the details of their hostess' intimate life: that Maurice had at first 'rogered her silly', and even now, on returning home after some time away, was wont to take his wife whenever and wherever the mood seized him, which was sometimes as many as three times a day – a salutary lesson to other married men, whose desire for their consorts too often fails in direct proportion to the length of time they have been wed.

'But my dear Andy,' said Charlotte, 'you must not allow Maurice's husbandly enthusiasm to deter you from paying me your respects; he has now been absent for five weeks, and I am deucedly in need of . . .'

Even I could not but blush at this, and fell into a sudden coughing fit, for it seemed to me that however used Mlle Femelle was to her cousin's familiar talk, it might unsettle her to hear such an open invitation so crudely expressed.

We sat for a while over our wine, until at ten o'clock Charlotte suddenly rose to her feet and announced that she was excessively fatigued with polite talk, and hoped that I would accompany her to her room, where conversation of another sort might be substituted for mere tittle-tattle. (That she said this without giving offence is only one mark of that extraordinary charm which made frankness of expression something to be admired in her, rather than condemned).

I rose from my place at Mlle Femelle's side with no lack of enthusiasm: Charlotte had always been the most delightful of bed companions, and I was happy to be in a position to renew that intimate acquaintance which had formerly given me so much pleasure. I must admit, however, that I could not but glance, as I left the room, in the direction of my late companion – the prospect of pressing a kiss upon those soft, bare lips was . . .

However, I did not repine; nor could I miss the fact that Sophie was warmly engaged with M. Lebaissant, whose arm lay negligently along the back of the sofa upon which they were seated, and whose other hand lay among the folds of her skirt as they conversed in the most intimate manner. Poor Mlle Femelle seemed likely to play the kitten without a tail.

Charlotte and I parted at the top of the fine white staircase, she informing me that her room was upon the right hand of my own, and the third door upon the left hand side; I kissed her hand, upon which she whispered, 'Twenty minutes, my dear, to let the house settle . . .'

On entering my room I immediately stripped and made use of the tub of warm water placed there in order to bathe myself, paying especial attention to those parts which I supposed would shortly receive the intimate caresses of my friend – for though it was but a few hours since my warm bath, the weather was sufficiently close to have roused a light perspiration. (Perhaps uncommonly in an age when odour and lack of cleanliness were the most efficient prophylactics, many ladies and gentlemen bathing but once a month, and then with no thoroughness, I was scrupulous in the matter, not only through a personal sense of delicacy, but through the experience that the cleanlier the person, the more intimate the attentions an enthusiastic mistress was willing to offer.)

As I was drying myself, the door opened and Sophie entered.

'I see you expect the evening to offer some entertainment?' she said.

'You know,' I replied, 'that Charlotte and I are old acquaintances, and out of common politeness . . .'

'Don't waste your time cozening me!' she said with a laugh, 'you are both as ready for the act as two cats upon the tiles . . .'

'And for the matter of that,' I said, 'I suppose that you will be assisting M. Lebaissant in his studies into the more intimate characteristics of the British female?'

'It is a matter of mere politeness,' she said, and, examining the tub and concluding that I had no more than slightly sullied the water, without more ado peeled off her gown and made a toilette as complete as my own. I will confess (having put on a dressing gown, no doubt the property of my friend Maurice, which had been left upon the bed) to seating myself and watching with pleasure as my friend passed the sponge over her person. This was a scene too common to be embarrassing for either of us; we had both, for as long as we had known each other, maintained a connection which was now much closer than that between siblings – and the many amorous adventures in which we had participated only made the keener our appreciation of each other's qualities.

'You are in beauty this evening, my love,' I said, 'and were it not for fear of disappointing Charlotte . . .'

Sophie smiled at the compliment, and gestured to a fresh towel, which I placed about her shoulders, taking the opportunity to place a kiss upon a breast which was as brisk and saucy as it had ever been. We then permitted ourselves to lie upon the bed and exchange a kiss or two, and even a more familiar gesture – until with a sigh my companion rose and, kissing me upon the lips, donned a gown (I suppose of Charlotte's) which had been provided for her, and made to the door.

'We will meet again,' she said, with a wink; and was gone.

The clocks were now striking the half hour after ten, and it was necessary for me to light a candle before making my way to the door, opening it, turning down a corridor upon the right hand, and counting the doors until the fourth lay upon my left. The handle turned; the door yielded to my pressure; and I found myself in my lady's chamber, the dim shape of a four poster ahead of me, the curtains drawn – a thing which slightly surprised me, since modesty had never been one of Charlotte's faults.

I stepped towards the bed, and placing the candle upon a side table drew back the curtains –

when to my astonishment I saw before me not the luscious body of my friend Charlotte, but the slimmer, paler body of Mlle Femelle, spread like a starfish upon the sheets. It is always true that candle-light pays a compliment to any person upon whom it falls: but in this case, the sight was a quite remarkably pulchritudinous one. The mademoiselle's body resembled rather that of a person in a medieval painting than anything else – for the middle part was long and lean, her waist willowy, the deep, dark knot of her navel marking its centre. Her breasts were small and round, marked at the centre by little brown roundels; the only remarkable thing (though no news to me) being the cleft which lay between her thighs, where rather than the bush which normally disguises the passage to heaven, the lips themselves were laid open to the view – the candle-light darkening them to a smudged brown – between which a darker aperture seemed to cry out for a caress more intimate than that which my attentive fingers had already afforded. Indeed so enticing was the idea that without a second thought I threw off my gown, precipitated myself without ceremony onto the bed, and planted the most enthusiastic kiss at the very centre of her being.

That this was welcome could immediately be apprehended by the reaction of the lady, who far from recoiling – as so young a person might be expected to do – positively thrust her loins up to meet my lips and the probing of a tongue which now sought for sweetness in the void, while at the same time throwing her arms about my hips (for we lay, I should have said, head to tail) and began to plant kisses of her own in the neighbourhood of those parts which offered a visual confirmation (if one was necessary) of the enthusiasm with which I was complimenting her.

It would have been superfluous for me to be surprised (had I been able to spare energy for thought, when all my attention was upon emotion and enjoyment) at the sophisticated reaction of the young lady – who now took my instrument between her lips and was sucking upon it with a tender application almost unbearable in its sweetness; she had after all accepted my earlier, watery caresses without repining – and it could not be supposed that that had been her first encounter with a person of the opposite sex.

It became clear, indeed, that she had been well taught – for the caresses she offered spoke of an industrious attention to the fine details of pleasant companionship; moreover, her own person was so enchanting that it was all too easy to lose oneself in the delight of devouring it. Never had I found such sweetness couched within the female concavity – the light, musky flavour which lay about those smooth lips darkening (as it were) to a delectable honey sweetness, which fell upon my tongue as I probed beyond them and into the depths.

That this (together with an attentive grazing of the hard little nodule of flesh which stood on guard in the vicinity) gave as much pleasure to Mlle Femelle as to me, I could not for a moment doubt; for she spread her limbs almost to dislocation, inviting my hands to play about her thighs, and even part the cheeks of her small, pear-shaped buttocks, and tickle with the tip of a finger the bud of that other aperture whose portals are as sensitive as any area susceptible to the arts of love.

In a moment, a gasp and an imprecation in French (somewhat muffled from the fact that the lady's mouth was stopped by a morsel of my flesh – that is, one of my cods) together with a paroxysm which shook her entire person, persuaded me that she had reached an apogee – a thought which together with the sensual pleasure I had received brought me nearer to my own climactic than was comfortable and I therefore, not without reluctance, prized myself from her attentive grip, and reversing my position placed my cock (now so horny as to seem made of a more impenetrable material than mere flesh) within the passage which my tongue, together with the natural juices aroused by the general lasciviousness of our mutual play, had now made so slippery as to banish any resistance so narrow a portal might have offered to an engine sufficiently large to be somewhat beyond the average in circumference.

Once the natural office of a prick was under way, our mutual movements took up an entirely natural rhythm; and the sensation offered – together with the friction of enchantingly pert breasts against my chest (the nipples so hard that they seemed almost to scratch my skin) – was so bewitching that in order to delay the inevitable final spasm I was forced to concentrate my mind upon the political repercussions of the treaty recently negotiated between England, Russia and France to secure the autonomy of Greece. Even this intellectual exercise finally failed me, upon the young lady, thrusting her tongue between my lips, wriggling her belly insistently upon my own, and parting the cheeks of my arse with determined palms to insert a finger into my anus, at the same time closing her legs about my body so as to trap me in a cage of warm, living flesh.

The sum total was that I was shaken with a convulsion so violent that I almost fainted; and recovered only upon hearing the voice of my hostess, who I now saw to be standing at the bedside, and who (I was forced to conclude) had been watching the entire passage of our amours through the curtain upon that side.

'I trust you will forgive the familiarity,' she said. 'But it is perhaps a small price to pay for so delightful an experience. I trust that you did find it delightful?'

I could not deny it – but was somewhat surprised when Charlotte, removing her gown and revealing herself to be otherwise entirely unclothed, placed a knee upon the bed and laid herself at our side. If I was expected, having enjoyed a moderately expressive passage that afternoon, followed by an experience of love as intense as any I had previously experienced, now to pleasure Charlotte . . .?

But I need not have troubled myself; for – somewhat to my surprise – her embrace was offered not to myself, but to the young lady whose body still lay beneath my own, for Charlotte bent her head and took between her lips one of the nipples of that rounded breast nearer her.

I naturally lifted myself immediately from a position which could only obstruct those embraces first practised (if we are to believe the historians) upon the island of Lesbos; and while I could not but be somewhat jealous at observing that Mlle Femelle seemed quite as pleased at the attentions of my friend as she had been at my own, I would not for the world have obstructed their pleasure by showing any sign of displeasure or disapproval. It has ever been my view that we must all find what joy we can in whatever direction our tastes lie – and while I recognised with sorrow that my exhaustion prevented me from participating in what might have been a charming orgy (for sadly while a lady may re-engage herself in lascivious play without delay, this is not, as my male readers will recognise, possible with us) my view of their coupling, which upon another occasion might have been excessively stimulating, in this case merely lulled me to sleep at their side!

I should perhaps be somewhat ashamed to admit that I slept so soundly that the enthusiasm of the ladies' coupling did not wake me; I even failed to waken later in the night (when no doubt I might have roused one, the other, or both to a warm encounter). My eyes did not open until the sun shone into the room on the following morning, when I found myself the odd man out in a bed where the two other figures were still entwined, each in each other's arms. I slipped from the room to my own, dressed myself and descended to the breakfast room, where an attendant served me some stirred eggs and coffee; and whence, in half an hour, came Sophie, looking (I thought) somewhat tired. We left a kind message for our hostess, with whom we had no need to stand upon ceremony, and kept our own counsel as, after engaging another servant to drive us into Fowey, we took our gig and returned to Penruddock Monachorum.

Chapter Four

Sophie's Story

I noticed, as Andy stood aside to allow Charlotte to leave the room before him, that she exchanged behind his back what seemed a significant glance with the charming Mlle Femelle, and inferred that some plot might be afoot – it had seemed to me from the first that that young lady was by no means as innocent as might have been supposed from her mild expression. However, it was no matter for me (although, as the reader has already discovered from the previous chapter, I was not wrong!) – and I must confess to being more concerned with the attentions which M. Lebaissant was now paying me. I was not entirely displeased when, Mlle Femelle soon afterwards having made her excuses and slipping from the room, he took the opportunity of pressing a kiss upon my lips, while at the same time slipping a hand within the bodice of my dress in order to caress a breast – which he did with that perfect mixture of assurance and sensitivity I have always marked in the French race, perhaps the most adept in Europe at paying a compliment to a lady, if not always the most vigorous in carrying it to a logical conclusion.

In this case, the gentleman's desire to follow up his advantage was clear; and indeed he whispered into my ear the hope that he might be allowed to stroll about the delectable fields of my body during the course of the night (as he put it). I was by no means averse to this, for, apart from what Charlotte had said about his natural abilities as a lover, he was a decent young man possessed of considerable natural charm – just the right sort of lover for an evening's play; he would no doubt like myself regard a passing pleasure as no more and no less than that, and would therefore be unlikely to be the source of any subsequent embarrassment.

I therefore smiled upon his request and promised to accede to it, at which he gave me another kiss, this time fixing upon my lower lip with a most lascivious, slippery motion.

First, however, I felt the need to refresh myself, and so went to the room set aside for my friend and me, where I found him concluding his own toilette. That we passed a little time in friendly toying need surprise no one: we have been familiar in the way of such pleasantries as long as we have known each other, and have often exchanged certain teasing preliminaries before taking ourselves off to other lovers.

Indeed, I could not but recognise in this present instance that Andy seemed less eager to take these pleasantries to a conclusion than to employ them as a preliminary appetiser, before a more substantial meal – nor could he have denied, had I put it to him, that his riding-muscle was less adamant and eager than I have known it; from which I inferred first that he was rather less keenly interested in spending the night with our friend Charlotte than might have been the case – and second that he somewhat regretted the impossibility of a connection with Mlle Femelle; which, when I twitted him, he confessed – nor could I reprove him for it, for we are not responsible for our emotions in these matters (so that, for instance, it had never occurred to me, on occasions when he had left my bed for that of material he found more provoking, to rebuke him for it; jealousy is the most wasteful and useless of emotions).

He eventually left me for what I hoped would be a pleasant rendezvous; and in only a few moments, I too, in a gown left out for me by Charlotte, made my way to the room which M. Lebaissant had indicated as his own.

Having perused the previous chapter, the reader may not be as surprised as I was when, having first taken me in his arms, and after saluting me, and then with a loving gesture lifting my gown from my shoulders, M. Lebaissant revealed himself to be naked as a needle – not only lacking hair upon his chest or legs, but also between the latter, where all was bald as an egg – or, rather, two eggs.

When I took the liberty of questioning him about this, he remarked that about two years previously there had been a plague of lice in the house in which he was living in Paris. It had proved remarkably difficult, even with the most modern chemicals, to be rid of those occupants – and the local physician had recommended the attention of the barber, who had shaved both men and women completely, denuding them of every hair upon their body, from the top of the head to the ankles.

But M. Lebaissant now had a splendid head of hair, as I observed – indeed, released from the ribbon which had held it in place, it fell about his shoulders as generously as that of any girl; so . . .

Ah (he confessed, as he took my hand and led me to the bed), he had discovered the truth that the removal of hair from the intimate parts of the body contributed greatly to the delicacy of the emotions felt there during passages of love – while as a matter of course detracting not at all from the natural vigour with which he was able to pursue the normal end of such passages.

So saying, as he laid himself down at my side, he took my hand again and conveyed it to those parts of which he had spoken – where indeed while a silky smoothness was to be found all about, the central column was as strong and upright as could possibly be.

I was entirely unable not to take in my hand the candle which stood upon the bedside table, and by its light examine the phenomenon before me. There was unquestionably something strange about the sight of such baldness – for only a slight darkening of the skin lay upon the triangle above the root of his admirable prick, while below it his cods were entirely lacking in their usual nest of hair: and on my touching them with my tongue proved that the simile I have already used was a correct one – for they were like nothing so much, to the touch of my lips, as two slightly warm, shelled, boiled eggs!

What the gentleman had said was confirmed immediately by the shudder which went through his entire body as I took first one then the other of these objects between my lips, and as I went on to test the skin about the surrounding territory with an exploratory tongue I could not doubt but that the absence of any decorative curls or concealing mist of hairs added much to the sensitivity of that part of the body to a caress – nor did it make it more unpleasant for the attentive lover, for nothing is less enamouring than to find a loose hair between one's lips. Here, there was the possibility of no such disturbance of the caresses which were exchanged with increasing enthusiasm, while it was possible to enjoy the remarkable smoothness of the skin about those parts, which in a natural state seems softer, more pliant than the skin of any other part of the body.

M. Lebaissant, having expressed the desire to inspect my person more intimately, lit another candle, and I now lay upon several pillows, which supported my back. He lay with his head and shoulders between my thighs, the better to compliment that area with his fingers and lips – though breaking off to assure me that I could not imagine how much more sensitive those compliments would be had I the courage to follow his example – and that of Mlle Femelle, for he assured me that he had succeeded in persuading her to follow his example, though Charlotte herself had to the present time declined to take the step.

He hesitated for a moment, and then, opening a cupboard at the bed side, produced a razor, soap and a brush, and positively asked if he could not assist me into the state of which he had spoken!

The reader will readily understand my state of mind! I have been ever accessible to notions which might make keener the pleasure of love making, which in my view is one of the chief reasons for living; yet could I place myself at the mercy of an unknown young Frenchman with a razor? Could I offer my most intimate parts for such an operation as he suggested?

I once more bent to inspect his own person: certainly there was no sign of the slightest scratch either upon his cods, the creases between them and his thighs, or upon his lower belly – surely he must be most adept with the weapon which he had even now taken suggestively in his hand?

Not at all, he remarked when I made the point – for Mlle Femelle regularly assisted him by renewing the baldness of that area of his body, which, although formerly unpractised, she did with the utmost skill: and had indeed done so that very morning (as I might have inferred from the fact that my lips had been unable to descry even the faintest roughness where the stubble of growing hair might be expected).

Having heard this, I found myself, almost despite my better judgement, assenting to the proposition; at which the gentleman's pleasure was unalloyed. He immediately lit two more candles, and, persuading me to lie with my buttocks upon the edge of the bed and my thighs spread widely apart, he placed two upon the floor nearby, and the others upon two chairs, so that the utmost light fell upon the area in which he was to operate.

Of the operation itself I hesitate to speak – not because it was uncomfortable (indeed, the application of the soap, its stirring into a lather with the brush, and even the delicate scraping of the razor were positively inspiriting) but because any woman will have her teeth set somewhat upon edge by the very idea. All I will say is that M. Lebaissant was so skilled an operator that not a single drop of blood was shed, nor was the slightest graze inflicted even upon the most tender part; and that upon his ceasing, when I could bring myself to examine my parts, I most confess to tolerating the sight without disgust.

Even if I had felt any doubt, the gentleman himself would have dispelled it. I could not but observe, as he proceeded with his task, his iron self-control – for under the stimulus of a close attention to a not unhandsome female's cunny, his cock could be seen to swell even beyond its former state of expansion, and to buck from time to time (I presume as a compliment to myself); yet his hand did not for a moment shake. However, on wiping the remainding soap away with a towel, and having applied to the whole area some fine and sweet-smelling powder, to soothe any itching which might follow the operation, he permitted himself to give way to emotion, and upon all fours began to kiss again and again the denuded area which he had revealed – to lick the skin all about the centre, and first caressing the portals, finally to thrust his tongue between them and into my very soul.

I cannot deny that the emotions these actions

aroused were keener, as to apprehension, than any I had previously felt; the cool air which moved about my lower parts was in itself inspiriting, while the feelings aroused by his tongue moving upon flesh which had always previously been protected by a furry coat were keener than I could have imagined; so that I found myself taking the poor gentleman's head between my hands and forcing it into my belly as though I wished to urge him into a channel similar to that whence he had been born!

Further, it must be confessed that when, after we had enjoyed such mutual caresses for as long as we could bear, and the normal process of copulation occurred, the sensations enjoyed were equivalently keener; the velvet skin about the base of his prick was brought now into juxtaposition with an equally bare plane of my own, with no interposing material preventing the exchange of emotion.

I would not go so far as to recommend every lady to follow my example; indeed, I only maintained my shaven state for a relatively short while – and the endurance of a prickly return to normality was the least pleasant aspect of my changed appearance; yet a lady who does not at least once in her life make the experiment is certainly missing an experience which I can recommend as a remarkably interesting one.

M. Lebaissant proving as experienced, confident and kind a lover as any I had known, we continued to enjoy ourselves and each other for much of the night; and it was with regret that next morning I slipped from his bed while he yet slept to greet Andy – whose night had been passed, as I supposed, in equal pleasure – and return home. I enquired of him at one stage of the journey whether he did not contemplate a visit to the barber; and after a moment's puzzlement he realised that I was aware of that unusual characteristic of Mlle Femelle's person – and raising his eyebrows enquired whether M. Lebaissant . . .? To which I replied in the affirmative, but failing to reply to Andy's statement that such a radical game could surely not be worth the candle – and failing too to confess to my own changed state, which I supposed that my friend would no doubt discover upon some future occasion.

(Indeed, that occasion was not long delayed, for within a day or two he came as was his wont to my bed, and upon slipping his hand beneath the sheets in order to give me a preliminary caress, burst into laughter as he discovered my state – which however, upon closer examination, excited him to a degree which made the subsequent coupling memorable.)

It was within a week or so that that admirable newspaper *The West Briton* yielded another paragraph which was of interest, and which was the prompter of another adventure: I read to Andy the announcement that

> 'Mr Graham, aeronaut to His Majesty (by special appointment) will make his one hundred and sixteenth ascent with a magnificent silk balloon (wind and weather permitting)

from an enclosed and eligible piece of ground upon the edge of Bodmin Moor on Tuesday next, April 27th, at three for four o'clock in the afternoon. The splendid balloon and car are the same with which Mr Graham had the honour to ascend in the presence of His Majesty from Windsor in September last, and also with which Mr and Mrs Graham ascended by appointment of Government from the Green Park, London, on the day of his Majesty's coronation.

'It is the largest balloon in the kingdom, more than one hundred feet in circumference, and is capable of holding nearly thirty thousand cubic feet of gas, and will conveniently carry two persons four miles above the clouds. To witness the ascent, two shillings each, children half-price, mechanics &c one shilling.

I noticed that my friend grew a little pale at the mention of the possibility of rising several miles above the clouds – and indeed, upon my concluding the paragraphs, derided the whole idea; he had heard, certainly, of such ascents – but the idea that they could be successful was impertinent to the heavenly Powers.

This forced me to laugh, for my friend is by no means normally complimentary to those Powers, and upon this occasion without doubt invoked them simply as a means of denigrating Mr Graham's scheme. I, on the other hand, found the very idea of rising even above the flights of the birds extremely exciting, and said so.

'Easy to say!' remarked my friend, 'but I cannot see you mounting the basket and rising into the air with nothing more substantial to support you than hydrogen gas, though doubtless that is safer than the mere hot air which some aeronauts employ.'

'On the contrary,' I remarked, 'I would be more than pleased to make an ascent should the opportunity afford itself.'

Somewhat short-temperedly, my friend continued to doubt it and I to assert it until we ended in making a bet in the sum of twenty-five guineas that – should Mr Graham permit it – I would accompany him on his ascent.

Both Andy and myself are not without a strong vein of obstinacy, and the wager having been made I was determined to carry it through. We therefore lost no opportunity of driving into Bodmin, where as we expected we found Mr and Mrs Graham established at the only decent inn and introduced ourselves – enquiring whether there would be a possibility of my taking a flight with him.

He showed some surprise at this, for his wife had been (we were assured) the only female who had ever flown in his balloon. She was a handsome woman in her thirties; he an equally handsome man of perhaps forty and two or three, but in fine condition, wiry and slim, with a dashing black curled military moustache and a vigorous air which expressed itself (as it seemed to me) in a glance which caught my eyes and was sufficiently appreciative of my beauty – I must not be modest – to make Mrs Graham a little jealous at the alacrity with which he assented to my request. She was, however, mollified by Andy's offer to cover the entire expenses of the ascent, thus leaving the monies paid by any observers as simple profit for the owners of the silk sphere.

Having shaken hands upon it, we returned to Vycken, where during the next two days Andy once and again enquired whether I was not having second thoughts – while in fact I was looking forward to the whole affair with considerable interest (though if the absolute truth must be told, not without a degree of apprehension – just sufficiently keen to give a zest to the proposition).

We arrived at the field upon the edge of the moor in time to see the great balloon beginning to billow and fill with the gas which was being pumped into it from two cylinders which lay upon the ground nearby, Mrs Graham overseeing the operation while Mr Graham circulated about the field shaking the hands of the ladies and gentlemen – particularly the ladies – and receiving their compliments. Upon seeing us he immediately made his way over and greeted us, enquiring solicitously whether I was ready for the Great Adventure, as he called it.

On receiving my assurances, he escorted me to the wicker basket which was attached to the balloon with silk strings. This was round, like a tub or barrel, the sides about four feet high; it was bare of any comforts – indeed there was room for none – save for a bottle of good champagne and a couple of glasses. A pair of steps made it simple for me to climb into it, followed by Mr Graham; it was a snug enough fit for us, and we were just able to turn about without too great an inconvenience.

The only discomfort likely to occur, Mr Graham told me, was in the descent, for this could not always be contrived so that the basket fell upon soft grass; however, he and his wife in their many ascents and as many descents had never suffered greater injury than a bruise or two, and he was confident that the same would be true upon this occasion.

By now the balloon had been filled with gas, and had risen above us; we felt the basket beginning to strain at the ropes which bound it to stakes driven into the ground, which even now Mrs Graham was, one by one, releasing – until only one held us, and finally, that was thrown off; and with a cheer from the crowd we began to rise steadily and with increasing velocity into the calm air.

I leaned over the edge of the basket to wave to Andy, whose face bore an expression combining something like jealousy, surprise that I was actually fulfilling the conditions of my bet, and concern for my safety – though he waved back with every assurance of confidence.

Mr Graham meanwhile leaned forward too, in order to wave to the crowd. While doing this, he had to press against my back, and I fear that it was at that moment that his admiration for me (evident at our first meeting) was sparked into something more intense, for while at first the pressure of his belly against my back was entirely innocent, I felt before long the stirring of something which could only be expressive of that emotion which is to be expected from a man whose body is perforce thrust against that of an attractive woman.

That I was conscious of this he was of course immediately aware, and for a moment attempted to draw away – but the constricting circumstances of the basket made it difficult; and indeed on my attempting to move to make it possible for him to relieve his embarrassment, the only result was that my buttocks rubbed against that very part of his body which was the signal of his emotions – and I fear that he took this for an invitation, for while continuing to wave with his right hand at the crowd below (the individuals now rapidly appearing more like ants than people), he thrust his left hand down and brought it around my waist, pulling me even more snugly against him.

I fear that I must now admit that the excitement of the ascent, the clarity and briskness of the air (so clear as to have almost the effect of wine) and a certain attraction to gentlemen of Mr Graham's adventurous sort, failed to lower my spirits to that degree which would have persuaded me to administer a rebuke; and when, upon clouds intervening to lose us the sight of the ground below, he took up my skirts and began to draw them upwards, I could not find it in my heart to stop him – even upon his discovering in the most obvious manner the fact that I wore no under clothes, a fact which (together I believe with my unexpectedly shaven state) drove him to such a culmination of excitement that he began feverishly to attempt to divest himself of his breeches – something excessively difficult at such close quarters, but which I was able to assist him in, once the necessary belt and buckles had been released, by passing my hands around behind me and pushing the waist of that garment downwards.

There being no room for any nicety in love making, there was but one obvious probability, which I adopted: that of remaining where I was, and leaning over with my arms upon the edge of the basket, while he – by necessity also remaining in his former position – introduced his prick into its proper quarters from behind. This he did with such careless excitement that for a moment he battered at quite the wrong entry; however, a slight elevation of my rear set this right, and now, a certain motion was possible – though once again, the basket was so slender in circumference that the vigorous swiving which might have taken place in normal congress with such a vigorous man was impossible. For me there was an advantage in this, for Mr G. was forced to restrict himself to a motion which was more governed and therefore more long lasting than might otherwise have been the case; and we were soon both in a delightful paroxysm of pleasure, our cries sufficiently loud to astonish those few birds who soared to an equivalent height.

A scalding rush of delighted liquor having signalled the triumph of nature over desire, I felt the bushy hairs of his moustache upon my neck as he pressed a kiss upon it; and he was polite enough to hope that I had not found the episode unpleasant.

Far from it, was my reply; it had merely added zest to a delightful adventure: and indeed I was now able to admire the towering clouds which surrounded us, parting occasionally to offer glimpses of the countryside far below, the landscape of which (through ignorance of any maps of the vicinity) I was incapable of recognising.

Through a contortion, Mr Graham now was able to take up and uncork the champagne, when we drank a couple of glasses, toasting each other and success to the venture. We were by this time at such a height that the cold air was a little too brisk (especially since our lower parts were still in an unclothed state, for my skirts were so bundled up that it was impossible to straighten them). Reaching up, Mr Graham untied a cord, and opening (as it seemed) a small aperture in the fabric of the balloon, released some gas, whereupon the machine began to descend, and I soon became conscious that we were passing downward through the clouds with almost the same velocity with which we had formerly risen. Mr Graham now announced that we must prepare ourselves for landing, and doing his best to recover his breeches (but failing to do so) advised me to hold on to the edge of the basket, and by no means to attempt to jump from it until it had come to rest.

The ground now seemed very close – and fortunately consisted of open fields, a few cows quietly grazing, ignorant of the great craft which was passing uncomfortably close over their heads. There was a bump, and then another; then the basket fell upon its side, and I saw Mr Graham's body tumble past me and fall upon the ground. I suppose that his grip had been less firm than mine, or perhaps he had simply been too intent on attempting to steer the balloon by means of the cords attaching it to the basket. At all events he was now no longer with me – and, relieved of his weight, the balloon surged upwards, carrying me up with it as its only passenger! I looked over the edge, to see Mr Graham lying upon the ground, his feet entangled in his breeches, staring anxiously upwards for a moment before becoming aware that a bull, whose peaceful sojourn had been disturbed by his descent, was showing a greater interest in him than was concomitant with safety, and rising to his feet making for the nearest gate as fast as his encumbering lower garments would permit. Sadly, a cloud intervened before I could see whether the bull or he won the resulting race.

I must now admit (though I would do so to no one less sympathetic than my constant readers) that I was somewhat concerned for my safety. Though the balloon was not ascending with great rapidity, ascending it certainly was; and I knew nothing of how to control it – even if control was possible (and Mr Graham had seemed to rely entirely upon the natural propelling force of the wind, without attempting in any way to steer the craft). I could do nothing, then, but wait.

This, I had not too long to do; for after perhaps ten minutes the natural lifting force of the gas seemed to decline, and the balloon again began to descend. Not far away to the south and west was a town, which I recognised from the remarkable spire of its church as Lostwithiel; and the balloon, it seemed, was now intent upon delivering me within the boundary of a ruined castle which stood upon a hill nearby. Indeed, it moved relentlessly downward towards this ruin, which was completely circular and much overgrown, and in a few moments the basket bumped against a crumbling rampart, and the cords supporting it caught in the branches of a high tree. Taking what was no doubt a risk, I decided to step from the basket onto the ramparts of the castle – and did so with remarkable ease, except that the stonework, crumbling from centuries of ruin, fell away under my feet, and I toppled headlong forward, saved from precipitation to the courtyard below only by my clothes becoming caught in the branches of the same tree which held the balloon captive – so that I now found myself hanging helpless and upside down, unable to move, much less release myself.

I was about to cry out as loudly as possible, in case someone might be in the neighbourhood and could release me, when I heard a rustling noise nearby and, after a moment of fear that some wild animal might be about to attack me, I heard a man's voice enquire, somewhat unsteadily (I thought) whether I was injured.

I was not, I replied; at which the gentleman – for his voice announced him as not being of the labouring classes – advised me to remain still, that he would attempt to aid me. He continued to sound somewhat shaken: but upon a moment's thought I recognised why this might be so, for it occurred to me that since I was suspended upside down, and could feel a certain coolness about my lower limbs, it was entirely probable that these were completely open to view, my skirts obeying the laws first observed by Mr Newton, and hanging down about my waist. This could be expected to render any gentleman somewhat unsure of the propriety of coming to my assistance.

I shortly felt a pair of hands close about my ankles and lift me bodily; but this had no effect upon my entangled clothing, which it seemed impossible to disentangle; next, I heard a rending sound and, with a muffled apology, those hands now seized my own and lifted them, at which my position was reversed, and I found myself first raised once more into an upright position. Then he lifted me not only from amid the branches but from my tattered gown, which it had evidently been necessary to tear away, so caught up was it into the tree.

My anxiety turning to relief for a moment overcame me, and I almost fainted – though I must confess that the counterfeiting of unconsciousness also struck me as an admirable way of relieving my saviour from the embarrassment of clutching a naked woman in his arms (especially since, as a glance from below my eyelashes revealed, at least the upper part of his own body was also unclothed).

I felt myself laid gently upon some soft sward, when I was released, and half opening my eyes saw my rescuer's back as he took a few steps from me and bent to dip his hands in some water collected in a bowl which lay nearby, bearing some resemblance to the holy water stoup of a church. I saw immediately that what I had apprehended was the case: except that it was not only his upper parts which were bare of clothing, but his entire body – my first view of him being of a long, lean back, a handsomely set spine dividing at its lower end into two comely spheres, supported by legs sufficiently sturdy and muscular to be the envy of many other men.

The gentleman now turned, and I was reluctantly forced to close my eyes again as he knelt at my side and laid his water-cool hands across my forehead – at which I stirred and opened my eyes, smiling into his own and immediately thanking him for his assistance, while reassuring him of my well-being.

As our eyes met, a dark blush fell across his features; and on my eyes lowering I was conscious that an appendage, which had no doubt been to that moment pliable and loose, was beginning to thicken. Observing the direction of my glance, the young gentleman quickly turned away; at which I caught at his arm and bade him not to disturb himself, to which he replied with the compliment that no gentleman could look upon such beauty as mine without the natural phenomenon which I had observed.

He then excused his nakedness by admitting that he regularly took himself to this remote place, when spring came, in order to bathe his body in the sun – a habit which he had brought back from a tour in Europe, where such behaviour is more common than in England. (I had already inferred this by the fact that his skin was a uniform brown colour, without those ridiculous white patches resultant from covering the centre of the body when in the open air.)

My rescuer now introduced himself as Jack Fortescue (I later discovered he was entitled to the sobriquet 'Honourable'), and I gave him my name; after which he kindly offered me his shirt, a fine silk garment which lay nearby, and which when I donned it gave me an almost respectable appearance. He meantime climbed into his breeches, somewhat to my regret, for he was a handsome figure; and having thus made ourselves moderately respectable we left the ruined chapel of the castle (for that is what it was) and made our way down the hill, leaving the tattered balloon still clinging to the tree into which it had fallen, for Mr Graham to recover as best he might.

Not far from the foot of the hill was an elegant manor house, where I was given a dish of tea while Mr Fortescue ordered a carriage to be prepared, for he intended (he said) to drive me back to Vycken: which indeed is what occurred – although by the time we arrived it was almost too dark for my young friend to see the road. We found Andy at home, waiting with confidence for my return – for (he said) it was impossible that even so harum-scarum an adventure could result in any injury to a lady so accustomed to unusual escapades as myself.

It was necessary for Mr Fortescue to stay with us for the night; and spending the evening in conversation we discovered that he was the squire of his parish (his father having died some time since) and was usefully knowledgeable about some of Andy's constituents – he was aware of course of my friend's position, and though of the opposite political persuasion was far from permitting that fact to interfere with a normal friendly relationship.

With some apologies for the lack of proper accommodation, we settled our new friend down upon the sofa in our small living room. I made a point of carefully explaining where my bedroom lay, and was awake for some time, believing that he might feel inclined to make a visit (and by no means repining at the thought, for the glimpse I had had of his body had convinced me of his desirability as a lover, and I was prepared to test his ability in that way). However, more than a little exhausted by my adventures, I fell asleep before he came, and waking in the morning was forced to the conclusion that he had decided to spend the night alone (though his involuntary reaction to my naked state had convinced me he was no eunuch).

He greeted us in friendly fashion next morning, and at breakfast invited us to attend the ceremony of beating the bounds, which would take place on the following day in his parish; it was (he said) an occasion of much interest to those who had never seen it – and, not only from a natural desire to respond to his politeness, but I confess from a continual interest in so charming a companion, I was pleased to accept; as, after a little persuasion, was Andy.

Chapter Five

The Adventures of Andy

None of the aspects of Sophie's aeronautical expedition were a surprise to me, for her courage has no more been in doubt than her capacity for discovering, in any crisis, a gentleman willing to assist her – and usually one in whom vigour and good will are combined with a prepossessing figure and face and a degree of admiration for herself.

So I was never in doubt that she would return safely from her flight, though I could not have foreseen Mr Graham's leaving her so dramatically, nor indeed her wreck at Restormel Castle. That romantic ruin (which once sheltered no less a hero than the Black Prince) can scarcely have seen in any previous age so remarkable a descent from the skies!

Mr Fortescue, who courteously drove her back to Vycken, was an agreeable young man whose devotion to Sophie was perhaps not quite so great as she initially believed, for he remained during the whole night upon the *palliasse* we arranged for him in our sitting room (I can say this with confidence, for, although the exterior walls of our cottage were of thick granite, not only did the stairs creak to a cacophony, but the interior walls were scarcely three inches thick, so that one could almost hear the breathing of a neighbour, let alone those excited gasps and exclamations which normally accompany the kind of activity which – from the brightness of her eyes – my friend had anticipated).

On the following morning breakfast was eaten in a somewhat more decorous manner than might have been the case had Mr Fortescue succumbed to my friend's charms; and only Jack's (for he invited us to address him by his forename) invitation to us to witness, on the following day, the ceremony of beating of the bounds cheered my friend, for while the celebration of a rustic custom offered little interest for one whose tastes are severely metropolitan by nature, another opportunity was thus to be offered for seducing him (and given her usual determination and charm, she was likely to succeed, even should his initial interest not be strong).

I will confess that my own fascination with local folk customs was well within the bounds of ecstasy – and indeed I was disposed to leave the field to Sophie, who would surely have more chance of success if alone with her new friend than if accompanied by myself; but making an opportunity to speak to me alone, Jack persuaded me that the occasion might offer me some objects of curiosity. Enquiring first whether I was betrothed to Sophie, or even more formally connected, and receiving a denial of the fact, he hoped that he had given no offence by not making more studious advances to her – for (he said) he fancied that she had expected them. But he must conserve his energies for the ceremony of the morrow, he went on; and on my raising an eyebrow he grinned and avowed that I would not be disappointed should I decide to accompany him.

So, on the following day Sophie and I rode out to a place one mile from Jack's home, to the eastward side of Restormel Castle, where already there was a group of local young men and maidens gathered about a stone which bore the legend 'Lostwithiel 1 M'. The company was all of ages (as I guessed) between seventeen and twenty-two or three. I looked around for children for, as far as I understood, the custom of beating the bounds was to take youngsters about the parish, and bending them over the milestones to administer a light blow to their buttocks which in goodwill would remind them of the boundaries within which they lived.

However, there were no youngsters of a tender age present, and when almost immediately upon our arrival Jack announced that the ceremony should begin he called out in the following terms: 'Have we an A?' A silence followed, whereupon he called, 'Have we a B?', to which again there was no response; and it was not until he reached the letter E that a young man held up his hand and confessed to possessing the name Ellacott, at which the question was asked, had he a beater? At this a young lady who had been jostling near him stepped forward with an air at once bashful and full of confidence, whereupon Jack procured from a nearby assistant a thin stick or switch cut if I am not mistaken from a hazel tree, and handed it to the girl with the words 'Beat thou the bounds!'

Two of the young men then took Mr Ellacott and, loosing his breeches, downed them. Then bending him over the boundary stone and throwing his shirt-tails over his head revealed a pair of pale buttocks (greeted by the girls present with a certain amount of nervous giggling). The young lady with the switch now stepped forward and administered a dozen blows to her friend's arse (not, I believe, with untoward violence, for, though each stroke left its red mark upon the pale skin, the victim neither cried out nor made any response other than a sort of wriggling which – despite his position – seemed redolent of pleasure rather than pain). The company clapped and counted in unison until the twelfth stroke had fallen, when to the cry 'Bounds are beaten!' the chap was up-ended and fell, a tangle of naked legs and disarranged clothing, upon the grass at the roadside.

I could not but note that on young Ellacott's rising he was careful to pull his shirt down between his legs before resuming his breeches, from which (whether with justice or not I cannot say) I inferred that he was in a state of some excitement; and indeed on our setting out to walk to the second stone, he and his friend, arm in arm, fell further and further behind us, until looking back I found they had vanished (as we were passing a wood which would give friendly shelter to a couple who wished to be more familiar with each other than public circumstances might permit).

On my remarking upon this to Jack, he replied that by the end of the afternoon I might well find our company more or less seriously depleted as to numbers; and on my asking whether it was only the male members of the company who were to be introduced in such an interesting manner to the boundaries of their parish, advised me to wait and see; and indeed at the next stone, it was a Miss Gurney who stepped forward, with a certain blushing charm, and turning towards it threw up her skirts without hesitation, revealing a delightful pair of plump, pleasing rosy cheeks which drew a round of applause from the male company – somewhat to the irritation of her friend, who despite being of tender years showed symptoms of jealousy which promised ill for their future relationship. I fancy he laid on with rather more enthusiasm than might have been expected by his victim, whose squeals however still seemed to me to be less expressive of agony than might have been expected from a genuine victim of ill treatment.

It was on the third stroke that the sound of hooves was heard approaching – a not unexpected phenomenon, since the milestone about which we were gathered was upon the main road between Lostwithiel and Liskeard, and thus some traffic might be anticipated. I expected the ceremony to be broken off – but no, the strokes continued, so that when a coach drawn by four horses rounded the corner and passed us close by, those passengers fortunate enough to be at the window had an admirable view of the proceedings – and indeed a cheer fell upon the air as the coach vanished.

This somewhat discomfited the victim, who was sufficiently irritated by the mirth of her punisher to lay hold of the switch on rising and with it direct a number of blows at his clothed posterior – at which he feigned more terror than he can have felt, and immediately fled, pursued by his friend, until they both disappeared behind the hedge which bordered the field beyond the lane in which we strode on.

'It is strange,' mused Jack as we walked on, 'how always at this spot we are overtaken, each year, by the Regulator – and how it is always a young woman who at the time is stretched over the stone!'

I did not find it especially strange – and neither, I fancy, did Jack, who on my enquiry revealed that the Regulator was one of two coaches which plied between Falmouth and London, the other being the Defiance. 'And I fancy,' he said, 'that there is to be trouble between them, for their competition is becoming more fierce than can long continue without tempers coming to a boil.'

As we walked, I questioned Jack as to the custom of beating the bounds, which he said was immemorial, though it had recently been revived after a period during which through the puritanism of a local parson it had fallen somewhat into desuetude.

'It may certainly be the case, as old Mr Jennings argued, that it is the remnant of behaviour common in a period less civilised than our own,' he said, 'and he did go so far as to permit a sort of travesty of the ceremony to be presented outside the church – but it was a sight too decorous for the livelier spirits among us, nor did anyone in the town believe that such a polite ceremony could properly mark a young person's entry into our fellowship with sufficient enthusiasm. Happily, our present parson is less concerned with the conventional proprieties, and holds to such old customs as this, the election of a boy bishop on Feast Days, carrying catkins on Palm Sunday, picking wrinkles on Good Friday, and so forth.'

'But these,' I said, 'are surely ceremonies less provoking than one which calls for so open a display of parts? – and surely some of the town boys and girls show a little hesitation in taking part?' I asked.

'A few are perhaps dissuaded by their parents from doing so,' he replied. 'Those parents who for some reason think it proper to dissuade their children for as long as possible from participation in those rites which conduct them from childhood into adult life. But even so, some of them sneak off and ask me to arrange a private ceremony of the sort, for they do not feel properly citizens of the place until it has taken place.'

'I begin to feel somewhat out of things,' I said, at which he gave me a look between sympathy and amusement – and at the next stone was astonished to hear him announce, 'We have an A!' – and to see him turn to Sophie and hand her the switch; whereupon he and another seized my arm, and in a moment I felt cold air about my fundament which spoke of the exposure of my bare bottom, while against my belly was the cold stone of the marker!

'Don' 'ee bever, now!' came the cry of a maiden – and from another 'Tes too boldacious!' – at which Sophie (understanding the meaning of the unexpected adjective without ever having heard it before) cried 'Not at all!' – and laid on.

I will not say that what followed was positively painful, and I was certainly aware that my friend was capable of much more violence than she demonstrated; nor can I say that the experience failed to convince me of the warming effect which it had had upon the young people who had previously undergone the treatment. And far from 'bevering' – the local word for shivering – I was all aglow by the time the third stroke had fallen.

'His bum be all bassomy!' came a cry from one girl – to which the response was a 'Shush!' from the others; though I could not but be conscious (not to any great shame) that they were all agog to see whether the rump of a 'foreigner' (as they called those from outside the county) was any different in complexion from that of their own men. Their conclusion, I believe, was that it was not.

To my amusement rather than embarrassment, I found that, as had obviously been the case with the other men, my yard, while not in such a state as to render me entirely ready for congress, was certainly through the effect of my beating swollen somewhat above its normal size, and I had some trouble in packing it away inside my breeches! I must confess that even had I been forced to divulge this, I would not have been unduly concerned, for the goodwill of the entire company was transparent. I had the idea of exposing Sophie to the same treatment, at the next stone; but nature intervened – for the sky had been getting darker and darker through storm-clouds beating up from the West; and before we reached the next boundary marker large drops of rain began to fall, which soon turned to a positive torrent – at which for a while everyone looked about them in some consternation, for we were well out in the country, and only the shelter of a hedge seemed to offer itself.

However, in a moment one of the boys signalled to the company to follow him; and upon doing so we found, at the end of a path which turned aside from the main walk, a small cottage to which the young man produced a key from under a flower pot near the front door. The place belonged (he said) to an aunt of his who was upon a visit to a sister of hers in Tywardreath town, some miles distant.

'Auntie surely wouldn' object to our shelterin' from the skeeny wind,' he said, and led the way in. We found ourselves in a small, snug parlour, plain but comfortable, with but a little furniture but (happily, in view of what later transpired) thick homespun rugs upon the floor.

The rain by now was falling with abandon, and even in the short run to the door we had all been soaked to the skin – and for a while stood about looking as melancholy as we felt. That is until Sophie, with that good sense which is one of her best attributes, remarked that we would catch our deaths should we allow our clothes to dry upon us, thus chilling us to the bone; and, giving an example, she peeled her dress from her and sat as naked as nature had made her in a chair next to a fire which the nephew of the place had by now lit.

It would be untrue to say that her example was immediately followed, nor that it was not to some degree regarded as 'bold', for as is generally the case the country folk show more modesty than would those of the upper station in life. But the girls were at last shamed by her cool demeanour – for she sat, breasts proudly jutting (lacking that false modesty which would have provoked some women to attempt to hide them by hugging a cushion, or some such) – and the envious glances of the boys – most of whom were young enough to have been her sons, or even grandsons! – provoked their female friends' jealousy. So in a short time first one and then the rest followed her example, and on Jack and I doffing our wet garments it was not long before the boys did the same, and with ease – for they wore merely shirts and breeches, while the girls were dressed in the lightest of clothing, which indeed through the wet had already clung so to their bodies that little was left to the imagination of the onlooker – and indeed (as the experienced will confirm) figures almost revealed are racier to the senses than any full revelation of nakedness.

The spectacle of half a dozen delightful maidens unclothed and in the first flush of youth was no more objectionable to me than (from their glances) to the other gentlemen present, most of whom I noticed had made a bundle of their shirts and placed them in their laps, no doubt thus hoping to conceal the nature of their interest in the spectacle before them.

We once more sat silent for a while, as though no one quite knew what to do; but then one young man spoke out. He was a fine, forward, muscular youngster who alone in the room did not concern himself with concealment, but sat, his thighs somewhat apart, and between them a prick which while still on the proper side of complete turgidity, through its nodding paid a sufficient compliment to all the females present, but in particular to my friend, who was seated opposite him.

'Why should not the ceremony continue?' he enquired. "Tis my turn next, for I'm Ford!' ('and the parson's son,' whispered Jack, at my side; which I had already suspected from his accent, which was superior to those of his friendly fellows).

'Since I have no perfect sweetheart,' said Jack, 'may I invite our visitor to remind me where I am?' Seizing the switch from Jack he handed it to Sophie, who I could see (being sufficiently familiar with her reactions) found him by no means a repulsive figure. I believe he apprehended this for, without more ado, he turned and, placing his hands upon the shoulders of the two youths who had been sitting upon either side of him, presented her with his rear – upon which, without further ado, she operated, no less to his pleasure than that of the girls in the room (who clearly considered him somewhat above himself, and supposed that he might profit from a beating – as could have been the case only were the cane wielded by a more implacable enemy than Sophie).

Standing as I was somewhat in front of young Ford, I could see the remarkable effect the strokes of the switch had upon him: which was that each one seemed to send a fresh pulse of blood through his veins and directly into his prick, which rose in jerks as each stroke fell upon his bare arse; so that upon the twelfth, when he straightened, a fine riding-muscle stood upright against his belly – and turning to Sophie he indicated it, and with a simplicity which could not give offence invited her to witness what she had done, and to ask herself whether it would be proper for her to decline to assist him in recovering from the state in which he found himself.

'Is it common practice?' she asked.

''Tis,' came the reply – and from one of the girls nearby, 'see, his pult gallops – he'm quiltering!' (which I later had interpreted as meaning that the young man's pulse was racing, and his heart fluttering with desire).

Sophie clearly felt that she could not deny responsibility for that state of affairs, and taking the young man by the hand looked about her – whereupon the nephew of the house stepped forward and whispered into her ear, when she led her partner from the room, doubtless to some bedroom of which she had been told.

Yet again, we sat and looked at each other for a while in silence, all the men (I dare swear) as aroused as I myself by the thought of what was progressing upstairs, but none knowing what to do. Finally, as might have been expected, it was Jack who broke the silence.

'Why,' he said, 'can we not offer Mr Archer the courtesy afforded to his friend? Come, Jessie, will you not oblige him?' (turning to one of the maidens, and by no means the least attractive) 'as you see, he is ready,' and he whisked my shirt from my lap, revealing my prick to be, while in no boastful state, certainly by no means in a condition of lethargy.

The young lady giggled and then, encouraged by her sisters, advanced and, sinking to her knees before me, bashfully laid a hand upon the instrument in question, whereupon it showed immediate signs of further growth and burgeoning.

'I'm afeared we've no other rooms,' the young nephew remarked; whereupon Jack replied that surely we were all friends? Jessie, who had been stroking my riding-muscle with her fingers in order perhaps to show her own disregard for the conventions, bent to place a kiss upon its head, which at the invitation released itself, bald and shining, from its topcoat of concealing skin.

The others began, I fancy, to feel somewhat out of things, and were soon paired off, there being (no doubt purposely) an equal number of men and girls. Jack himself laid claim to one of the most buxom, whose breasts were so generously proportioned as to threaten to smother him as she leaned over to kiss him!

My own partner was by no means modestly endowed as to her bosoms, and on my fixing my lips to a nipple which under their caress instantly swelled and hardened I found it no burden to fondle and kiss them, which I did with a sufficient enthusiasm to begin to repay her for coming forward – while an exploring palm discovered that between her thighs the muff which fell under my palm concealed a cave already so slippery as to reveal a provoking interest in what was going forward. No gentleman could have declined so strong an unspoken invitation, and falling to my knees and parting her thighs with my palms, I gently divided her lower lips with my fingers and with my tongue was able instantly to caress a phenomenon extraordinary in size – almost that of my little finger. It was immediately clear to me that this was the first time she had been paid such a compliment, for a loud squeal of pleasure split the air, and fixing her teeth in my shoulder she gave me a bite which made me jump.

I could not further prolong my attentions to her lower self, for so acute were the emotions my kisses had already aroused that a state almost of hysteria had resulted; so raising myself I substituted for my tongue that other feature most welcome to a lady's heart. There was no difficulty in doing so – not only through the glossiness of her flesh, but because there was no natural obstacle – the young lady clearly being no virgin. Nor however was she a practised votary in the courts of love, for she was clearly astonished that so close a communion was possible while she was sitting and myself kneeling between her legs: the lover who had taken her virginity had no doubt done so in the most conventional manner.

She did her best to receive me with enthusiasm: but of course in that posture it is impossible for the lady to move as freely as she may wish to do, and it was for myself through my own enthusiasm to contribute those motions which transmit pleasure through friction. Her puzzlement and even embarrassment lasted for only a moment, and was soon overcome not only by physical delight, but by the interest of the situation and the fact that she had only to glance down to be able to see with the utmost clarity my prick first entering then leaving her person – something which she had clearly never witnessed before, and a sight from which she found it impossible to avert her eyes, once it had been glimpsed. Indeed so keen was her interest that she could not resist carrying a hand to that area, and touching with a finger the gleaming column as it moved, shining with moisture.

I did my best to restrain my instinct, which was to plunge ahead with such enthusiasm as to complete the connection within minutes; but restraint was difficult not only through the eagerness and abandon of young Jessie, whose hands now played along my thighs, belly, breast and back – but through the tableaux by which we were surrounded, and from which it was not possible to avert my eyes: within two feet were Jack and his friend, he mounting her from the rear – and since they were side on to my view, offering me the most complete prospect of his prick entering and leaving her muff. The sight was only the counterpart of that which my partner was so closely observing, but was nevertheless a vision which could scarcely fail to contribute to my high spirits, which were further irritated by the fact that my friend was now busily exploring the cleft of my buttocks, her finger discovering the most intimate aperture there in a manner normally the prerogative only of the most knowing of lovers.

How could Jessie have acquired the knowledge that such a trick might not be unwelcome? I took my own hand behind, to catch at hers – for to be honest, the titillation she was providing was such that it would, if continued, bring our congress to a too premature conclusion. But to my surprise I felt a hand the back of which was covered with fine hairs – and on looking about caught the eye of a young person of my own sex, a dark, slim youngster who was lying propped up against the side of the sofa while his female friend's lips were busy about his nether regions. On catching my eye, he had the grace to blush, and was sufficiently discomfited to remove his finger from its probing – though only in order to insert his hand between my thighs and catch at my cods!

This was once again a lesson to me never to be surprised at the instinct which teaches even the most innocent the tricks of the oldest trade – or perhaps at the extent of the inquisitiveness of youth, for the boy concerned could not have been more than seventeen years of age, or even less; yet seemed more interested in the mechanics of my swiving than in the emotion which must surely have been conveyed by the pair of lips which even now were fixed to his own riding-muscle!

It would be supererogatory in me to bore the reader with a detailed description of the country copulatives at their exercise – yet I cannot refrain from stressing the fact that pleasure was the theme of the afternoon, for I did not see about the place even one pair in whom circumstances had aroused feelings either of shame or jealousy; and indeed while there were natural pairings, and in one or two cases couples remained faithful to each other, in other cases polymorphous perversity reigned, and it was even observable that a chap would as it were change horses in midstream, on the invitation of his partner (as shameless as he) leaving pleasuring her in order to transfer his attentions to another whose friend took his own place! The entire scene indeed was a tribute to innocent enjoyment; and upon our exhausting for the time our energies and lying in a tangle of disrobed limbs, Sophie and her young admirer descending from their own pleasure were perhaps a little envious, for it was clear from the proximity of the bodies that an enthusiastic debauch had taken place.

The young man indeed showed for the first time an instinct of resentment, and stepping over a couple of bodies bent over a girl who had fallen asleep with her cheek against the thigh of her satisfied partner, and shaking her by the shoulder seemed about to reproach her – though upon what grounds I cannot suppose, for even should she be his sweetheart, he had after all deserted her for my friend. Sophie indeed seemed about to intervene – but on waking, the young girl looked up with such innocent pleasure at the boy, and reaching up caressed his thighs and privates with such tender affection that his jealousy immediately subsided, and sinking to the floor he clasped her in his arms – whereat with that fortunate resilience of the female (who needs no time to recover from a bout of loving) she immediately set about rousing his spirits, so that in no time at all he was at attention – despite the fact that (as Sophie whispered to me) he had already twice sacrificed to Venus in her company. Such are the buoyant spirits of the young, further illustrated by the fact that, shown the example of their peers, the other members of the party soon threw off their lethargy and once more plunged into lascivious action, their enthusiasm even successfully communicating itself to their elders. Sophie was, I fear, somewhat dispirited because Jack turned his attention once more to another rather than herself, but was not displeased when courted – and successfully mounted – by the youngest member of the group. (With half an eye upon young Mr Fortescue, I must confess that I wondered whether a communication with him would be as satisfactory as my friend believed, for it seemed to me that he was perfunctory in the extreme in his attentions to his partner, and came a great deal too briskly for her convenience. However, that is something that Sophie must be allowed to find out for herself, should the circumstances permit it.)

It was now almost dark, and the rain had long since ceased, when Jack with some reluctance rose from the embrace of his partner and announced that the party must break up – even had we repaired to an inn for refreshment, the ceremony of beating the bounds would long since have ended, and the families of the participants would be curious as to the manner in which their time had been occupied.

'It may be,' he drily observed, 'that embarrassment will attend some who must invent a necessary explanation!'

We broke up, then, the cottage was put in order, the door locked. As we made our way homeward, Sophie was a little silent, and I suspected that though she had (and she assured me of the fact) nothing to complain of as to the warmth of the attentions of her rustic swain, she had clearly still not captured the heart of Mr Fortescue. He had however invited her to accompany him, on May Day, to the festival which would take place in Polpier, and to be his guest in the nearby manor house belonging to his uncle. This, she clearly supposed, would offer a further opportunity to make essay upon his affections – a battle she was determined to win.

Chapter Six

Sophie's Story

I am ready to confess that the little adventure which accompanied our beating of the bounds was by no means distasteful to me, not the least of its pleasure being my acquaintance with the parson's son.

In parenthesis, I have always noted – though I hesitate to put it forward as a rule, for fear of offending any readers who are members of the Established Church – that the sons of the clergy invariably make energetic and inventive lovers; and for that reason have always been a fervent antidisestablishmentarian, even though there is no evidence to show that ministers of the Church of England are particularly fervent in teaching their sons how best to administer the pleasures of the flesh. Indeed, I suspect that the opposite is true, and that human nature – with its instinctive reaction against any measures taken to curb a course which seems satisfactory to the senses – may be the reason for the observed phenomena.

But though the young gentleman of whom I speak was, considering his age and presumed inexperience, a remarkably elevating lover who adopted with enthusiasm any suggestion I cared to make for the heightening of our mutual pleasure, and though I was entirely pleased with his performance, it was not without a pang that on descending I found Mr Fortescue not only stripped for action, but clearly – through his enervated state – recently satisfied. The lineaments of his person, which I was able to observe on his participating in the brief orgy which followed, in no way fell short of my remembrance, either as to its chief and most prominent member, the suave platform of his breast and the flatness of his belly, or (on his revolving) as to the pert jutting of a handsome small arse, the curves of which so keenly affected me that I could almost feel the plump pleasure with which they would fill the palms of my hands.

The reader familiar with my past adventures will confirm that it is extremely rare for me to form such a violent predilection for a gentleman as to find my thoughts centred upon him to the exclusion of all others; but it is also the fact that very few gentlemen to whom I am attracted are not similarly drawn to myself, and that a mutual drawing together of minds generally results in a drawing together of bodies. Nor has 'love', in the romantic sense, much to do with the question. In common with the poet Shelley,

'I never was attached to that great sect,
Whose doctrine is, that each one should select
Out of the crowd a mistress or a friend,

And all the rest, though fair and wise, commend
To cold oblivion . . .'

In other words, I am for taking pleasure where it is offered. Though I make a point of avoiding, if possible, the beds of gentlemen to whom I have an antipathy, it is not necessary for me to hold a man in great affection in order to enjoy a lascivious passage with him. Affection is another matter: some of those for whom I feel it (though I must confess, few) are not among my favourite lovers; some I welcome to my bed with all the enthusiasm and interest which I can command (my friend Andy is a case in point).

In this case, I must admit that the attraction was a matter of simple lust – though Mr Fortescue was an amiable companion who I was delighted to call a friend. At all events, I was determined to gather him into my arms at the earliest possible opportunity – though of course without any action which would lay me open to the complaint of being lacking in the proper instincts of a lady.

That he was not entirely indifferent to me was clear from his inviting me (and Andy) to visit the village of Polpier in order to observe and take part in the festivities of May Day, which he said were celebrated with uncommon enthusiasm in that village.

We were to stay with Jack (as I may call him, for familiarity had by this time led to our addressing each other by our Christian names) at a manor house at Landavedy, on the hill to the west of the village – or small town, for it was a place of some six hundred souls, mostly engaged in the fishing and agricultural industries. Jack had inherited the farm at Landavedy from an aunt, and while he let the land to a Mr Randall, who farmed it with industry and enthusiasm, the house itself remained at his disposal, and he was given to staying there often in the spring and summer months, through its nearness to the sea, of which he was as fond – for swimming – as anyone not born in close proximity to it could be expected to be.

Landavedy Manor is delightful – a long, low-lying building with cool rooms and views over the English Channel. Andy and I were each provided with our own room (Jack having asked whether we wished to share a bed, and having been assured by myself with perhaps more vehemence than was strictly necessary that this was not the case).

The village consists of a collection of houses which seem to have been dropped rather than placed in position within a deep valley between tall, abrupt and rugged hills, between which a rapid rivulet dances in and out among the dwellings till its voice is lost in the waters of a tidal haven thronged with fishing boats and guarded by a peak of serried rock.

The people of the place seemed extremely friendly, and greeted Jack with enthusiastic pleasure – especially the young men and women among them, our friend being (as we had already discovered) clearly of such a disposition as to make an amiable relationship with himself easy of access. The villagers were busily decorating their houses against the morrow (for our first view of the place was upon the thirtieth of April) with bunting and ribbons. On my commenting that they seemed to eschew the more natural materials offered by the rich hedgerows, I was told that early upon May morning the children and younger adults would go forth into the countryside and fetch home branches of narrow-leaved elm, or flowering whitethorn buds, both of which are locally called 'May', and which would be used to put the finishing touches to the decoration.

Retiring to Landavedy Manor, we had a good dinner, and Jack, producing first a bottle of liquor made from Dutch gin in which the fruit of sloes had been steeped for some months – a drink as delightful as it is intoxicating – announced that he had a favour to ask, which was each year required of some knowledgeable stranger.

It was the custom (he explained) that on every May Day a May Queen and May King were selected from among the virgins of the village (male and female) who were of a proper age to taste the fruits of love but who (as far as the closest possible observation could tell) had refrained 'til then. Crowned with all ceremony beneath the may pole, they were then expected to celebrate the rites of love together to 'bring in the May'.

This was a couple, he said, naturally drawn to each other – for a mutual interest was a prerequisite of their taking part in the ceremony. However (he said) most of the people of this village were (however enthusiastic and naturally adept in making their living) ignorant of any attempt to educate their children in what was expected of a bride and groom, and it was necessary that some demonstration should be given if they were to join together without embarrassment or impediment (the latter being likely, it was believed in local superstition, seriously to injure the prospects of a good harvest). Each year, therefore, someone must introduce the tyros to the pleasures of love upon the morning of the Feast, in order to circumvent the problems already advertised.

'I hope that you may be persuaded,' Jack said, 'to help us in this manner?'

So kind and hospitable had he been, and so welcoming the villagers, that it would have been churlish in the extreme to decline the honour. I therefore immediately acquiesced – as indeed did Andy. There was however some small difficulty in his case, for Jack, after a little mumbling, explained that, through age-old custom of the place, he himself had what he called the *droit de seigneur*, a French term which related to the days when in areas of France the local overlord had the right to take the maidenhead of every virgin living upon his territory.

Things were, Jack explained, not so ordered here; nor indeed would he wish to force himself upon any young female; but, since the local society expected it, he must conform to the general rule that the Lord of the Manor of Landavedy should himself escort the May Queen into the realms of love.

With something of an ill grace Andy accepted the explanation; and with an inward sigh, so did I, wishing, I must confess, that I was the young person who would be introduced to the pleasures of love by that remarkably personable young gentleman, our host. However, my own maidenhead had ceased long ago to be a negotiable property, so I must simply endure a situation that could not be cured.

Having finished dinner, we sat late – indeed so late and with such good conversation that, before I knew it, the clock was within ten minutes of midnight – upon which Jack remarked that we should set out.

On my expressing surprise, he merely hurried us into the lane and down towards the village, which – the evening being considerably advanced – seemed remarkably lively, it usually being the case that villagers in remote quarters of the country retired early (candles at the time of which I write being too expensive for most people in the lower station of life to afford, and rush lighting being of so indifferent a quality as to make it a positive denial of pleasure to attempt to sit by it).

However, as I have remarked, there seemed to be uproarious meetings in almost every house. On my questioning him, Jack remarked that this was all a part of the May celebrations, which had been from time immemorial an important festival in the county, second only to those of Christmas and Midsummer.

As we passed into the little main street, a clock in the distance struck the hour of twelve, and from a public house fifty yards away immediately was expelled a small but lively crowd of youths, some bearing fiddles, others drums, which sprang straightway into a remarkably cacophonous tune which bore no resemblance to music I had ever heard! This band immediately set out down the street, knocking upon each door as it was reached, whereupon the said door would immediately be thrown open and the company greeted with a bowl of some kind of liquid.

On our enquiring what entertainment this was, Jack remarked that it was the first greeting of May – and on my expressing an interest in the bowls of liquor, he called upon a housekeeper who was kind enough to offer us a taste of what was called 'junket', made of raw milk and rennet with sugar and cream – by no means unpleasant. But this was not all – every housekeeper in the place had also laid in stocks of heavy cake (composed of flour, cream and currants), and also of sloe and elderberry wines and great jars of metheglin or mead – so that the band of young men, as we followed it, became by the minute merrier and merrier, and was joined by a number of girls, none of whom seemed inclined to sobriety. On reaching the quayside, where a brisk wind from the sea was enlivening without being sufficiently cold to be disturbing to the system, the band stuck up more recognisable music, and dancing began – four-handed, six-handed and eight-handed reels, riotous quick-steps, all danced with a joy and abandon untiring.

The behaviour of the young people, while delightfully free and open, was to no serious extent lascivious – though, as I remarked to Jack, by now in London a much more considerable degree of freedom would have been notable. He replied that it was considered improper to indulge in corporeal pleasures until the night of May Day itself, after the May King and Queen had taken joy of each other.

It was by now one o'clock, and having taken part in one of the dances, for form's sake, we retired to Landavedy Manor and our beds, from which it was to be necessary to rise early in order to continue our observation of the rites of May. Indeed only some five hours later, I was aroused by the sound of singing and shouting, and the day being clear and sunny I rose and walked down towards the village.

Halfway down Landevady Lane, beside the stream, I heard, then saw, a group of youngsters coming towards me, each appearing to carry a bucket, and singing in concert a song which had as its main burden the words 'The first of May is dipping day!' On their coming up with me, I gave them a greeting, which they laughingly returned. They pointed at me in what seemed an accusatory manner and asked, 'Where is your May?'

I did not properly know how to reply, though, after noticing that each of the six boys and girls wore a piece of hawthorn about their person I soon learned that it was the custom to duck with water any person found without such a distinguishing feature about their dress!

There was some movement to forgive me, since I was a stranger and unaware of local ways; but one youth in particular, a dark handsome boy with fine black ringlets hanging about his shoulders, was unregenerate in arguing that only evil could come of not keeping to the custom – and finally, though without violence, upended his bucket, drenching me from head to foot with water.

This was no great trial, for I had on only a light dress (the morning being as mild as such spring mornings can be in the west of England); and it was almost worth the slight inconvenience to witness the manner in which the three boys' eyes widened at the spectacle I now presented. The material of my dress was plastered against my body, making each contour more notably smooth than before, especially where the wet cloth was spread over my bosom, the nipples of which were roused by the cold water into sharp points.

One boy in particular – that darkest and most handsome of them – seemed to find it almost impossible to speak, being, as I took it, caught between fear of having offended a lady whose sensitivities might be considerably more tender than those of a village maiden, and a shyness born of his having been unlikely ever to have been in the presence of one such. Indeed, stepping forward, he made a clumsy bow and hoped that I had not been offended by their 'village fun' as he called it.

My smiling response put the small group at its ease, and in a moment the boisterous young people set off in search of other victims, leaving me to return to the house (fortunately not far distant), where meeting Jack in a corridor he remarked that I had obviously received my May greeting, and, on my suggesting that he might have been so good as to warn me, said that that would not have been according to custom. I could not but be conscious that his eyes were no less drawn to my bosom than those of the young admirers of the village, and hoped for an embrace; but he passed on.

By the time I had changed into some dry clothes, a positive procession of youths and maidens had come up the lane and into the little yard of the house, where a rough band was performing upon May whistles known as feepers or pee-weeps – made of sycamore branches, the bark of which had been removed and shaped into a pipe which let out a somewhat melancholy peep.

The May having been brought home (as they termed it), the villagers dispersed for a day's work – for being but humble they could scarcely afford to give over ten hours' labour for merry-making; and Andy and I spent our day quietly.

At six of the evening Jack came to escort me to the village. I had, at his request, dressed myself simply – and he wore merely a shirt and breeches, without the handsome topcoat he usually affected – for, he said, it would be easy to overawe the young persons we were to educate, and a first impression must be persuasive and kindly if everything was to go off well.

Upon the quay a large number of people were assembled, including many of the elders of the village as well as the youngers (though no absolute children). On our being seen, a signal was given, and the moment we had taken our places upon a natural rock or promontory above the Three

Pilchards Inn a little procession appeared from the direction of the hills. Four young men bearing upon their shoulders a pole decked with May and with ribbons set this into a barrel filled with stones placed just before us. To my surprise, upon its upward point was set a carving which could only represent one thing – viz., the erect masculine organ.

This drew no reaction at all even from the ladies present, and the whole ceremony indeed was taken to be a most serious one, the villagers regarding the May Pole with as much solemnity as it had ever been regarded before the days of King Charles, when it was the centre of similar ceremonies throughout the whole land – but now seems only to be seen in such remote places as this.

Below the May Pole an elder of the village now stood forward, a fisherman with a great white beard dressed in a long garment of knitted wool, holding by one hand a maiden and by the other a young man – who I recognised as the dark fellow I had met that very morning when I had received my ducking. These were as simply dressed as we – the young man in a white shirt and trousers, the maiden in a simple white shift; and they stood before us as one might expect a bride and groom to stand before the altar.

But now we too stepped forward – whereupon the old man mumbled a few words in some strange tongue (which I later found to be the ancient language of Cornwall, which few now spoke, but a few tangled phrases of which were used at ceremonial occasions such as this).

Upon a word which sounded like *omgara*, and which I later found to be the instruction to love one another, we stretched out our hands, which were taken by the young couple, the girl (I could see from my eye's corner) without enthusiasm, the young man with rather more warmth. The motley village band (never far from the centre of the crowd) struck up its bawling again, and amid applause – some of it, I am bound to say, accompanied by what sounded very like ribald remarks, though in so thick an accent (or perhaps so strange a language) as to be incapable of my understanding – we were escorted into what seemed a barn, but was actually a loft for storing nets. These had been piled into one corner, and a large mattress (consisting of several laid together and covered with a single covering) lay upon the floor.

I must confess not to have expected to perform so delicate a task as had been entrusted to me in the same room, and upon the same bed, as Mr Fortescue was to recline with the maiden entrusted to his care. Moreover, though I am not easily embarrassed, I must confess that the occasion demanded more *sang froid* (as the French put it) than I felt fully possessed of. Nor did the young gentleman seem likely to be of much assistance for, while his eyes were bold, their brightness did not for the moment support action, and for a while we both stood like ninnies, merely looking at each other, and avoiding any glance at the bed which occupied much of the floor of the room (and was therefore indeed difficult to avoid!).

However, there was no use in simply standing,

and indeed our companions had paved the way, for without ceremony Jack had thrown off his clothes and without further ceremony had precipitated his companion onto the mattress, where he was was at that very moment in course of lifting her shift above her head (revealing a body sufficiently attractive to take the eye of any young man, and which certainly took the eye of my companion). Bold action always being the best solution either to indifference or to misdirected attention, I took the step of reaching for the hem of my dress and lifting it over my head, which left me bare as a needle, and immediately an object of the most particular interest to the young man, whose eyes played over my body with an even keener apprehension than they had when it had previously been almost as fully exposed to his gaze through the adherence of wet muslin!

He still made no move, however; and once more it was my responsibility to take a further step, which I did by stepping forward, pulling his shirt free of the waistband of his breeches, and passing my hands beneath it pulling him to me in an embrace which could leave him in no doubt that I would be sympathetic to any approach he cared to make.

The signal was immediately recognised for what it was, and his grasp became warm and full and so close that I found some difficulty in breathing. Nor was there any doubt of his interest, for against my upper thigh (we were much of a height) I felt the pressure of something which could only be an indication of fervour – but which could be of no use to either of us while the closeness of our embrace was continued; so I did my best to free myself, and finally did so by attempting to draw his shirt over his head – when reluctance to release me was finally overcome by his desire to be free of any encumbrance which separated my skin from his own. Nor did my suggestion – conveyed by palms slid downward from his waist – that his breeches should also be removed fall upon an unwilling sensitivity, and in less than no time the offending garment had indeed been disposed of. Before any further movement or remark could be made, we were once more in a close embrace – though this time a not inactive one, for moved by a passion which needed no instruction the young gentleman began to press kisses upon my brow, my lips, my ears, my neck, my shoulders and, on my showing no sign of repining, upon my breasts, which he evidently found exciting to a positive fault, for he seemed ready to consume them like exotic fruit, licking them with his tongue, mumbling them with his lips, and even nipping them with his teeth – though happily with a tenderness which ensured that no damage was done!

My own hands had, meanwhile, not been inactive; on his lowering his head to my bosom they had slipped from the nape of his neck, where delightful black curls lay, along the length of a spine dinted with tiny protruberences, to the bifurcation which marked the swelling of a tight, round arse the globes of which, when I stretched to encompass them with my hands, fitted my palms to perfection; and on my fingers brushing their convex surface, a gasp shook the young man's entire body, and he straightened up so suddenly as almost to strike me beneath the chin with the top of his head!

He was all confusion at this, and made to apologise; but I stopped his lips with my tongue – and in turn I now lowered my head and planted kisses upon two charming tits, at the centre of which were tiny pellets of flesh sufficiently hard as almost to graze the lips! The muscular surface of his breast was covered with skin which, though so brown as to suggest a lifetime of working in the open, was smooth as velvet and entirely as pleasant to the touch as that of the swelling breasts of any girl (and I speak as one to whom the embraces of my own sex are not unknown, though by no means as habitually enjoyed as those of men).

It was now my privilege, sinking to my knees, to examine his person further. If his breast was as hairless as a girl's, so indeed was his belly, only the slightest sprig of tender hair lying there, though thickening slightly below where a prick as adamant as iron now pressed against my cheek. That a young lady should ever take that object between her lips had never, I believe, occurred to my new friend – as I could tell from the incredulous gasp he gave and the delighted tightening of every muscle about his body, but particularly those of his arse and loins, which took place the moment the action was performed, his prick itself leaping with such astonishment as positively to jump from its unexpected place of retirement and thwack against his belly! – whence however he did not object to my recovering it with my fingers and replacing it in the soft, warm receptacle from which it had so ungratefully escaped!

That the young man was not entirely devoid of good sense was now evidenced by the slow shuffle with which he began to move backwards towards the bed, upon which he collapsed so suddenly as again to break all contact between us. However, I now laid myself at his side, and, rejecting his attempt to clasp me once more in his arms (for it was my duty to offer him the utmost extent of pleasure I could, in order that later he might communicate it to his Queen), I pressed him upon his back to the sheets and once more bent to my pleasant task.

There is surely nothing more pleasing in life than making love to an innocent young person of the opposite sex! That parents and guardians should so fail in their duty to their children as not to ensure that their education in this area of life is complete fills me at once with pity and horror. If I had my way, every school in the land would instruct young persons in the arts of love from the earliest age. The young gentleman I now had the pleasure of instructing, for instance, must have been of the age of seventeen or eighteen, and yet had clearly been offered no previous advice upon the subject of conversation between the sexes – though at least he had, perhaps, been encouraged thoroughly to cleanse himself, for his entire body was sweet and clean (though this may have been from continual bathing in the sea, which here in Cornwall continues through the chilliest winter months, obviating the necessity of heating water for baths – a luxury which can neither be afforded in terms of time or coal). It is, by the way, my experience that many country people are more cleanly in their persons than those of the town, the interstices of whose bodies are too frequently cloyed with stale scent, if not worse. But his were certainly free of that muck with which both ladies and gentlemen too frequently dab their persons, often using perfume – as it seems to me – to disguise an odour grown too clinging from lack of the application of hot water and soap.

But I digress.

My young gentleman, while a stranger to such caresses as I offered, failed to lodge any objection to my continuing them; and indeed relaxed so completely as to suggest to me that his talents as a lover might be great – a reluctance to tolerate a lascivious toying being an early signal of lack of sensory appreciation in a lover. There is of course also the possibility, especially should the lady concerned be slim and light, that any undue movement or jumpiness while she is atop her lover might result in her being thrown off – and I have known some unfortunate accidents, viz. one wittily commemorated in a couplet, by my friend Andy:

That elegant man my Lord Quegg
had a body as bald as an egg:
His mistress one night
in a flux of delight
fell off him and fractured a leg.

But once more, I digress.

My young friend clearly found my endeavours entirely satisfactory, though I speedily discovered that the action which most delighted him was in my applying my tongue to that most sensitive of places immediately between the anus and the cods, and passing it over and around those cods, then up the entire length of his prick (which, as I see I have failed to remark, was an instrument as impressive for thickness and length as in rigidity) until, reaching its engorged helmet, my lips for a moment could lie about the whole head, pursing in a final kiss before descending to repeat the journey. This journey having been undertaken a number of times, indeed the tightness of the aforementioned cods, together with an audible moan, the springing of a single small globe of moisture from the tiny aperture which threaded the length of his cock, and a sudden tightening of the muscles of the anus (which with a forefinger I was at the time tickling) betrayed the swift approach of a climax – whereupon I applied finger and thumb just below the helmet, and by an immediate pressure avoided too speedy a consummation – another axiom in which a proper education should instruct every young gentleman eager not too quickly to pass the apogee of pleasure before his partner is satisfied.

As I waited for the wave of pleasure somewhat to subside from my partner's body, my eye fell upon the two figures which reclined within feet of where we lay; I had of course been conscious of their presence, but my attention to my task together with my pleasure in it had distracted me from any close observation. Now, to my astonishment, I saw that Jack merely lay asleep at the side of his young friend, his cock squab and limp, a little snail's trace of liquid falling from its tip across his belly the only sign that excitement of any kind had recently affected either it or himself.

Not surprisingly, the girl at his side was perplexed and even angry – she had evidently been observing our activities with an envious eye, for all she had been the object of (as was clear from the situation) was a sudden attack, and a victory – for Jack – equally hurriedly enjoyed, leaving her perfectly unsatisfied.

She could not but see that I apprehended her distress, and as our eyes met a tear sprang to hers, together with a mute appeal which positively demanded a response from any female cognizant of the circumstances.

Stretching out my hand, I reached for hers, and, as Mr Fortescue continued his slumber, drew her towards us. My male companion was somewhat amazed at this, and I believe was about to protest that it was much against the custom of the village when I stopped his lips with a kiss, and persuaded the girl to recline at our side, her head towards his feet. By gently thrusting his head downwards, I suggested that he should pay the delightful child the compliment which I had lavished upon him.

While I do believe such an action would not have occurred to him before the present time, he was as quick off the mark as any naturally interested young man – and if in the first place driven more by inquisitiveness than anything else, he proved (once by a little cry of pleasure she had signified more than assent) eager to give pleasure – almost too eager, as it seemed to me, to transfer his attentions from my person to that of our new companion! Placing his cheek upon one slim thigh, he set his lips and tongue immediately to work – and the result was entirely satisfactory: indeed within a very short time a natural instinct had led him to just that area of the girl's lower parts most profitably complimented by kissing, and her pleasure was expressed in a cry of delight so marked as to seem almost one of pain. Yet he did not for a moment cease his ministrations except (and it immensely amused me that he should be so quick to devise a scheme which countless lovers had previously discovered) to reverse his body – somewhat to my personal inconvenience – and throw his leg over his friend's body so that, kneeling astride her person, he was able to continue his caresses while placing his own portions in just such a position that they were suspended above her – to which her lips, tongue and fingers could give most delight, that is had she for a moment been aware what was expected of her.

Well, if Jack had not the wit properly to instruct a partner, it was clearly my duty to do so; and, leaning so that my lips were at her ear, I whispered a hint to the young lady, who was so ingratiated by her lover's pleasuring that for a moment no sense could be made of any words spoken to her; but on my taking her hands and conveying them to his prick, she was quick to incline it downwards so that she could first shyly kiss its marbled surface, but then positively consume it with kisses – which had the effect of his redoubling his own efforts to give her pleasure.

The spectacle was one as warming as it was delightful: two young persons at the height of beauty engaged in the act for which they were created provide a subject which has entranced the finest artists throughout the ages. I am as susceptible as the next person to the appeal of the subject, and if I had been looking forward to the final embraces of my pupil I now felt sadly deprived of them.

However, as I raised my eyes, I saw that Mr Fortescue had awakened from his doze, and that the sight which had met his gaze had had its effect even upon so recently collapsed a prick; for that instrument was now once more in an engorged state, and indeed was being rendered if anything yet more adamant by the flattering application of his own fingers.

A mixture of lust and anger at his failure properly to instruct his pupil drove me to action: and, raising myself, I threw my leg over his body and mounted him with all the swiftness and determination with which a jockey mounts a recalcitrant steed, impaling himself with (I must boast) perfect aim upon his cock.

No doubt the result would have been the achievement of a meridian as speedy as that provoked during his passage with the young lady had he not so recently been relieved of goatishness; now, however, he was at least somewhat able to endure the act for somewhat longer, and, rising and falling in the saddle, I was able to prolong the action at least until I myself was satisfied.

In the meantime, observing my action, the young person at my side (knowing no better, or perhaps requiring no better example) had undertaken a similar action. Suddenly sitting up, she had thrown her partner off his balance, and as he sprawled upon his back had taken up an attitude similar to my own – which her lover made no protest at; and indeed, in a display of natural lechery which promised well, made himself free of her breasts, which now hung like apricots within reach of his caresses.

Jack, for a second time brought off, fell into a state of exhaustion which made further adventure out of the question; the young people, however, almost immediately recovered, and – for I understood we were expected to occupy the whole night in our instructions – I was able to demonstrate to them a few more tricks which would enliven the passage towards harbour, to show them some of the many ways there are of coming into port, which both the fisherman (as he was) and his mistress eagerly embraced and were happy to spend time practising; for falling at last into a light sleep, when from time to time I awoke during the hours of darkness, I saw by the light of a candle their bodies in any number of poses – some of them so adventurous as to prove impossible of persisting, others tried and trusted by lovers for generations but rediscovered in experiment by these latest recruits to Eros's army.

Before dawn, I did fall into a deeper sleep; and awoke to a kiss – which proved to be from the lips of the young lover, as a gesture of thanks for my assistance; a congratulation in which he was joined by the pretty young girl at his side, now drawing on that garment so ungraciously stripped from her by . . .

But on looking about me for Jack, I found him absent; he had slipped away while I slept, no doubt ashamed to have had his own lightly regarded task taken over by myself, and fearing the rebuke I would certainly have administered had he still been present; for I was full of concern for those other maidens who, almost raped, as it were, by so sudden an approach as his, might even to this day be unaware of the niceties of amorous embrace.

The thanks of my friends sweetened my temper, however; and before the village had properly awakened, we slipped from the room, and away. I took myself back to Landavedy Manor, where I found Andy already up and gone, and got my possessions together and departed; for any further encounter with our host could only, I felt, be embarrassing. If I could not entirely dismiss from my mind my former admiration of my host, I could comfort myself that I seemed to have lost nothing by missing his embraces.

Chapter Seven

The Adventures of Andy

After witnessing the little ceremony on the quay at Polpier, I made my way back, somewhat short of temper, to Landavedy. One would really have thought that Mr Fortescue, in view of the fact that I was no less his guest than Sophie, might have deferred his own part in the ceremony and made me free of it. However, what could not be cured, I must endure – and while he no doubt enjoyed the first-fruits of the extremely pretty girl whose hand he had taken, I went to my lonely bed – for apart from any difficulty of persuasion, the only female in Fortescue's house was three times my age and several times my weight, and did not commend herself as an intimate friend.

I decided immediately to leave the manor early the next morning; for I did not trust myself not to bring up the topic in conversation with our host, and that could only lead to tears. So rising at five, when the sun was already well up, I saddled and rode for Penruddock, leaving a note for Sophie that I had been called away. (Her bed was unoccupied, from which I supposed that her night had been a hardworking one, and that her task was still continuing – pleasantly enough, I trusted, the young man with whom she must occupy herself seeming sufficiently virile to satisfy a temperament which I knew to be volatile).

Arriving home – as I may call our cottage – by ten o'clock (having paused at Lostwithiel to break my fast upon a crust and a bowl of milk), I found the house as I thought unoccupied – but, venturing to look into Purity's room, discovered her still abed (when the cat is away, the mouse will naturally be expected to remain somewhat longer in her nest).

It was by no means an unattractive vision which met my eyes: the young person lay upon her back, the blanket beneath which she slept thrown aside from the upper part of her body (no doubt from the warmth of the night), one hand lying across her breast, the fingers however parted so that a pink nipple showed between them, while the other breast was quite uncovered save for a curl of jet black hair which lay across it, emphasising the whiteness of the bosom – still further enhanced by the brownness of her shoulders and arms, exposed daily to the elements.

The blanket lay across her waist – and yet somewhat below it, for the deep dint of her navel was exposed, and the shallow hillock of her small, round belly, which rose and fell so rapidly that I felt it necessary to tear my eyes away and regard her face, for surely such an agitation of breathing could only result from wakefulness and the knowledge that she was observed?

Her eyes however appeared to be entirely closed, though a low sigh escaped her sleeping lips, which seemed to smile; and her hand slipped from her breast, which now lay completely exposed, and no less beautiful in its nakedness than when it had been partially concealed.

My eyes once more gliding down the length of her body, I took a quiet step forward and gently laid a hand upon the edge of the blanket nearest her person, lifting and folding it back until she was entirely open to my delighted view. It was not, of course, a landscape entirely foreign to me; yet this was the first time I had observed it at leisure – for in the heat of battle the terrain is explored only so much as is necessary to the occupation of it, and those passages of love which I had enjoyed with Purity had been notable more for the skirmishing than for any scouting of the topography.

No cartographer however could have failed to admire the landscape which now lay before me: the shapeliness of the hills – first the gentle curve of the lower slopes of the two most notable, rising to twin peaks which resembled little pebbles, then the low-lying swell of a more subtle foothill, to the south, its centre marked by a dark and shadowy pit, a little fold of skin lying about its declivity . . .

Then, below, the beginnings of a dark thicket, at first no more than brush or furze, but gradually becoming a curling tangle of undergrowth below which could be discerned the opening to a lush cave, the outer walls of which were of a gentle pink, though shading almost to a purple within.

No gentleman imagining himself in my place will doubt that, having been deprived of a promised satisfaction the previous night, I was roused by the vision; nor was my enjoyment of it lessened by the knowledge that were I to attempt a closer inspection than the merely ocular, my approaches would give rise to no protest even should the lady wake during the course of it. I therefore silently doffed my shirt and breeches, and kneeling at the side of the bed placed a light kiss upon the entrance of the tempting grotto.

At first there was no discernible result – other, I mean, than my own pleasure, the slight saltiness which met my palate, and the further swelling of my prick, now somewhat uncomfortably pressed against the side of the bed.

But upon my applying my tongue first to the outer lips of the cavern and then, softly parting them with my fingers, to the inner walls and that small nut-like protruberance which was suspended (as it were) from the front roof of the cavern, there was a stirring, and the loins of the sleeping maid were thrust upward as though imploring more lively attention – which I did not hesitate to give, licking and thrusting with my tongue until, after a rather shorter period of time than might have been expected, a shiver was followed by a shuddering and a final leap, signalling the acme of pleasure; and the reader will not be surprised that, on my raising my head and glancing upward, I met a pair of wakeful and delighted sparkling black eyes.

Purity made no exclamation (her taciturnity upon such occasions was a delight, for nothing is less attractive to me than the continual stream of endearments some women feel it a necessity to expel from lips which would be more rewardingly occupied elsewhere). Raising herself upon her elbows, she puckered forth those charming, pink lips, upon which it was my pleasure to plant a kiss – while with her hand she confirmed the obvious: that while I had accomplished her pleasure, my own was still to come. Her smile was at once an acknowledgement of my condescension and a promise that it should be rewarded; and in a moment she had turned about, and now was upon all fours, her head and shoulders buried in her pillow – those mischievous eyes however still aglitter – while her rump was elevated, a plump and pleasing pear-shaped arse poised in just such a position as was both tempting and convenient.

I wasted no time in clambering upon the bed and disposing myself behind the delightful minx in just such an attitude as was invited, whereupon with that candour for which she was marked she reached for my prick and placed its tip just within those lower lips which were ready to receive it (for my attentions had rendered them, no less from my saliva than from the extrusion of those liquors which were the signal of her own satisfaction, lubriciously slippery).

There was no need for me to thrust home: for with a delicious wriggle and the slightest movement rearwards, she swallowed me whole (as it were), at the same time giving a little cry of pleasure which reassured me – had it been necessary – that her own enjoyment was not diminished as a result of her previous indulgence (she was not one of those women whose artificial squeakings and pantings counterfeit a pleasure they do not feel).

My former experience with the girl had taught me that once roused, she was no laggard; and thus my own instinct – which was towards an immediate satisfaction, so roused was I – need not be frustrated, and with a very few strokes I unburdened myself of my immediate passion, though not of my affection for young Purity (whose nature, no less than her person, was sufficiently warm to engage my sympathy); so drawing her up, I embraced her as she sat astride my knee, my now shrinking manhood slowly withdrawing from the warm cave into which it had been so generously welcomed.

Somewhat tired from my early rising and from my journey, and having made sure that the girl was provided with a bed infinitely more comfortable than the straw hassock which had formerly been her lot, I had no hesitation in curling into a sleep; nor did Purity see any reason why housework should predominate over the opportunity for a little further rest – and so we lay entangled for the duration of an hour or so, after which at my wish (though with some little complaining) she rose and made me a dish of food.

While I was eating it, a knock upon the door announced Treweers, who brought a letter from Frederick Couch Esq., of Liskeard, whose name I recognised as one of those who had originally proposed me as Member of Parliament for the borough for which I sat. His letter was brief (the man was curt in expression as in manner): 'Should you not, as our Member and a magistrate, do something about the enclosed?'

'The enclosed' was a cutting from *The West Briton* of that week's date:

> 'The farmers of Liskeard are complaining much of the depredations committed on them since the establishment of a beer-shop in the town, which we are informed is kept open long after the time prescribed – frequently with music and dancing. We are assured that dancing &c was kept up the week before the last until four o'clock on the Sunday morning.'

I sent Treweers immediately to the post with a reply that I would of course look into the matter; and indeed it somewhat intrigued me – particularly '&c'; what amusements could the gentlemen of Liskeard find so enlivening as to make them perilously loud until four in the morning? I therefore took myself off that very afternoon to Liskeard – no more than a couple of hours' riding, at a decent rate – and there put up at Webb's Hotel, a place I remembered well as that in which I spent my first night after election as Member of Parliament (and from whose balcony, indeed, my triumph had been first announced to the world).

Wilkins, the landlord, raised an eyebrow when, having dined, I bought him a glass of his own brandy and then enquired about the beer-shop.

'And who might have been complaining about it?' he asked, and, on my telling him, he laughed.

'I'm not surprised to hear it!' he said. 'Old Couch

is a thorough-going Methodist – by which I don't mean that there aren't members of that sect as liberal in their tolerance of the pleasures of others as they are determined in their own indifference to them. Couch however – well, the moment he hears the sound of laughter he sends for the hangman. He will have planted that complaint in the *Briton* with the help of a donation towards the editorial expenses.'

'So what of the beer-shop?' I asked.

'Why not go and see for yourself?' said Wilkins – with a wink which seemed to suggest that I would not find any research to be done in the matter either arduous or uninteresting. Having given me directions, he returned to his bar – and I took myself off through the town, remarking as I did so that no young man could be blamed should he feel that Liskeard needed a little spice in order to make residence there tolerable. Oh, in some ways it is an admirable town – with for instance a handsome church, the second largest in the county. But one cannot spend all one's time in church, and there was little else to offer either by way of amusement or elevation of the senses.

The address which I had been given was at the southern end of Torhay Street, which dived at a steep rate from the top of the town to the bottom, so that in descending it one's stride naturally quickened until the hill decanted one almost without effort into the doorway of the beer-shop.

There will be some among my readers whose idea of this particular beer-shop will be founded upon quite a false premise. In general, the term does not raise great expectations as to elegance or even cleanliness. The house in whose doorway I now found myself was, however, to the outside view eminently respectable, its windows clean, its woodwork freshly painted, its step white and brisk with scrubbing, and its brass knocker – which I now plied – positively sparkling.

It did not seem to me that the noise which issued forth from the windows was such as to give concern to neighbours, and my feeling was confirmed by the speed with which the door was opened to my perfectly ordinary knock. A pleasant-looking servant in a clean apron, without asking my name, gestured to me to enter, and on my doing so took my hat and cane without remark, then pointed me to an open doorway through which I stepped.

The scene which met my eyes was almost metropolitan in its air of civilised enjoyment: two young men sat before a couple of glasses of claret (though there was certainly beer also in evidence), while at a piano forte another accompanied a young lady in a song of perfect respectability. Two other young ladies sat by the card table, occasionally exchanging a courtesy with the players.

On my entry, a middle-aged woman of impeccable dress welcomed me with a smile and offered me a glass of claret, which I was pleased to take.

'Whom have I the honour of addressing?' I asked – to which the reply was given that Mrs Tregunter presided over the establishment, and that I had her ear.

I introduced myself.

'Bless you, sir' – came the reply – 'I am perfectly

aware who you are! – you are familiar to me through the depictions in the public prints. Moreover, I had until recently in my employ the two young women who entertained you on the very first night of your election, though they are now returned to their previous house in Plymouth.'

Had I been by way of blushing, I might have blushed at that – for the truth was that my political Committee, to celebrate my victory, had procured from Plymouth two ladies whose virtue was purchasable for ready money, and whose presence in my bedchamber had proved to be for use rather than decoration.

'So,' I said, 'beer and wine are not the only . . .?'

In reply, Mrs Tregunter gestured me to follow her from the room, and, passing through a curtain which hung across the passage outside, we walked to the back of the house. In the meantime, I took the opportunity of mentioning the reason for my visit.

'Ah, the squib in the newspaper,' said Mrs Tregunter. 'You will find however that if you enquire of the nearest houses – and you see that we are some distance from them, my garden intervening – that my neighbours have no complaints, partly because indeed the distance is such as to render even loud sounds unprovocative, and partly because in one way or another I have sweetened their tempers. Besides which, I can if necessary explain Mr Couch's reason for making his complaint . . .'

That would not be necessary, I said, having already concluded that what I had heard at Webb's was no less than the truth.

We now turned into a parlour which indeed contained three young gentlemen of just such an age as high spirits might under other circumstances provoke to rowdiness, but who were sitting quite quietly, conversing with four young ladies whose dress was such that the real purpose of the place immediately became clear (had I not already guessed it). I do not mean that they were in any way indecent in their appearance, but that they paid no tribute to puritanism, their clothing being sufficiently loose to reveal figures undoubtedly provocative.

'Daisy, my dear,' said Mrs Tregunter, 'this is Mr – ah, Mr Incognito, who is to be the guest of the house. Will you entertain him? I am sure,' (she added, *sotto voce*) 'that these gentlemen will not object, since you are a distinguished visitor, to your preceding them in taking your pleasure . . .'

'Not at all, Mrs T.,' said one of the young men, having caught her word; 'we'm in no hurry!'

I made them a little bow, and the fine-limbed blonde who had stepped forward – perhaps the youngest of the four (and fortuitously, just the one which I would have chosen for pleasure) – invited me with a gesture to join her in one of those pleasant chairs which so winds about (in the shape of an S) that, when one sits upon half of it, one without effort can turn to face one's companion, an intimate conversation thereby being made easy no matter how many other people be present – though in this case, the three other couples, having glanced up, merely smiled and returned to their own conversations, which were warmed by appreciative gestures on the gentlemen's part and graciously received by the ladies, who clearly regarded the fondling of a breast or a thigh as a proper compliment.

Daisy, who was a charming girl, began our conversation by remarking that it was clear I was not a product of the county, and asking whether I was not from the capital? On my admitting the fact, she volunteered the information that she had grown up in the village of Richmond, and had been brought to Cornwall by a friend some eighteen months ago and had decided to remain when the gentleman concerned had gone back to the east.

I did not enquire as to the circumstances (it being a cardinal rule when talking to ladies of her profession to accept any information volunteered, but to make no enquiry as to their antecedents, for fear of causing embarrassment).

'It is something of a holiday for me to be in the fresh air,' she remarked, 'for the country (you know) is only a matter of ten minutes' walk from this door, while in town . . .'

I still made no comment, but it was now clear to me that Daisy had been a member of some similar establishment in London, as indeed her general deportment had already led me to suppose; and it may be that Mrs Tregunter had employed her chiefly because of her past experience, for I had already noticed that she kept a keen eye upon her three companions, being ready no doubt to correct any infelicity in their behaviour.

'Moreover,' she went on, 'the young gentlemen

here are far less trouble – in Bond Street it was a common occurrence to be asked to produce the whip, or to turn one's back – if you take my meaning; here, the demands are simpler and the recipients of our favours more appreciative.'

I was about to respond with a non-committal remark when the door opened and another gentleman entered. Greeting him with a smile, Daisy rose and allowed him to take her seat, at once bringing him a glass of wine.

'You had a pleasant hour, I trust, Mr Dawson?' she enquired, at which the gentleman assured her of his complete satisfaction. She then bent to my ear, and asked me to be patient while she cleaned the room and changed the sheets before I took my turn. I assured her that there was no cause for undue haste, and she then left us, having ensured that our glasses were full.

The gentleman at my side introduced himself as John Dawson. In turn I gave him my proper name, there being no reason on earth for concealing it from him.

'You are upon business here, sir?' I asked.

'In this house, you mean?' he replied with a smile – upon which I remarked that his business in the house was presumably identical with that of other gentlemen, and that I was enquiring more generally.

'I am a teacher of dancing,' he said, with a somewhat defensive air, 'and have for a space of two weeks been instructing the young ladies of the district.'

He was slim and moved with a peculiar grace,

though without the least effeminacy. He was (I should have reported) somewhat of my own age, that is in his middle twenties, though with a pair of sidewhiskers carefully cultivated – as I believed – to make him appear somewhat older, in which they signally failed.

'Mine is not by any means a disagreeable calling for one whose interest in the fair sex is considerable,' he went on.

I supposed not.

'But,' he went on, 'there is a particular problem, arising from the present popularity of the waltz. The polka, the gavotte, the country dance are supportable – but, to be enabled – nay for it to be obligatory – to take within one's arms a pretty young thing of seventeen or eighteen, bosom heaving, eyes flashing, – 'tis something too heating for any man of blood!'

'And so,' I said, 'you bring yourself to Mrs Tregunter's in order to take the edge off your appetite?'

'You have it precisely,' he said; 'though it must be admitted that from time to time a complaisant woman makes it clear that there is more than one sort of dancing to which she would be amenable, and it would be disingenuous of me not to admit that upon such occasions I, too, am complaisant.'

There was a pause.

'This is your first visit to this house?' he asked. I admitted the fact.

'It is extraordinarily well run,' he said, 'and quite equal to the better sort of establishment to be found elsewhere in this country or in France.'

I did not think it necessary to explain to him that I had had some experience in running just such a house of convenience; but instead enquired what experience he had had of the French brothels, to which he replied that he had spent a year in Paris studying the dance, and had as a matter of course made himself familiar with some of the houses of pleasure there.

But was that not an expensive pastime?

Happily (he responded) he had a comfortable income at his command – and in any event, while those fashionable houses to which the nobility had recourse were beyond his means, those of the middle sort were perfectly agreeable. 'And,' he said, 'there are now, you know, some two thousand registered houses in Paris, so that it is easy to find one which suits one's tastes and one's pocket.'

This was something of a surprise to me – certainly it had not been the case some eight years earlier, when I had last been in the French capital.

'Oh, yes,' Mr Dawson said when I questioned him in the matter; 'the legality of the bordello there has resulted in prostitution becoming a respectable business, and the ease with which money is to be made has resulted in a considerable growth of the industry, which is particularly well regulated. There are strict rules which apply to the working ladies – each must have a room of her own with her own means of making her toilette, and she must be medically inspected once a week. The average charge is now five francs, but as a matter of course one is obliged to leave a gratuity which might amount to ten or twenty francs for a young lady whom one finds attractive, or who is particularly attentive.'

And the houses themselves – were they luxurious, or plain?

They accord with the scale of prices one was prepared to pay (replied my new friend).

'The house to which I usually repaired, just off the Rue Royale,' (he went on) 'was as I might say of average comfort. One was received by the mistress of the house with the words "*Si vous montez voir les jolies filles, cela vous n'engagez à rien*", and ushered up a set of stairs and into an ante-room where a curtain was drawn aside revealing a door in which was set a circular piece of glass about the size of a crown piece, through which one might reconnoitre at one's ease a small but well-lit and elegantly furnished drawing-room, occupied by the ladies of the establishment.

'These ladies are usually to be seen seated on sofa chairs, elegantly attired in different coloured silks, with low bodices and their hair dressed in the extreme of fashion, the whole group being arranged artistically, as in a *tableau vivant*, and the individuals who comprise it representing the poses of different celebrated statues, selected with the object of showing to the best advantage their individual and peculiar attractions.

'From this room of observation one may select a girl – or if one pleases, one may enter and enjoy their society, only with the necessity to buy a bottle or two of champagne, and at leisure decide whom to invite to accompany one to a bedroom. Myself, I was attached to a little mulatto girl whom I invariably engaged, and whose attentions I still miss . . .' He paused with something of an air of regret.

There was nothing surprising to me in his description, for it was much the manner in which our London houses are run – though, as I have already mentioned, the Parisian mode of business had evidently been much improved since my last visit, and of course their legality resulted in the absence both of disease and of the violence which too often attached itself to the profession in England.

'I was unable through lack of funds to enjoy the company of the most celebrated *grandes horizontales*,' Mr Dawson continued; 'though I often saw Marguerite Bellanger driving in the Bois, and once kissed the hand of Leonide Leblanc, the mistress of the Prince d'Orleans. But the twenty-five gold louis necessary to purchase even a quarter of an hour in their private company were quite beyond me!'

I would have questioned him further about the *grandes cocottes*, whose way of life was most interesting to me, had Daisy not at this point approached and whispered in my ear that if I wished it we could retire. 'For,' she said, 'I fear that I am the only girl free at the moment, the others being already spoken for . . .'

Assuring her that nothing would give me greater pleasure than to accompany her, I rose and made my excuses to Mr Dawson, hoping that we might meet again, but being informed that he was leaving next morning for the larger town of Truro.

I then accompanied Daisy from the room, up a narrow staircase and into a surprisingly capacious bedroom in which stood not only a sturdy bed but two large movable mirrors which could be placed at the convenience of the occupants, and a tub of warm water with freshly laundered towels.

Assisting me to remove my clothes, Daisy invited me to sit upon a chair, and taking a cloth and some soap attentively washed my lower parts, with the excuse that it was a rule of the house (and an extremely sensible and ingratiating one, as I remarked to her). On her removing her own gown, which she next did, it was clear at our first embrace that she had also bathed, for her skin had that cool and slightly damp feeling which spoke of the recent application of soap and water.

Taking me by both hands, Daisy now raised me from the chair and leading me to the bed encouraged me to stretch out upon it, when she began to press kisses upon my shoulders, breast, the hollows of my arms, my belly and thighs – and eventually by a natural progression lifted my prick (by now in a state of attent uprightness) in her slim fingers, and framing its tip with her lips gulped it to the root with a professional smoothness and ease which evoked admiration even in one for whom this service had been performed by the most adept.

It is always a source of astonishment to me, when I think of the matter in calmer circumstances, how completely one is able to forget, in the presence of a skilful mistress, those other gentlemen to whom she has been equally kind, and who she has pleasured in just such a manner. It must clearly be the case, as a matter of course, that Daisy had taken between her lips a number of pricks so large that perhaps even she would hesitate to estimate the total – and some of which no doubt were the property of gentlemen less attractive (if I may be allowed what may seem a boast) than myself. Yet does it occur to we men, in such a situation as I now found myself, to repine at the fact? It does not – or if it does, it is necessarily a criticism of the performance of the lady serving us – for she who best knows how to give pleasure will by conveying it make the recipient unconscious of every moment but the present one.

Miss Daisy was certainly capable of that; and for the following minutes I allowed myself to be conveyed to heaven by gestures and actions of the utmost lasciviousness – so entrancing indeed were her attentions that it was almost impossible to decide, at any one moment, to what precise part of my body she was giving particular attention, for between navel and knees all was aflame – until at the point of bursting, I gently lifted her head and asked permission to return the compliment by offering her some comfort?

She smiled at this, but with gratitude rather than amusement; however (she said) she must ask to be excused – without giving a reason – and invited me once more to recline, which without further argument I did, though I felt as always somewhat deprived of an element of pleasure, for it is always my satisfaction to feel that a partner – even one whose services have been bought –

should enjoy my company as I enjoy hers.

Miss Daisy's skill however soon put this out of my mind: for now she threw her leg across my body, and lowering herself engulfed my cock within the slender embrace of her Venus trap, and gently rising and falling seemed so to caress it with her lower lips that the climacteric, when it came, shook my entire body.

She performed the remainder of her task with the cool proficiency of the complete professional: washing my body again, and carefully drying it; assisting me to dress; and always with a tender care of which no criticism could be made – though perhaps there remained a touch of remoteness, of which now (my passion spent) I was naturally more aware.

Showing me to the door, she bade me farewell with some warmth, and some gratitude for the two guineas which I pressed upon her. Mrs Tregunter, downstairs, hoped I had been properly accommodated – and when I replied in the affirmative, declined to accept a fee, and asked whether she might take it for granted that I would be taking no action about the complaint received

Though this smacked a little of bribery, I had no hesitation in saying that I would not – for indeed it was perfectly clear to me that the accusation had been made upon false grounds, and that Mr Couch deserved no support.

I then took my leave; and as I turned the corner, glanced back at the house – to see in an upstairs window the silhouette of two young ladies, apparently unclad, in a passionate embrace. Making my way back to Webb's I conjectured (not with any emotion other than slight regret) that Miss Daisy was at that moment probably enjoying those sensations, which she was so adept in raising in the members of a sex in which she appeared – like many ladies of her calling – to have only a professional interest.

Chapter Eight

Sophie's Story

I found on returning to our house that Andy had taken himself off to Liskeard upon some constituency matter. He had left *The West Briton* – a newspaper which it is always my pleasure to read through, for the local news – in a state of crumpled disrepair which irritated me: why cannot men leave their newsheets in such a condition that they are fit to be read by other people? Merely (I must confess) to vent my spleen, I ordered Purity – who was in an extremely somnambulant mood – to heat a flat iron, and repair the paper somewhat; finding while doing so that my friend had actually torn half a page away.

I made an effort to control my temper, however – for there was nobody upon whom I could exercise it but Purity, and there is nothing to be said for venting one's spleen upon a domestic.

After a light lunch, I settled down with the *Briton*, which as usual communicated nothing of excitement, but was soporific in its record of dances and meetings, births and marriages and deaths.

One announcement, however, did interest me:

> 'Mr John Dawson, professor of dancing and fencing, has the honour to announce his arrival in Truro from London, and at the same time begs most respectfully to say that he has profited by the instruction and experience of the most able professors. Mr J. D. has acquired all the new and fashionable dances, the celebrated gallopades, Spanish dances, &c &c. He has also entered into treaty with M. Geroux, ballet master of the Italian Opera, who is engaged to supply the earliest intimation of every change in the fashionable assemblies. Mr J. D. therefore hopes to merit a portion of public patronage, and appointments for private instruction can be made by calling upon him at number eight, Quay Street, Truro.'

This announcement was not so interesting in itself, as in its reminding me of the sophistications of town, which I now realised I somewhat missed: the adventures of the past weeks had been of a somewhat extraordinary kind, and it occurred to me now that I felt the lack of that common social intercourse attendant upon a decently interesting life.

If such were to be found in this distant county, it must be in its largest town, which was Truro; a few days spent in that place would soon reveal whether it would provide that contrast with my present life that I suddenly felt to be necessary. If it did not, I could return here with nothing lost, if nothing gained; if it did, then I could recreate myself for a short period, and return all the fresher.

I therefore packed a small trunk, informed Purity that I should be absent for some little while, wrote a note to Andy similarly advising him, and, having had the horses put to the smaller carriage, set off to drive myself (the weather being settled and the distance not too great) to Truro, a matter only of some thirty miles.

At midday I found myself approaching the village of Grampound, where there is little to be seen except a cluster of cottages, a broken bridge, and an inn where I bespoke some bread and cheese and a tankard of ale (for I am as partial to good ale, when it is properly brewed, as to the finest French wine). The weather was mild and the sun shining, and it was a pleasure to sit upon a bench and take my food and drink in the open, not far from a shed in which a fire heated a coffer for the washing of sheets, some of which were already being hung out to dry on the nearby bushes.

The task of washing these was clearly that of a pretty young maid who was sitting on a bench not far from my own, her face still red from the heat of the steam, and a pair of plump breasts partially revealed from the necessity of releasing the neck of her shirt, which she had opened as wide as decency permitted, no doubt in order to facilitate cooling her heated flesh.

I now found myself watching a little pageant of man and maid, for the young washerwoman shared her bench with a young man of not unhandsome appearance – and one not unadmiring of her beauty; yet who, far from wooing her actively, sat glum and silent, making not the slightest effort to compliment her with his lips, or even to offer to caress with his palms those fine breasts from which – were I a man – I would find it difficult to keep my hands! Surely the lad was either satiated by the compliance of some other young woman, or a complete fool! Yet he was not that, for I could not but notice that his eye sparkled upon meeting my own, and that on my pretending to look away he continued an inspection of my person which in the end betrayed itself to his companion, for whom his admiration of this female stranger was the final insult. She now fell silent, and in a while the lad got to his feet and disappeared into the inn, when the poor girl sat for a while, and it took no uncommon eyesight to see a tear upon her cheek.

The sight of a member of my sex in distress ever being mournful to me, I took myself over to her and enquired whether I could be of assistance – and being something of an expert in the examination of witnesses in the matter of love (and overcoming the slight resistance which attended her suspicion that I had been making eyes at her friend) learned soon enough that – as I had supposed – the girl was besotted by the lad, but met with the most complete blank.

My first words were to express what I felt – that he was a fool to disdain the company of so pretty a maid, the freedom of whose person might be craved by a man of much higher station.

At this she blushed, and said that she had made

no such offer as the freedom of her body; on the contrary, it could not be expected that Jem (as was his name) should be rewarded for his company by more than permission to kiss her cheek.

I must confess that I smiled at this – for not only did it betray the most complete ignorance of the humour of men, but I could imagine too clearly my own response were I a man, and wooing her. Not only her plump lips but those delightful breasts called out for caresses, and I had no doubt that other, secret sweets awaited a wooer, and were that wooer denied access to them the denial would but turn him on to some other and kinder lass (the first having ignited a fire which must be quenched, if not at that stream, then at some other).

I attempted to put this to the maid, but met with the argument that once a man had been permitted the freedom of a girl's person, he would regard her as dross, and soon enough desert her. I could not deny this was a possibility; but was forced to ask which were best – to have seized the opportunity to capture a lover, and in the end lose him, or to remain a virgin, losing not only the first wooer but perhaps the sole opportunity of a husband?

That my argument was specious I must have admitted, had I been tasked with the criticism; but I believed I had discerned in Jem's eye at least the possibility of constancy, and so pressed my argument – in the end being questioned as to my own actions, were I in Molly's place (for that was her name).

A moment's thought and a couple of questions brought forth my answer; and Molly after some further persuasion consented, only pausing for so long as to enquire again as to my forecast of the probability of success. She then on my advice took herself into the shed, piled some wood upon the already blazing fire, and began rubbing at some of the remaining washing.

In a moment, as had been foretold, Jem reappeared and, as he passed, I took the opportunity of wishing him a good day, to which he returned a more than civil answer, and happily accepted my offer of a tankard of ale, which he immediately fetched from indoors, then freely agreeing to sit with me for a few moments while he drank it.

It was not long before I took the opportunity to congratulate him upon his keeping company with so fine a young woman as Molly – a compliment which he accepted without more enthusiasm than would cover a groat.

'But she is exceedingly handsome,' I remarked, 'and no doubt is possessed of all that warmth and expressiveness which makes the company of a pretty woman so rewarding to the enthusiastic male.'

Jem looked puzzled at this for a while (my language being very different from that to which he was accustomed) and finally after a pause asked whether I meant, Was she a roistering lass? Upon my replying that indeed that *was* my meaning, he was forced to admit that his experience was that she cared not at all for the pleasures of the flesh, apart from an occasional exchange of kisses. As to the rest, she guarded her chastity as a miser his gold.

But had he pressed his suit with sufficient vigour? I asked. Was it not possible that should he take advantage of a promising opportunity, the citadel would fall?

He had already done so (he said) short of violence.

Violence I could never countenance (I said); but to make a firm offer was not necessarily to be violent. It might be that his previous efforts had been made at the wrong time of the month (at which he blushed and stammered). My view was that he should try again – and soon, for so delightful a maid would surely not long be without a lover.

'Aye,' he replied, 'indeed 'tis the case that Jim Puckey is already making eyes at her, and him without a dung fork to call his own.'

I had clearly struck the right key, and now suggested that, since Miss Molly was at that moment not more than a few feet away, and hidden from the public view, there could be no better time for action than the present.

He thought for another silent moment, and then, draining the remains of his ale nodded, got to his feet, and without more ado strode into the hut where the girl was about her washing. I will admit to the reader what I would not vouchsafe to a less sympathetic audience: viz. that I took the trouble now to march to a small window at the side where I could observe what followed.

The first thing clear to me, through the mist of the steam from the hot water in a copper container over the fire, was that on my advice (the heat of the fire being an excuse) Miss Molly had entirely undone her shirt, and turned it down about her waist, thus leaving the top half of her body entirely bare. What was revealed was pleasant enough to make me smile in approval, while no gentleman whose eyes fell on these pert, pretty breasts, with the most charming pink nipples in the world at their centre, could surely resist an allure made yet stronger by the liquid (from the steam) which swam upon the surface of the skin, making it gleam and shimmer.

Young Jem was certainly not of such a puritanical disposition as to find the sight revolting – and, striding at once round the fire, he first (I am sure more from an unconscious sense of propriety than anything else) saluted her lips with his own, then buried his face in those enchanting bubbies, taking first one then the other as far between his lips as could conveniently be. The expression of her face at this liberty went far to convince me that she was not likely long to resist such blandishments – let alone the liberty which followed, for, falling to his knees, the lad (with a confidence far greater than I would have expected of him) took the waist of her skirt and without difficulty (its being held by only a single tie, which soon was undone by his nimble and hasty fingers) drew it to her knees, revealing first a tight round belly whose plumpness proved irresistible first to eyes then to lips, then a fine bush of black hair upon which he laid first a cheek, then a pair of fingers, and finally those same lips.

And what of Miss Molly? Any nervousness she might have felt was soon dispelled by the delicious sensation which only a first experience of such intimacies can convey – and was further discouraged by her meeting my eyes, when, upon my smiling in an encouraging manner, she leaned forward and positively tore his shirt apart, pressing it over his shoulders so that she could pass her hands beneath it and thus caress his breast. (This, incidentally, revealed to me four scratches running across his back from shoulder to small, which seemed to suggest that the young man was not entirely devoid of experience with the fair sex.)

It would be improper of me, as a on-looker whose presence could only be excused by a wish to oversee matters on Molly's behalf, to describe in detail the familiarities which followed. Suffice it to say that, pausing only to close and bar the door, Jem without further ado divested himself of his clothing, revealing to Molly what I believe to be her first view of an entirely unclothed man. This by no means upset her, for on catching sight of the chief mark of difference between the sexes (now in so rampant a state as to be unmistakably either a promise or a threat) she did not hesitate to catch at it, and, perching herself upon the edge of the table on which the clothing was folded, threw open her thighs and enabled him immediately to present the sword to the scabbard. Without demur she assisted him to sheath it, handling with considerable interest the pommel and appurtenances, and being clearly no less pleased at the sensation offered by the application of the instrument than at the interesting spectacle first afforded her.

Needless to say, I did not stay to observe them further; but left while the young man's motions were still provoked and provoking, paid my reckoning, and left – confident that I had been of service both to the man and the maid, who I trusted were now to be relied upon to make as happy a life together as any pair in the county – or, if they were to be doomed to a disappointment in each other's characters, at least not to die that most regrettable of deaths, that of a virgin.

At Truro a few hours later, I drove into the yard of the Red Lion – one of the pleasantest inns in the country – handed my horse into the custody of a dependable ostler and bespoke from the host an excellent set of rooms upon the first floor, looking out onto what I took to be the main street of the town.

I was ready for some small luxury, and ready too to be waited upon with more style than could be commanded by little Purity, pleasant and well meaning though the child was. I cannot say that that service was the equal in sophistication of that to be found in the best of our London hostelries, but it was certainly directed at making a guest comfortable and ensuring that her belly was full – and, as to further corporeal comfort, my accommodation consisted of a roomy sitting room, with armchairs built to support the bodies of giants, and a small table at which I could entertain three or four friends in private, should the opportunity present itself. The bedroom was equally commodious, and held a large four-poster bed in which I could equally conveniently entertain three or four friends should the even less likely opportunity present itself.

By the time my baggage had been brought up stairs, and one of the hotel's maids had unpacked my clothes and disposed them in presses, it was nine o'clock of the evening, and I simply ordered up some pie and beer, made a frugal but satisfactory supper, and retired for the night, finding the bed even more comfortable than it appeared.

Next morning I was awakened by a knocking and the appearance of a maid with a dish of chocolate and some newly baked bread. She drew back the curtains of my bed and wished me a very civil good morning; I was happy to sit up and partake of some nourishment, after which I made my toilette and took myself into the town, where I walked for an hour or two, recreating myself upon the banks of a river where numerous little skiffs passed to and fro, small vessels loaded and put off their cargoes, and shoals of small boys in a state of nature hurled themselves into the water with an enthusiasm which matched their youth and vigour.

The windows of the shops offered no extraordinary temptations – there was a pretty elegant disposition of last season's fashions, but, as far as the shopkeepers of Truro were concerned, my purse was safe, and the limit of my expenditure was two pence spent upon a dish of tea.

Returning then towards the Inn – for my meal of the night before had been sufficiently light to commend me to an early luncheon – I passed the assembly rooms, where there was a fly poster bearing the same legend as the advertisement I had read in the *Briton*, Mr Dawson's name however being in somewhat larger type, and in smaller letters beneath it, 'For further information apply at the Red Lion Inn'.

After luncheon, finding the maid in my room busily dusting, I took the opportunity of enquiring about Mr Dawson, and learned that he was expected that day, but had not yet arrived. He was evidently in a fair way of business, or else was concerned to give the impression of success, for he had taken a set of rooms similar to my own, but immediately above, and these, while by no means expensive when compared to the cost of a similar establishment in town, were not cheap by the standards of the country.

The afternoon I took as easily as the morning; there was after all little enough to interest me in the place – though advertisements for a couple of balls shortly to be held promised perhaps some entertainment, and there was always the opportunity of observing the people of the town, for as ever I was interested to observe local manners and men. The latter were however mostly plump to an excess, and for the most part elderly. The gentlemen to be found in the streets had an air of concern only for themselves – there was no pleasant gossiping on the corners or in the coffee houses: indeed, there was only a single coffee house in the place, and that of no great elegance, and occupied only by gentlemen talking about their business affairs rather than (as in London) by those with time to waste in idle banter.

Those younger gentleman who were to be seen – as I observed from the window of the coffee shop (in which I was, by the way, the only female so that I must suppose that the ladies of Truro were disinclined to enter it) – while often possessed of that animal grace which is usually at the command of those of tender years, for the most part altogether lacked grace of address. Where they greeted members of the other sex they did so with all that casual banter which might normally pass between brothers – and was often enough even rougher than that. They tended also to lounge together, whispering and laughing, and evidently exchanging comments about those ladies unfortunate enough to have to pass them.

If the ladies who passed to and fro seemed to despise these young tyrants, I was not surprised; and indeed they looked askance, turning up their noses and with every good reason ignoring the obvious slights and slurs being made upon their persons and characters. In fact, the relationship between the young was so peculiar as to make me consider that this was the rudest place I had yet found in England, which could be dignified with the name of civilised society.

Back at the Red Lion, I took my supper early, and retiring to my room read for an hour or so in Miss Austen's *Emma* before summoning Betty, and having removed my dress ordered her to take it away for pressing with a hot iron, and climbed into bed – glad to pull the curtains about me, there being an unpleasant draught from the window.

I must have immediately fallen into a sleep, and

was awakened at some later hour by a noise which I thought came from the room next door. Surely I was mistaken? But no, unmistakably someone was moving about, for the ancient floor boards now and then creaked under his or her weight. I now considered that the intruder must be Betty, returning my dress. However, in a moment, I heard the door of the bedroom open, and between a chink in the curtains saw a flutter of light.

Raising myself to my knees, I peered through that same chink – and was astonished to see that a gentleman, tall and by no means unhandsome, had set down a candle upon the bedside table and was in the last stages of removing his breeches! I opened my mouth to utter – but then paused, for, before I could do so, he drew his shirt over his head, stood for a moment entirely divested of covering (and no unpleasant sight, I may say), then swiftly extinguished the light by clapping his hand upon the flame, threw back the curtains and allowing me only a moment's time to retreat to the far side of the bed, in a moment was reclining at my side.

I was stayed, and had nothing to say: and, while I was still considering a position which even the most assured young woman would surely find somewhat embarrassing, I realised from the regular breathing of my companion that he was already lost in the arms of Morpheus – that is, sound asleep! After a moment's consideration, I concluded that the best thing I could do was to follow his example; explanations could wait for the morning – and for me to divulge my presence at that moment, when 'twas pitch dark, would lead to a confusion which might be both noisy and disconcerting. I will confess that my thoughts were for a time somewhat disturbed by the recollection of the person of the gentleman who now lay at my side, and in that state of dress (or, rather, undress) normally provocative of sensual activity. However, it was not long before I fell into a sleep from which I only awakened after dawn – for, upon opening my eyes, I found the light already streaming into the bedroom, and illuminating (since one of the bed curtains had been left undrawn) the bed.

This bed, as I have mentioned, was a large piece of furniture, though by no means as massive as that great one of Ware, which I was once shown in an inn at that small town between London and Cambridge. There had therefore been no necessary contact between my own body and that of my still unconscious companion, who remained at that moment deeply asleep.

He was a fellow of perhaps rather fewer years than myself, dark curling hair falling about slightly sallow but delicately formed features, long black lashes depending from the closed eyes (which were not without those wrinkles at the corners which marked some humour in the character) and, below a moustache less than impressive, a mouth which was characterful and somewhat stern. In short, from his face the young man was by no means unattractive – and my memory of the glimpse I had had of a long back and the jutting (as he had bent over to snuff the candle) of a pair of admirably firm and hairless buttocks convinced me that his person matched in charm the delineaments of his face.

He lay now upon his back, the sheet falling half across a breast notably well formed, the paps marking with their red buds a skin as white as that sheet, and surrounded only by a slight mist of tiny hairs. I was amused to see that below, the sheet rose in a billow which suggested that the gentleman was in just such a state as marks a sound sleep, disturbed by a pleasant dream (for my gentlemen friends tell me that on wakening from dreaming they often find their members extended as forcibly, and congested as firmly, as though provoked to that state by the most lubricious actions of a female companion).

It may be that some of my female readers may find the action which I now describe somewhat unladylike: however, they will grant that curiosity, besides killing a cat, sometimes provokes an unwise action – and the fact is that I could not resist lifting the sheet to discover whether the rest of my companion's body was as well shaped as that fine shield of a bosom. I may immediately satisfy the curiosity of any reader who shares my own by admitting that it was.

There are those ladies so immune to the charm of the other sex as to suppose that when one has seen one piece of male apparatus, one has seen all. Even a restricted observation – of perhaps two or three gentlemen – will condemn such a statement as absurd; while a lady of wide experience (and readers of my memoirs will allow me to place myself in that category) can only express astonishment that anyone could make such a claim.

I would not be so silly as to argue that appearance is all: the most handsome equipment may be faulty – a canon with a barrel of iron may misfire, and the most elegantly tooled piece prove incapable of firing at all – while the rudest blunderbuss may stand up to any demand made upon it, and even a rifle with a twisted bore may be capable of firing shot after shot without more than a moment for recovery of the aim!

However, any sensitive female will at the very least look with curiosity at the latest exhibit upon which her eye falls: will examine the angle, the length, the thickness, the form itself with attention – and may perhaps be forgiven for conjecturing what advantages may be demonstrated upon the object's being put to use. It was with just such an emotion that (to return to my narrative) I now lifted the sheet and saw before me the pleasantest sight in the world – a well-shaped organ, neither so short as to be squab nor so long as to be out of balance with a sturdy girth, and lying back against the belly with an air of assurance which led me to suppose that in action it would be as vigorous as it appeared burly.

Perhaps I will be forgiven for imagining the sensation of that admirable prick being put to its proper use; and if I confess that, lying back upon my pillow and closing my eyes, I turned and as if in sleep threw out an arm so that it fell across my sleeping companion's breast, I comfort myself that I was doing no more than any spirited young lady in my position might have done.

That this had some effect was noticeable from an immediate pause in my companion's regular breathing, which stopped as suddenly as if in death! Then I felt his hand fall upon my arm, and had little doubt from its moving along the length of it that, before glancing in my direction, he was testing whether I might not be a gentleman (for it was still the custom in some country inns, upon the place being full, to thrust gentlemen, unknown to each other, into the same bed).

The smoothness of my skin and the absence of hairs upon it must have suggested at least that I was not of the male sex – and to make the matter sure, I now turned upon my side and, with a sigh as though still in sleep, threw my leg across my companion's body, so that the whole length of my own person was stretched along his.

At the sensation, I heard a little moan spring to his lips, and, as I confess I hoped, the softness of my body against his together with the provocation of his already being ready for action was sufficient to provoke immediate action. In a moment I felt his lips seek out my own, while raising himself slightly he turned me upon my back, and I felt against my thigh the positive impression of that fine instrument I had already observed. At this I no longer felt it necessary to counterfeit, and allowed myself the liberty of running my hand along the gentleman's side and over one tight cheek of his pert back side, which feeling the pressure lifted sufficiently for me to open myself more comfortably and more conveniently to his laying his trunk between my legs; when it was the work of but a moment for me to raise them, making the most common form of intercourse not only possible, but inevitable; not only inevitable but instantly achieved!

Whether he believed me still to be unconscious, I could not say; but whether he did so or not – and I suspect the latter – he showed no reluctance to proceed, and did so with just that firm swinging motion which through a fine and searching rhythm convinces one that it could go on for ever. This in fact began, after some time, to seem quite likely – for, despite my reaching the apogee of my own pleasure, the gentleman showed no sign of achieving his own, continuing to plunder my treasure until a second wave forced from me, despite myself, a little shriek of pleasure.

I now placed both my hands upon his arse, and, forcing its cheeks apart, thrust with my fingers at his very fundament – which in most cases will bring a man off with little delay; in this case, however, it had no more effect than the energetic thrusting upwards of my loins, with which I was careful to match his own downward motion. Yet a third almost painful climax shook me, and despite myself I was forced to plead for mercy, in a voice so hoarse with emotion that it seemed not my own: 'No more, sir, I beg – no more!'

At this, he faltered, and in a moment – clearly without being satisfied – lifted himself from my body (now a welter of perspiration), and in a low voice remarked: 'You see, my dear, the reward of a maid too eager to offer hospitality to a guest!'

'I fear I must disillusion you, sir,' I remarked

(panting somewhat from my exertions, though his own seemed to have left him entirely in command of himself). 'I am not a maid, but a fellow guest.'

'My dear ma'am,' he stammered, 'a thousand pardons. I thought . . . I was under the impression . . .'

'Sir,' I said with a smile, 'you surely cannot suppose that I allowed myself to be raped? I assure you that I could dispose of any gentleman whose attentions were unwelcome, either by voice or by action!'

He could not but smile at this, and fell back upon the pillow, his chin supported upon a hand.

'It is true,' he said, 'that you seemed nothing if not complaisant – a fact which convinced me that it was a servant who had, not for the first time, placed herself at my disposal on my arriving at this inn.'

'Your mistake was natural,' I replied, 'and the only quarrel I can have is that the mistake which placed you in these rooms might have furnished me with a less attractive companion than yourself.' And, taking his hand, I pressed it to my lips. 'My other quarrel however *is* with yourself.'

He raised an eyebrow.

'I am sorry that my person is so unattractive as to preclude your own more complete enjoyment.'

'Ah!' he said, immediately taking my meaning, 'please do not suppose that any lack of beauty or vigour in yourself is responsible for that. It is merely the case that the self-control which I have been forced to acquire through my profession has made me capable of deferring a complete surrender of my forces almost indefinitely – and indeed have convinced myself that the seeking is in all respects as enjoyable as the finding, though I am by no means averse to reaching the goal when that is convenient. Had we been previously introduced, and our enjoyment been the leisurely result of an evening's conversation, I assure you that . . .'

'I hope nevertheless, sir, that you will allow me . . .' and I placed between my lips a prick which though of a fully extended size was at first somewhat soft and limber, and persuaded it soon enough into a state of hardness so adamant that only its warmth and the faint throbbing of blood through its veins could have convinced a stranger that it was not an ivory similitude of the reality, so entirely smooth and perfect was it in form!

The pleasure of sucking upon a handsome cock is much undervalued by those ladies who for reasons of modesty or hygiene have never experienced it. It is perhaps worth my spending a paragraph in conveying the reality: which is that, in the first place, modesty must be no bar to any exchange of compliments between lovers, while in the second, provided the gentleman exercises a proper degree of attention to cleanliness, there can be nothing more distasteful in this action than in any other. But greater than either of these considerations must be the delight which the compliment gives not only to the recipient but to the donor.

I have pondered upon this for some time (the entire mechanics of the activities of love being of interest to me); and while I cannot pretend to have come at the entire truth, must aver that the pleasure of what the Italians call *fellatio* is almost equally in the giving and the receiving of pleasure. It may be, as some doctors aver, that the faint memory of the pleasure of sucking upon our mothers' breasts is a part of that which we receive through a similar action in our maturity – for it is the case that there is something infinitely touching in the sensation aroused by the passage between the lips of so warm, so smooth, so living a piece of flesh. Again, nothing is so pleasant in a passage of love as the knowledge that one is giving pleasure to one's lover – and the gasps, the involuntary shivers, the little jumps which the machine gives as one passes one's lips over its surface are in themselves testimonies to this.

But also equally pleasant is the realisation of the power the action gives one over one's companion: the pleadings with which a man will attempt to persuade us to continue should we pause; the manner in which he will lay his hands upon our heads to attempt to direct us; the involuntary raising of the buttocks, the thrusting which must be controlled if it is not positively to injure us – all these are marks of how great our influence must be during such an operation (and signify, if I may suggest it, how opportune such a time is to make almost any request, for it will almost certainly be granted if we should show only the slightest sign of desisting!).

To return to my narrative. My companion had now clearly been persuaded by my words to permit himself to reach his apogee; for there was no mistaking the pleasure with which he received my attentions, while the caresses which at the same time I allowed myself to give to his cods were equally delightful to him – and in a relatively short period of time, the tightening of the muscle between my lips suggested a culmination, which very shortly followed, and was as generously displayed as might in the circumstances be suspected, my bosom and his belly both being drenched (he having been polite enough at the final moment to lift my head from its position, for fear that I should be offended should he spend between my lips).

It was now time for a polite introduction, and it was not with immoderate surprise that I heard the gentleman present himself as Mr John Dawson, professor of the dance and of fencing!

Chapter Nine

The Adventures of Andy

I was sitting in the retiring room behind the magistrates' courtroom at Lostwithiel, waiting to preside from the chair for only the second time as magistrate (a position I held by virtue of my Membership of Parliament) when a knock came upon the door – and rather than the clerk, who I expected to see, there entered none other than Colin Ford, the only son of the Rev. Michael Ford, Vicar of the town – who (the son, I mean, rather than the father) I had last seen bollock naked in the cottage to which we had retired during the interrupted ceremony of beating the bounds!

I greeted him with pleasure, for he was a likely and forward boy, and, though he had at first seemed somewhat above himself, this was only the result of his nervousness at meeting so great a man as myself (as he foolishly believed!); our mutual participation in the larks of the afternoon had soon reduced me in his eyes, however, to the more approachable rank of a companion in pleasure.

I hoped (I now said) that he did not present himself before me in my official position as magistrate. The answer was both yes and no, he replied

– for while he certainly had not come to face me as a delinquent of any kind, he was about to appeal to me as a magistrate and indeed a Member of Parliament – a gentleman therefore of some consequence and influence.

'The fact is,' he said when I had given him permission to speak out, 'that I am in the way of wanting to wed, or rather of needing to wed, for I have got Maisie Bennett of this town with child, and must marry her.'

This remark gave me at once an even better opinion of the lad than I had previously held, for, all too often when the untoward result of an improvident union becomes apparent, a clean pair of heels is the only sympathy shown to a maid by the swain responsible. My good opinion was not diminished when in reply to my questioning I discovered that he professed to love the girl. Did I know her? I enquired – had she been his companion during our romps at the cottage?

'One of them,' he replied, averring that the said Maisie was not one of those jealous females who objected to sharing the qualities of a young man with her friends – something less uncommon than one might think, in the country, especially where there was a shortage of young men.

So what was the matter? I enquired. If both he and the girl wished to wed, what could be the obstacle?

It was (he said) that his father would not countenance such a marriage, having in mind a union with the daughter of a certain Canon of a nearby parish, who would upon his death inherit a considerable estate – sufficiently considerable in the Rev. Ford's eyes to soften those hard features and mellow that harsh voice which (even were it not for his passion for Maisie) would for Colin disqualify the Canon's daughter as a possible spouse.

But if he was fixed upon the idea (I said) why did they not simply marry, and to hell with the Vicar?

'Because', he said, 'I am but nineteen; so his permission must be obtained.'

This assertion somewhat startled me, I must confess, for the lad's activities at our last meeting were sufficiently enthusiastic and determined to suggest a greater experience than a lad in his teens might have been expected to possess. Would I, in short (he continued), intercede for the couple with his father? – who, it appears, was in favour either of paying young Maisie to keep the child and conceal the identity of its progenitor, or of having it placed in some decent home sufficiently far from the town to preclude damaging gossip.

I would have thought that Mr Ford would have been sympathetic to his son's predicament (I remarked); it seemed that he was not altogether antipathetic to pleasure himself, since he showed a lenient attitude to the various and often licentious revels of the youth of the town.

'Indeed', replied his son, 'and it is not as though he is himself entirely innocent of those activities which . . .' But the good boy, conscious that he should not tell tales out of school, forebore to go further, leaving me to understand that the reverend gentleman's own indulgences were nevertheless insufficient to persuade him to overlook similar ones in his child.

I naturally promised to have a word with the Vicar – and at that moment was summoned into court, where I dealt summarily with two poachers and a petty thief before there was ushered into the dock (protesting both verbally and physically) a remarkable figure: a girl who, as far as could be seen from glimpses of her face, before which a cloud of pitch black hair fell in abundance, was young and sufficiently handsome, and whose gaudy dress seemed to suggest that she was a traveller or gypsy. Into the dock with her, protesting less and adopting a servile attitude, was projected a thin-faced youth who was introduced as Roger Glasson, otherwise known as the Ferret – while the woman was said to be called Betsy Bunting.

The evidence of two woman and a disgruntled middle-aged gentleman brought before me revealed that the young woman had for the past fortnight been telling the fortunes of spinsters, widows and susceptible gentlemen, and on one occasion had been heard to boast that she had obtained fourteen shillings the preceding day by such ingenious deceptions. Under various pretences, she obtained from several of her dupes trinkets and articles of wearing apparel, which she was to return the following day with valuable additions! It was unnecessary to add that she failed to keep her appointments, to the no small chagrin of the expectants.

My own view of the situation was that here was

a pleasant, naughty wench whose activities did little enough harm, and indeed somewhat increased the merriment in the world – while her victims were surely almost as culpable (through their silliness) as she. Moreover, the gentleman witness, who had a distinctly sheepish air, seemed to be concealing something. I was by no means sure that cozening him of his watch was the sum of the lady's dealings with him, and I adjourned the court with the intention of questioning her myself – and had her brought before me in the retiring room, where we were left alone, at my request (it being my view that the presence of my clerk, a gentleman of repellently unctuous appearance, could only deter her or any other witness from open conversation).

On entering, the young woman – for it could now be seen that she was no more than eighteen or nineteen years of age – was of a distinctly handsome appearance; standing before me, she now lifted back her hair from her face, revealing it to be somewhat swarthy, but mischievous rather than wicked, humour shining in a pair of lustrous black eyes, and shown in the lineaments of rich, curved lips. With a smile, she now unwound the knitted cloak which she had kept wrapped around her while in the dock, and letting it trail from one hand showed herself to be attired in a blood red dress of some light satin, which billowed about her person, entirely concealing her body yet somehow suggesting that it was infinitely promising in its fullness.

Invited to be seated, she stepped forward and, rather than taking her place in the chair which was available to her, preferred to perch upon the side of my desk, at which her long skirt, proving to be slit to the waist, fell aside so that one leg was revealed almost to the thigh – and very brown and shapely it was, the calf richly curved and full, the thigh clearly muscular but finely shaped.

I got little from her in the way of pretence, for when I taxed her with the little thefts she admitted them freely, merely arguing (in terms which I myself might have used) that anyone blockheaded enough to be taken in by her wiles deserved to be deprived of their small goods, none of which were worth more than a penny or two. It was clear that her friend the Ferret disposed of these at local markets, and that she bore him no particular affection.

'I allow him a sniff of my goods now and then,' she said, 'to keep him in order; but he's no particular friend of mine. I prefer a *gentleman* . . .' and, as if unconsciously, she advanced her leg somewhat, so that to that stretch of thigh which was already revealed was added another two or three inches. 'And I know,' she went on, 'how to express my gratitude for consideration.' And, making no more ado than other women would of offering a hand in greeting, now got to her feet and whisking her skirt above her waist revealed herself completely bare from hip to foot – a sight which I must admit to being not in the least repellent, but which I did not allow to move me (my duty as a magistrate precluding me from taking advantage of such a bribe).

At my failing to rise to her bait, she smiled. 'Aha!' she exclaimed, 'you won't buy without examining all the goods,' and without difficulty (her clothing I believe carefully constructed for just such a display) somehow contrived to throw off her dress altogether, now appearing like Eve, and just as attractive as any portrayal of that ancestor of ours that I have yet seen, the apple she offered being most temptingly juicy.

'Come, now, sir!' she said, 'what harm in a tit for tat?' and, once more perching upon the side of the desk, she placed herself in just such a position as would have been convenient for the satisfaction of any little favour I cared to ask.

Seeing that I continued unmoved by her blandishments, something of scorn seemed to enter her eyes.

'Shall I send Roj to you?' she said, 'he'll open his arse freely for a magistrate, or any other gentleman with something to his advantage . . .'

I reached out then and, taking her hand, carried it to my lips – for though she was no doubt a villainess, there was something saucy about the girl.

'My dear,' I said, 'I understand too well how you make your living, and can take no objection to it beyond hoping that you spare the deserving poor – which from your expression I do believe to be the case. Nor would I hesitate to embrace you were we to meet in any other circumstances, for as to your beauty no gentleman of feeling could have any doubt . . .'

At this, she leaned forward, and without so much as a by-your-leave thrust her hand between my thighs – where to tell the truth there were signs of an interest which I was determined to carry no further, but which brought a smile once more to her full lips.

'Let us return to the court,' I said, 'although I would advise that you resume your clothing, if my clerk is to avoid an apoplexy. In the meantime, here are two guineas; take a room at the Talbot hotel, and I may have a commission for you later,' (for the vestige of an idea was already passing through my mind).

I disposed of the case in no long time, releasing the prisoners – something to the scandal of the complainants – on the condition that no further offence should take place. I then took myself off to the vicarage, where I was immediately granted an interview with Mr Ford, whom I found in his study, reading. He put down his book with uncommon alacrity, and although it bore the name of that distinguished divine John Donne, I could see (for I was familiar with the work) that it was not a volume of his sermons, but a copy of those lascivious verses written when the Dean of St Paul's was a young wit, and which are as strong in the conveyance of physical passion and pleasure as any other verses in the language – viz:

> 'Licence my roaving hands, and let them go,
> Before, behind, between, above, below . . .'

and further

> 'Full nakedness! All joyes are due to thee,

As souls unbodied, bodies uncloth'd must be,
To taste whole joyes . . .'

But I digress. On my putting my embassy to him, Mr Ford heard me with patience, but declined to discuss the possibility of young Colin's marriage.

'You will forgive me, Mr Archer,' he said, 'but I consider the matter a private one, and that is my final word upon it. Now, you will join me in a glass?'

But I declined politely, made my excuses and left.

I now knew my course, and made my way immediately to the Talbot hotel, a sufficiently pleasant coaching inn upon the corner of the main road called Fore Street, and but two minutes' walk from the vicarage. There, I enquired for Mistress Betsy, and for my pains received a somewhat strong look from the landlady's eagle eye, and an equally strong wink from that of her husband. The girl I discovered was playing the lady in the best room of the house, and I must smile at the ease with which she did so, for she greeted me as politely as any of my acquaintances might.

Gratitude for my leniency led her to suppose that I had set her up here for a particular purpose, for no sooner had I entered than once more she was divested of her dress; and I must confess that only the business I had in mind persuaded me to relinquish the idea of a tumble with her, for her strong and lithe body, full-breasted yet without a trace of undue pulchritude, was of just such a nature to interest me strongly.

Somewhat with a puzzled air, she was persuaded to resume her convenient clothing while I explained my plan – when the promise of a further two guineas and the prospect of a good joke against the clergy (for whom she appeared to have no love) speedily persuaded her to agree to what I suggested. A word with Bennett, the landlord, secured his concurrence in my plot – he had no reason to love Mr Ford, who had recently been making a fuss about the conditions of his licence, and the freedom with which his bar was used by members of the church choir before evening service, which added an unpredictable quality to the singing of hymns and psalms.

Having fixed things to my satisfaction, I now found the Ferret, hanging about downstairs. He was readily persuaded by a present of a shilling to take a message to the Vicarage that a lady required his presence at her bedside, for the purpose of making her last confession, she being taken severely unwell.

A word with Bennett secured the use of a small room next door to Betsy's (in which it was usual to accommodate, I suppose, the servants of those occupying the main room). In half an hour Mr Ford was announced, and I immediately took myself next door while Betsy, pausing only to divest herself once more of her clothing (with a celerity which was startling to see, despite the fact that I had already twice witnessed it), threw herself into bed. A chink at the door's edge, where a hinge had been removed, enabled me to see what followed.

Ford entered quietly, no doubt prompted to do so by the fact that he believed he was coming to hear the confession of a sick – even a dying – woman.

He approached the bed, where Betsy lay quiet, until he was within reach, and indeed had seated himself at the bedside with a concerned attitude, when she stretched out her hand and gripped his arm – revealing as she did so one full bosom, upon which Mr Ford's eyes clapped themselves with an almost audible thwack.

'Oh, Vicar, my thanks to 'ee for coming – oh, but I must make my confession quick, for I am mortal sick!' she said – in a display of rural histrionics which would not have deceived me; but perhaps the Vicar's judgement was clouded by the fact of her sitting up, upon which her entire bosom was presented to his view – a sight by no means likely to be repugnant to any red-blooded gentleman, even one of the cloth, and certainly not to one who had (through the death of his wife many years previously) but few chances of scratching the itch which is common to all men, whether they care to admit it or not.

With a facility born no doubt of her manner of life, Betsy then embarked upon a detailed account of a number of lubricious encounters which surely imagination could not have evoked, even when prompted by generous payment? She had obviously lived a very full life, and began at the beginning, with an apology for having at the age of fourteen seduced her brother (on the grounds that sleeping in the same bed with him had become a temptation too great to be borne). She then went on to speak of a liaison with an uncle, whom she had happened upon one afternoon when he was swimming in the river, and who, finding her spread-eagled upon the ground at the spot where his clothes had been deposited, had not allowed the closeness of their relationship to persuade him against a romp which had left him (as Betsy said) more exhausted than his companion.

Her adventure with the keeper of the game on the estate on which she lived had been consequent upon his discovering her father in an act of poaching.

'Oh, sir!' she cried to the open-mouthed parson, 'how many pricks would you not suck to prevent the calamity of a parent's transportation?' Mr Ford was I believe ready to protest that such an action was unlikely to be demanded of him – but, before he could do so, Betsy had progressed to her experience with the squire's son, who returning from Italy had raped her upon sight; but she confessed to making only token resistance – and, on discovering that the young gentleman had during his travels conceived a liking for sodomy, had not hesitated to offer him her rump. 'For, you know, sir, 'tis by no means unpleasant once you have the taste for it.'

The vicar, as was no doubt his duty, opened his mouth to protest at this – but whatever he had in mind to say was lost as Betsy proceeded with the tale of her entering the service of a merchant in Plymouth Dock, where she was expected to join with another female servant in pleasuring him of a Saturday night – his taste being in part for the witnessing of acts of love between the two young women. And, 'While nothing can take the place of cock,' she said, 'Sall and I by no means found each other's company unpleasant, for which I am heartily sorry and repent, sir, and hope for forgiveness.'

'My child . . .' began the Vicar.

'Oh, sir,' went on Betsy, now leaning so far from the bed that the sheets slipped almost below her waist, 'you as yet know but half: I have made my living from the game since I left home – and I fear without remorse, for I must confess I love a rough and tumble; and though I truly repent after each bout, I am too easily tempted to the next. Why, sir, would you believe that even now I cannot keep myself from . . .' – and in a moment she had slipped entirely from the bed, fallen to her knees before the dumbfounded parson, and was undoing the buttons of his canonical gown, which I suppose he commonly wore upon such excursions as this, and which could certainly be claimed as a most convenient dress in which to encounter a lady of this sort, for upon the buttons being undone she found the remainder of the vicar's clothing to consist merely of a sort of childish clout wound about his loins – into which Miss Betsy now plunged her hands, in a moment drawing it aside to reveal a prick which, while nothing to boast of as to size, certainly expressed by a determined pouting an interest in her narrative.

At the sight of it, with a display of emotion that no doubt seemed entirely convincing to her companion (but which must surely have been acted?) Betsy threw up her hands, then in a single motion had clapped her lips around the clerical appendage and was addressing it with such a thoroughness and warmth that it would have been difficult for any man to make a motion to prevent her. As it was, Mr Ford sat quite still, his eyes turned upwards so that only the whites showed, ludicrously suggesting an attitude of devotion directed towards a form of satisfaction unsanctioned by the Church (at least in recent centuries, though if we are to believe ancient accounts the Borgia Popes were not entirely averse to it).

In a while, the consciousness of where he was and what was happening seemed to dawn upon him – as did the possibility that the woman to whom he had been summoned was not as sick as had been given out. For a moment it seemed that he might draw away from her. However, perhaps conscious of this (through that instinct which had made her living, no doubt), Betsy redoubled her efforts, fixing with her fingers upon his cods and making playthings of them; then, relinquishing her hold, rising to her feet and pausing only to nibble at a pair of pendant nipples which hung upon a breast almost sufficiently full to be that of a woman, before throwing one leg over the parson's lap and sinking upon him with a sigh indicative (whether genuine or not) of delight.

The parson made no effort to dislodge her, and indeed upon her beginning to rise and fall upon his knees (and more important, upon his now concealed prick) his expression became even more impassioned; then, with a sudden and most unexpected turn of events, he lifted her bodily from her position and – rather than rejecting her advances altogether, which had been my fear – turned her about and thrust into her from the rear, at which an expression of unquestionably genuine pleasure could be seen upon her face, which continued to beam as he continued to shove!

Now, it seemed to me, was the time for my entrance: opening the door, I came through, my gown over my arm, as though making for the place of convenience beyond – and showing upon my face my astonishment at the sight before me: the Vicar of the town, his trousers about his ankles, apparently playing the part of Ulysses with Patroclus!

'My dear Mr Ford!' I exclaimed.

The Vicar was quicker than I had imagined to come at the truth of the situation – at least in respect of the fact that I intended blackmail, if he was mistaken in conjecturing the object of my effort. He raised a hand.

'One moment, Mr Archer!' he said, and with two or three bucks of his ample back side completed his business, when withdrawing from his former position he resumed the proper use of his clout (not without some small difficulty), and then complained that I need not have gone to such lengths to place him under such an obligation to me as would persuade him to give me his vote!

I was quick to assure him that such was not the reason for the subterfuge in which I had indulged, but that I wished merely to persuade him to accede to his son's request to allow him to make an honest woman of his mistress. He looked for a moment grim, and indeed began to assert that his parishioners, forced to choose between his word and those of a whore and the assertion even of a Member of Parliament, would . . . But then he hesitated, and almost smiling agreed to my request without further conditions – indeed with such a readiness that I am not sure that Colin himself might not have had success in persuading him had he only persevered in his arguments.

'I trust, sir, that my passage with this admirable young person – for which I trust you are affording her an adequate remuneration – will now remain a matter between the three of us?'

'Provided that . . .'

'My word, sir, is my bond!' said the parson, and I believed it; at which he took his leave, and a very strange man he seemed to be (I reflected).

I now apologised to Miss Betsy for the indignity she had suffered, and hoped she had suffered no injury.

'Injury?' she said. Then, understanding me, she went on: 'Oh, no, he did not play the Greek with me! – the proper aperture was employed for his enjoyment, though for a moment I wondered whether my confession had prompted him to try the boys' way. But, sir, I confess that he managed to satisfy his own high spirits without bringing me to a conclusion. Might I suggest that you . . .? Of course without further remuneration being required . . .'

Whether she spoke from natural generosity of spirit, or (as I now believe) was a genuine lover of the game, as some strumpets are, I found it impossible not to accept the invitation and challenge, and the bed she offered was in any event more interesting than that at the magistrate's lodgings which awaited me; so without more ado I removed my garments and joined her. She proved a most substantial dish, being as strong as she was able, and as inventive as she was energetic. Indeed, her enthusiasm and invention was positively tiring: I was persuaded to have her upon her back, upon her belly, standing, kneeling, crouching – and only when I was out of breath and almost out of energy did she consent to permit me to expel that final gasp of energy which gave me relief, after which she was kind enough to profess herself satisfied (which was as well, for I certainly did not have the energy to pursue her any further). Her skill in the matter of love was remarkable – so that I believed all the stories she had told her confessor, and would have been prepared to hear more.

We then fell into a sleep, and if upon waking I found my purse as absent from my trousers as Betsy and her companion were from the inn, this was no surprise – and since I had taken the precaution of emptying the said purse of all but two guineas, was not so much of a loss that I was led to regret the remarkable encounter, which had proved both useful to young Ford and amusing to myself.

On my rising, I was presented with breakfast, a feast of innuendo from the landlord, some ill looks from the landlady, and a copy of that day's *West Briton*, in which I found an item relative to Lostwithiel, and of which – being occupied – I had heard nothing the previous day.

> 'A greater number of salmon fry have been caught this season in the Lostwithiel river

> than for many years past, and, on Monday night as one of the men was fishing with a trammel, something larger than usual struck the net, which, when drawn, proved to be a sturgeon measuring about four feet six inches. The fish is kept alive in a large tray of water.'

The reader can imagine that I made it my business to finish breaking my fast as speedily as might be, and to issue forth in order to cast an eye on this rarity. It proved to be an astonishing sight, as it measured according to the most accurate computation full five foot three inches in length. This fish was (I was told) relatively small, for the common sturgeon had been known to grow to a size of no less than twelve feet; in this case, it was suggested that the fish must be a young one, for its black snout was still long and thin (as these fish grow older, so their snouts grow blunter and shorter).

The fellow who was caring for the fish in its tank, the moment he was aware of my identity, came up to me and asked if it was true that such a fish must be sent to London to the King. I happened to know this as a fact, for there had recently been a debate upon the matter in the House, when some fellow had asked whether it was right that the statute of Edward II (under which the provision was made that all sturgeon caught in English waters belonged to the Crown) should still stand. Only a short discussion had been necessary before we reached a nearly unanimous decision that the law should remain unchanged, especially since the occasions of such a catch were so rare.

I was one of those few Members who examined the statute in full, from a curiosity arising out of the fact that sturgeon had been known to be caught, in the past, in the river near my friend Sir Franklin Franklyn's place in Hertfordshire (though not in recent times). And tucked into a small paragraph near the end of the document was a provision which I believe no one else had noted: that the reward of the catcher should be what monies the King cared to send him, and the right to choose any woman in the county to perform the act of *conjunction* with him (as the document put it).

Eager in the first place to ensure that His Majesty receive his proper tribute, I sent for the catcher – and after a pause for him to be fetched from some cottages by the river, two men appeared – or rather, one man and a boy, as it seemed, for it turned out that they had been fishing together when the sturgeon had fallen upon their line. On my enquiring which had actually been plying the line at the crucial moment, it turned out to be the younger, one Davy Rundall, who appeared to be of about seventeen years of age, and so shy that his friend Sam Fox – perhaps three or four years his senior – must speak for him.

They did not demur at the news that their catch must be sent to the King at Kensington Palace, and were pleased at the news that a purse of some sort was therefore in prospect; I immediately put the necessary preparations in train. The news that young Davy now had the *droit de seigneur* over all the ladies of the county was received with somewhat less enthusiasm; the two lads clustered together in a whisper, and the elder, Sam, then came up to me and made a request which at the time seemed so extraordinary that I will – if the reader will forgive me – leave it to my friend Sophie to convey.

Chapter Ten

Sophie's Story

Mr Dawson proved as energetic, attentive and elegant a companion outside the sheets as between them, and, as I had originally intended, I visited one or two of his classes; but found that neither was he able to teach me anything I did not know (in the capacity either of dance master or lover, since I hear the reader's unspoken question) nor were those other ladies and gentlemen who enrolled in his classes so charming in manner or conversation as to detain me long.

Though it was amusing to see the ladies attempting to interest him (for he was a fine figure of a man, and eminently attractive to those whose husbands had perhaps lost the first bloom of seductive beauty) there seemed nothing further in the town of Truro to detain me, and I therefore announced my determination to return home. Mr Dawson expressed himself to be sorry to hear of my decision; and certainly after a final dinner expressed his regret in a manner so persuasive that I was forced to regard his love making as an attempt to engage my emotions sufficiently strongly to make me reverse my decision to leave –

or perhaps even to tempt me into some kind of permanent arrangement with him. But (need I say?) he was neither of the class nor the intelligence to woo me into matrimony or any other long lasting companionship – though he was bold enough at one moment to propose the former; and I made my leisurely way back to our cottage – only to find Andy waiting with the news of which the reader will already be aware: the catching of the sturgeon.

I was interested to hear of the reward to be offered to he who had caught the fish (I mean that part of the reward which depended upon the complaisance of a selected female) – the more interested since it had a bearing upon my own circumstances. The young gentleman who had caught the fish had announced that the most beautiful lady he had ever seen was she who had accompanied Mr Archer on his previous visits to the town of Lostwithiel, and had requested her company upon the conditions laid down by statute! Since the reward had been announced, there was nothing to do but to comply with its conditions. Indeed, how could I demur?

As a matter of fact, I was as flattered as any female would be, even by being the choice of a mere youngster – though Andy warned me not to expect too much, for, he said, not only was the gentleman concerned scarcely old enough to be out of school (which did not signify, for some of the most spirited passages of love I have experienced have been in the company of young men exulting in the delight of first discovering the pleasant use to which a newly erected prick might be put) but he also doubted that the request was the boy's own, suspecting that it had been made at the request of a friend and companion who had been with him when the fish was caught, and seemed considerably more assured in the ways of the world than young Davy Rundall (as he was called). Indeed, Andy even conjectured that the latter might not keep any appointment made for him.

But at all events there was no way of escape from my obligation – even had curiosity permitted me to wish for one. A message was sent to young Mr Rundall that the lady of his choice would await him at the Talbot Inn upon the following Saturday night.

I took the precaution of arriving at the Talbot some hours before the time of the appointment, not expecting much of the house; and indeed it did not offer particularly salubrious accommodation, though decent and clean. The chief room (the same in which my friend had plotted the downfall of the parson) was fair enough, but I had some difficulty in making sure that provision was made for washing – not knowing the extent to which my young lover might be in need of this. Indeed, the difficulty I had in finding a tub was significant, for there was at that time little regard to cleanliness in rural places – the habit being to bathe only when circumstances seemed to demand it. Indeed, the landlady when sending out for the tub to a neighbour remarked by way of criticism that the latter was an exquisite, for she bathed once a week, 'whether she needed to or not'. This paragon was persuaded to part with her tub upon the recognition of six pence, and it was brought up and set behind a screen. I also bespoke a bottle of brandy, with which the young gentleman might be plied should he be in need of Dutch courage.

At seven o'clock in the evening, the appointed hour, there came a knock upon the door – and, on my opening it, I discovered not only the fresh-faced boy who I took to be the winner of the prize, but also the slightly older fellow who was surely that companion named by Andy, and whose eyes so impertinently played about my person that I had no difficulty in believing that it was indeed he who had paid me the tribute of naming me. Young Davy kept his gaze upon the floor, and when I offered my hand exerted no pressure upon it in greeting, but relinquished it immediately, as though it was made of hot coals!

Sam Fox, the elder of the two, had no compunction in taking my hand however, and even somewhat clumsily planted a kiss upon it; then introducing himself and his companion, hoping I would excuse his presence, since Davy had been too nervous to come on his own.

They seemed harmless enough lads; even Sam, who had forced himself upon me, was by no means rough or overweening, and, though evidently a countryman of little education and less style, had a certain rustic charm which commended him, being as well built and solid in body and limb as little Davy was slim and almost girlish. I therefore mentally shrugged my shoulders and invited them to take a glass of brandy, which they did, though holding the glasses like tankards, their whole palms clasped about them, and coughing so much as the liquor went down that it seemed likely it was their first taste of such a spirit.

It was clear to me from their appearance no less than from their general manner that both worked upon the land, for their disproportionately broad shoulders and brown faces spoke of it; and they had that peculiar combination of strength and gentleness which our best sort of labouring men have (I sometimes believe that the latter quality must derive from their having commonly to work with animals, where gentleness of character obtains so much better results than violence and tyranny; it may also be that the natural movement of such animals has its effect, for these men too, left to their own devices, move with a freedom and grace often lacking in your town fops).

Sam, the elder, was (as I have suggested) immediately appealing – his appearance bespoke considerable strength and solidity – while his black eyes twinkled with a humour which he was sparing in the expression of – I dare say through his not being sure of my attitude towards him and his friend. It scarcely seemed proper to speak of Davy, the latter, as a man, so young did he appear; in fact I wondered whether, should I carry through the conditions of the contract between us, I might not be accused of baby stealing, for he seemed no more than fourteen or fifteen years of age. He was as slim as his friend was broad, his hands and fingers narrow and slender, and his frame – as far as could be seen – lightly built. On my enquiring – which I felt bound to do – I was somewhat surprised to discover that he was indeed seventeen years of age – at that, two years younger than his friend.

Both lads, after three or four glasses of brandy, which they threw back in a manner more suggestive of the ale drinker than the connoisseur, lost something of their shyness; and when I finally asked whether it was not time that we approached the business of the evening, Sam was clearly delighted, though Davy at once resumed his earlier manner, looking as though the cat had not only got his tongue, but consumed it.

'You understand, sir,' I said to Sam, 'that the reward for catching the fish can only go to the one who reeled it in – which as I understand it, was your friend?'

'Aye,' he replied, though without enthusiasm, 'come, Davy, off with your togs!' – and, taking the younger boy by the shoulders, began without ceremony to remove his shirt. Davy made no effort to help, being as it seemed paralysed (whether by pleasant anticipation or fear I cannot say, but suspected the latter), merely rising to his feet to facilitate his friend drawing off his trousers.

The body then revealed was lean and pleasant enough to those for whom youth and smoothness are as commendable as age and roughness, and who find innocence a spur to desire as compelling as experience (the former summoning all the ingenuity of the latter to inform and teach it). Though without the muscularity attendant upon complete adulthood, Davy was nevertheless clearly a grown man, his manhood signalled (if modestly) by the twists of hair surrounding each pap, and the little cluster which lay between his thighs – though, no doubt through apprehension and the strange circumstances, his masculine accoutrements were unstimulated by enthusiasm, merely hanging prettily below his belly, as inoffensive and dainty as those which decorate the statues of youthful Greek athletes in our museums.

The same, I may say, was not the case with his friend – for, though as a matter of course he retained his clothing, I saw unmistakable signs of an enthusiastic response to my removing my own – which I did not hesitate to do; since he had decided to accompany his friend, Sam must put up with any inconvenience consequent on his envying the dish set before young Davy, who I now took behind the screen, and, persuading him to sit upon a stool by the tub, took some soap in my hand and applied it to the shrunken apparatus before me. This action, entirely unexpected by the boy, nevertheless clearly pleased him, for his little prick grew beneath the ministrations of my hand (doubtless made kinder by the slipperiness of the soap) into a finely shaped slender wand which was so appealing, so fresh, so handsomely clothed in its white and pink skin, that I could not but place a kiss upon its tip – at which I felt a shudder run through the boy's lower limbs (my hands were upon his thighs) and feared that my passage with him would be but a brief one!

Leading him by the hand, I now drew him from behind the screen (when I could not but notice Sam's smiling at his friend's appearance) and led him to the bed, encouraging him to lie upon it and (I believe to Sam's disappointment) drawing the curtains about it to conceal us, as I joined the younger fellow.

Sadly, as I turned, I saw that (perhaps through his friend's smiling) Davy's wand was now once again no more than a twig. Making no bones about it, I immediately gathered the boy into my arms, expecting that the warmth of my body against his own cooler flesh would have the result generally to be expected in such a circumstance. It was not however the case: not only did he lie there like a fish upon a plate, and with as little animation, but there was no suggestion of a renewal of that tumescence which I anticipated.

However, I had had such an experience before with a young and untried lover; and now pressed the boy back upon the pillow, and lowering my head without more ado took his shrunken instrument – sweet as a nut, I may say – between my lips and attempted once more to bring it to the requisite sharpness of apprehension which would result in the necessary extension. Every trick at my command was utilised: my tongue was applied first gently, then more astringently, the charming but limp limb was well lubricated with saliva, the resulting mucosity allowing my lips to slide over the surface of the skin with as tender an application as possible . . . but . . .

Nothing.

On my glancing at Davy's face, I found a look almost of desperation upon it; and realised that clearly there was a strong misapprehension of womankind (I could not believe, in particular, of myself) which might be difficult of resolution, and possibly beyond my cure in such circumstances and with so little time at command.

Drawing myself up, wiping my lips, and kissing his cheek as kindly as I could, I was about to suggest that we take our ease and see what a period of lethargy would do, when I heard a rustle, and looking up was astonished to see the naked body of Mr Fox lowering itself upon the bed on the other side of my reluctant lover. I was about to send him packing with a sharp word, when to my even greater astonishment I saw him lay a hand upon the reluctant prick of the younger lad, which immediately like a jack in the box sprang into an upright position, turning from a limp and useless object into one sufficiently proud and strong to do any work demanded of it!

I was, I confess, extremely sorry to see this: for while close friendship between any youths of a tender age must almost of necessity involve some experiment in carnality, and while I can have no objection to traffic of that sort between gentlemen devoted to their own sex, it invariably gives me some pain when young men of so admirable appearance as my two young companions demonstrate a preoccupation with each other which is likely to exclude them from all the pleasure of loving conversation with the opposite sex – and indeed necessarily precludes the latter from enjoying their company.

I lifted myself upon my elbow, and was about to announce that I would leave them to whatever sport they cared to devise, when Sam placed his hand upon my shoulder and with a persuasive pressure laid me once more upon my back, then encouraging his friend to throw a leg across my body and, in short, place himself in just such a position as was necessary for a proper consummation!

On finding itself in proximity to that part of my anatomy for which it was made, Davy's prick once more through apparent panic lost confidence, and for a moment declined to take its place; but Sam merely moistened his index finger at his lips, and searching out his friend's arsehole inserted it with what I presume was a lecherous delicacy – for Davy's cock now immediately resumed its sturdy verticality, and there was no further difficulty in its affording an entrance – whereupon instinct persuaded Davy to begin those movements normal in such a situation.

The show of pleasure upon his face was immediate and delightful – there could be no question but that he was enjoying himself, and was perhaps even (as his expression further suggested) surprised at it: I could not but smile at what seemed a combination of the two emotions, which puzzled him but certainly did not preclude his continued pleasure. Sam meanwhile must have felt somewhat out of the scene, but tiring of merely participating through toying with whatever part of his friend's anatomy came to hand, at length found it impossible to contain himself – and spitting upon his own prick and kneeling above his friend, inserted it into that aperture which his forefinger had previously titillated, and with only a little inconvenience to me from bearing almost the weight of two lads, ploughed his friend as the latter ploughed me – the three of us I believe equally conscious of the pleasant novelty of the situation, and through it, no less than through a normal friction, consummating our emotions without delay.

First Sam dismounted, then Davy; and after we had rested for a time, I felt bound to acknowledge the help of his friend, and congratulated Sam (who lay upon my other side) upon his actions. However, I could not but remark on the unusual manner in which Davy had been raised to that point of sensuality at which he was able to enjoy me. Was it the case that he and his friend were . . .

'Not a bit of it,' said Sam (and I translate the vernacular into a more readily understandable English, the original accent being so thick as to be almost impossible of comprehension). 'Or, at least, not as a matter of nature.'

He then went on to tell a sad and remarkable story.

He and Davy were neighbours and had grown up together, his mother taking the place of Davy's (who had died when he was a child); though he was only a couple of years older, Sam had accepted the part of an elder brother with enthusiasm, and the two boys had played together, talked together, and, as Sam believed, when the time was right, would court together.

As boys will, they had seen with interest the changes which occurred in each other's bodies as they passed from childhood to boyhood – Davy in particular watching with admiration and envy as Sam first exhibited the remarkable capacity of his private organ for extension, and the manner in which it could be milked of a viscous liquor, the jetting forth of which (Sam opined) was accompanied by a pleasure quite as keen and possibly keener than that given by any other activity known to him. Davy was younger and a period of time must necessarily elapse before a similar exercise was possible for him – but curiosity led him to examine Sam's organ, and the latter was not slow to appreciate the fact that the pleasure given by toying with himself was rather less than that which could be derived from his prick being handled by someone else – even of his own sex; and when Davy himself reached maturity, they did not hesitate to afford each other the fullest enjoyment that could be derived from mutual caresses.

However, Sam was not one (as he assured me, his eyes fixed now upon my breast) to restrict such pleasure to the company of a male friend, and soon was able to pass on to Davy stories of the amusement to be had in the company of girls, whose bodies seemed to have been designed by benevolent nature specifically for the accommodation and pleasure of the male organ.

Now Sam had a sister, Kate, of about the same age as Davy; the three had played together, and, just at the time when Davy was ready to look towards female company, Kate had begun to turn into a young woman of considerable attractions. 'Though she be my sister,' Sam said, 'she's a beauty, and enough trouble I had to keep my own hands off her bubbies' (for like most young people of their class, they had shared a bed). Unhappily, Kate's father (a violent and disturbed man) also took a keen interest in his daughter's sudden womanly appearance, and only the girl's threat that she would inform her mother deterred him from making his own attempt upon her virtue.

Fortunately, a young female neighbour had saved Sam from the sin of incest by enthusiastically coupling with him under the greenwood tree, and Kate now turned her eye upon young Davy – encouraged by Sam, who assured him that the pleasure to be found between a girl's thighs was inestimably greater than that which could be conveyed by the arsehole even of the most devoted friend (for they readily admitted to enjoying that pleasure so freely condemned by our puritans – and protested indeed that it was common in country society, and infinitely preferable to commerce with sheep or goats, who while perforce receptive were incapable of returning human affection).

But to resume. Davy took the liberty of kissing Kate one fine afternoon, upon which she happily thrust her tongue into the passage of his throat, and, while he was still considering whether she would permit him to caress her breast, had thrust her hand into his trousers and taken in her fingers that which a vigorous massaging soon much reduced in size and vigour.

The following day, chiefly at Kate's instigation, the two wandered off to a hedgerow below the town, where in next to no time they were bare as needles, and Davy was ready to try how the eye of the needle might best be threaded.

However, no sooner had they began to couple when there was a great roar, and Davy found himself in the hands of Kate's father, who (whether through jealousy of her virtue or envy of the lad's possession of her body) took him by the waist and threw him with such force against a tree that he fell almost unconscious to the ground. The couple had been betrayed by another lad, who had had his own eye upon Kate but had been repulsed by her in Davy's favour. It was this other lad who, larger and stronger than Davy, now helped to lash him with his face to a tree's trunk, whereupon the farmer laid into him with a cane plucked from a nearby tree, and administered a beating so fierce that . . .

At this point, Sam encouraged his friend to turn over, and there, down his back from shoulders to tight white buttocks, were pale scars which spoke of what must indeed have been a terrible beating – so fierce indeed that Kate had had to fetch Sam to help his friend, bleeding, to his cottage, where he lay upon his face for some days until his wounds had healed.

A month or so later, Sam's father was killed by a bull, while cruelly beating it to market. Neither Sam nor (especially) Kate repined; and the latter almost immediately made it her business to court Davy – but, to her sorrow and his despair, found that despite his devotion to her no encouragement on her part could make him ready for or capable of that act necessary for a proper union of the sexes.

Sam was no less distressed for her than for his friend; but the boys were utterly confused, discovering that Davy's prick would respond readily to the caresses of his friend, but remained unresponsive to those of Miss Kate.

Unfortunately she found it impossible to understand the nature of the difficulty, and while Sam tried to persuade his sister to permit him to share the bed upon which she and Davy attempted their courtship – convinced that he could be of just such assistance in their lovemaking as he had recently been in ours – she was repelled by the idea. Sam's devotion to Davy was such that he could not but offer consolation, and the two boys had fallen into the habit of assuaging their natural desires in each other's company, though for his part Sam still paid his attentions to the girls of the neighbourhood, some of whom however became so jealous of his friend as to repel his advances. Nevertheless, his friendship was such that he was never entirely free from the wish to solve Davy's problem for him, thus freeing the latter from the necessity (through sensual deprivation) of positively seeking out a male companion, which he properly regarded as a second rate solution to the lad's predicament.

When Sam heard from my friend Andy of the reward offered for the capture of the sturgeon, he saw the opportunity for his friend to try whether a full-blown woman (as he called me!) might be able to affect a cure – and this had been to a degree successful, for, though he had had to offer some help, Davy had at least for the first time experienced a successful consummation!

The question was now, of course, whether the connection could be effected without Sam's help. I therefore whispered to him an invitation to withdraw, which he did. Left once more alone with Davy, I took him again in my arms, and whispered to him that I was in no doubt that such a fine lad as he could surmount the obstacle which had denied him the pleasure he had sought with Kate. He was now by no means so shy as he had been, and indeed without prompting took a nipple between his lips and sucked upon it with considerable delight, while at the same time I felt exploring hands moving about my body – which, if more concerned with exploration than with the actual conveyance of pleasure, at least showed that the lad was already sufficiently cured of his shyness to take such an action.

But now, plucking his lips from my breasts and persuading him (with some reluctance) to turn upon his face, I laid my lips to the scars of the stripes with which he had been injured, and comforted each in turn, kissing and licking them, while at the same time caressing his sides with my hands. On reaching his buttocks, I felt him stir uneasily, and passing my hands beneath his hips was delighted to find that his prick, while by no means iron hard, was at least of a size suggestive of a distinct interest; and by joining to my kisses some small nips with my teeth upon the fleshy part of an enchantingly round, firm arse, I found in no time a considerable bulge beneath my palms – which grew implacable upon the additional stimulation which I offered to that tender orifice so familiar to his friend; when encouraging the boy to turn over, I was able to confirm with my eyes the fact that his prick was in such a state as no woman could fail to feel complimented by.

Calculating that to offer him the service of my lips would only be to repeat that courtesy the pleasures of which he had probably experienced with his friend, I instead parted with my fingers my lower lips, and lowered myself with deliberation upon his prick – fearful lest the nature of the action should renew his fears and thus result in an inability to maintain a proper stance. My fears however were groundless, for in a moment he was bucking beneath me like some previously unharnessed yearling, and showing such enthusiasm as seemed to indicate that his problem might be solved.

A cry of 'Well done, Davy boy!' was now heard, and looking around I found that Sam had been unable to resist the temptation to peep between the curtains, and was now standing upon the end of the bed and watching us, his own appendage standing up below his belly at such an angle as to indicate an extreme anxiety for congress! This, I would in the normal course of things have discouraged – but could not resist the boy's grin (and after all, he had been instrumental in his friend's recovery) – while Davy himself, without asking my permission, signalled to his friend to join us, whereupon he came forward and laid himself down so that he could examine with interest my body as it rose and fell upon that of his friend – something which he had not previously allowed himself to do with such obvious relish, and which intrigued him so much that he adventured his hand between my thighs in order to test just in what manner the connection took place (presumably it had never occurred to him that a lady could adopt such a position in love making).

Davy meanwhile had reached to take his friend's prick in his hand and was stroking it with a gentle and practised enthusiasm clearly the product of the hours they had previously spent together. Sam lifted his head for a moment and glanced at me, as though wondering whether he dare appeal for some attention – but then, thinking better of inviting an untoward familiarity, moved forward, turned to face me, and threw a leg across his friend's body, lowering himself just sufficiently for Davy to be able to reach with his lips that part most in need of their attention, while himself taking the liberty of placing his hands upon my shoulders and showering kisses upon my breasts.

It did occur to me how amused and intrigued my London friends would be could they set eyes upon the situation, for I was sure it would not occur to them that such an interesting combination of figures was likely to be seen in a rural inn! Nor, I think, could they have resisted the emotion of jealousy, for neither of the boys now keeping me an avid company were figures to be sneered at: if Davy was certainly slim and as yet relatively undeveloped (though as to the development of that part of him upon which I was still able to ride without fear of its collapse, that was sufficiently complete!), his friend Sam was as fine a young man as could be desired, his shoulders broad and muscular, his waist slim, and those buttocks which were now proudly parted above his friend's head as firm and elastic as could be (as I now confirmed by leaning forward and placing my hands beneath them, drawing the boy up and away so that his prick was plucked from his friend's lips and was now almost in contact with that other upon which I still rode).

I believe he saw what my intention was, and reaching behind him gave Davy's young nipples so determined a tweak with his finger that the latter gave a cry of mingled pain and pleasure, and almost at that moment I felt within me the scalding evidence of his pleasure. With a sort of frenzy of enjoyment and infuriation, he gave his friend a tremendous smack upon the back side – but, on my raising myself, wriggled from beneath me with a grin which showed no sign of anger as his place was usurped by his friend.

Sam, however, showed no sign of wishing to be ridden like a mare, preferring to ride like a stallion; and tumbling me backwards thrust into me with such determination that (not having reached my own apogee at the hands – or rather through the prick – of his friend) I could not but give a cry of pleasure; whereupon he redoubled his attack, and lifting my knees upon his shoulders gave me such a thorough bollocking that, although he came off within a minute or so, I was by that time entirely satisfied.

We were now all three so pleased with ourselves, and so exhausted by our actions, that we fell shortly into a doze, and from a doze into a sleep, from which I awoke only as the morning light came through the window – which showed me the two youngsters lying one upon each side of me, innocent as angels (though considerably more virile than those creatures usually appear). My stirring awakened them, whereupon both laid hands upon my person, silently imploring a recapitulation of pleasure, which I happily allowed them – and since it could not be determined which should have precedence, and they were experienced in the other form of copulation to which I have no objection, I laid Sam down upon the bed and once more climbed atop of him, but this time while lowering myself upon an instrument no less ready for the indulgence than the night before offered to his friend that other convenient aperture into which he introduced himself with apparent pleasure (and indeed with some pleasure to myself, for while the act is – as I have already reminded the reader – condemned by society, it is by no means devoid of interest to those to whom the pleasure derived is in itself a sufficient excuse for it, and who find it both agreeable and convenient).

This further somewhat acrobatic combination of three is not one I can recommend to the plump or inactive; but with two lithe and slim young men no such problem arose, while Sam's attentions to my back side were so careful and practised that they afforded no pain and a great deal of pleasure (a circumstance not so easily attained when the lover is unfamiliar with such an approach).

Both boys were properly pleased and grateful –

while my own pleasure was as considerable, and not in the least lessened as I watched them dress; each of us in our way had achieved satisfaction, and, in addition to the physical pleasure I had received, I had the additional knowledge that Miss Kate would soon benefit from my night's work!

Chapter Eleven

The Adventures of Andy

I was – as the reader, I trust, has also been – interested to hear of Sophie's connection with the two youths from Lostwithiel: the younger of the two seems to have profited from the confidence instilled in him by the episode, for he has subsequently been thrice Mayor of the town (one reason why Sophie, upon my advice, has spoken of him under a *nom de plume*, though the slightest research in the area will doubtless discover his name to the curious, for the story is well known in the neighbourhood, and has even latterly been boasted of by the chief protagonist).

My own present anecdote concerns that trade which is well known to have flourished in the county of Cornwall from time immemorial: that is, the business of smuggling brandy and geneva to our shores from the continent. It all began once again with a paragraph in that excellent journal the *West Briton*, which read:

'The schooner *Marie Victoire* (Captain Barnett), laden with coals, entered Fowey harbour last week, when she was boarded by preventive man Bright, who remained while she was unloading. He suspected deceit, but the sailors conducted themselves in such a careless and unaffected manner as to very much shake those suspicions. When most of the coal had been unloaded, Bright bored various parts of the vessel, and at length sent his gimlet into a cache of brandy. The craft was found to have a false bottom, and 276 tubs of brandy and geneva were found.'

I read the passage with interest, and with some sympathy for the smugglers, for while their activity certainly deprives the country of some revenue, when considered in proportion to the whole of taxation it is but little, while the damage done is restricted to a minimal loss from the Treasury.

No sooner had I put the paper down, than a girl brought me a letter marked URGENT, which claimed that my presence was immediately required at the town of Fowey, both in my capacity as magistrate and as Member of Parliament for the area. The writer was none other than Preventive Officer Bright, who wrote a most educated hand, and offered the opportunity, he said, of apprehending a major mover in the smuggling trade in Cornwall. He requested that my visit should, however, be kept a secret, and that I should for that reason take care to arrive if possible after nightfall, in case I should be recognised by any townsman of Fowey.

I was not only eager, as a matter of course, to fulfil my duty, but extremely curious as to Bright's letter; and therefore lost no time in leaving for Fowey. As I approached the town it was still daylight, although dusk was beginning to fall; and so I paused at a farmhouse near Castle Dore (long supposed to have been the site of that castle of King Mark's to which Tristan came, and where the fateful meeting with Iseult took place).

The farmhouse was sufficiently imposing and handsome to seem capable of offering decent hospitality, and since I only required shelter for a few hours I had no hesitation in knocking upon the front door, which after a while was answered by a pretty slut who, on hearing my request to speak to the master of the house, ushered me without delay into a sufficiently well-furnished sitting room, and vanished. In only a few minutes there came not the farmer but his wife – an extremely fine woman in her middle years clad not in apron and cap (as one might expect) but in a dress which would not have disgraced the owner of a house in a fashionable suburb of town. She introduced herself as Mrs Job, and enquired my business. She had entered the room confidently – but, on seeing me, started as though almost in terror, but then regarded me with the utmost keenness.

On hearing that I merely wished shelter until the hours of darkness, she readily consented (but continued to look me up and down with a curiously direct stare and an interest which would have seemed insolent had it not been for the slight smile which seemed to signal that she found the prospect pleasing).

'Perhaps you would care for some refreshment?'

she said, signalling me to a comfortable seat, which I took. 'I can offer a very good brandy, which will warm you after your journey.'

I was happy to accede, and while a maid lit a lamp Mrs Job left the room, to return shortly with a tray bearing glasses and a bottle, which indeed turned out to contain liquor which in a couple of swallows did its job admirably, coursing through my veins with a satisfactory warmth.

I confided in her my proper name, though at first hesitating to do so; however, there seemed no reason for concealing it from so respectable a woman – who turned out, on my enquiring for her husband, to be a widow of some nine months' date, and still to be in mourning.

I commiserated with her: it must be, as I said, a fearful thing to accommodate oneself to the loss of a constant companion.

It was, she replied, especially since in every respect the late Mr Job had been an admirable man, firm in character, vigorous in business and loving in the bedchamber (this last comment, though delivered with lowered eyes, was made without a blush). She then rose and fetched from a nearby table a representation of her husband made by the process called *talbotype*, or otherwise *photography* – something to which I had been introduced, in somewhat unusual circumstances, by its inventor, a Mr Fox Talbot (the curious will find these set out in Chapter Eight of our volume *Eros off the Rails*, first put out in the year of '92 by the diligent and mettlesome firm of Headline Publishers of London). The representation now in question showed a fellow leaning against a table, dressed in a fetching topcoat and carrying a hat and gloves – but the remarkable thing about him was his resemblance to myself!

'Ah!' exclaimed the lady, as I studied the picture, 'you have noticed! The first time I set eyes upon you I was startled almost from my senses, believing that my Zephaniah had returned from the grave! Oh, sir, do not repine when I say that I would give all I possess were that to be possible!' – and to my distress I saw a big tear start from her eyes, while she fell rather than sat upon a nearby sofa, and carried a handkerchief to her face.

Could any man see such sorrow without attempting to console the griever? I took myself to her side, and placing an arm about her shoulders raised a glass of brandy to her lips, which after a moment she consented to sip – fixing upon me, with an attentive look, eyes which seemed large enough to swallow me, whole. As the glass was lowered, her lips were left shining slightly with the liquor, and half parted in such a way as to be entirely irresistible. Whether or not the reader can blame me, I found it impossible not to plant a kiss upon that delightful mouth, feeling as I did so the wetness of the tears transferred from her cheek to my own.

It will be believed that the moment the action had been put in train, I wondered whether she might not reject it with contumely; but it was almost immediately clear that the contrary was to be the case – for her lips parted still further beneath mine, and in a moment I felt a sweet tongue playing about the tip of my own, while her hands were placed upon the back of my head, resisting any attempt on my part (had I thought of making it!) to draw away. It was only when we were breathless that our lips parted, when she buried her face in my shoulder, and I felt her slender body pressed to my own.

I must invite the reader to believe that I never in my life took advantage of a lady – however beautiful – in distress; but I must also confess (and my published works will confirm the fact, should any doubt it) that I have never refused comfort to those who were in need of it – and who should be more in need of comfort than a wife cruelly bereft of those marital consolations which make the state so delightful and satisfying?

Therefore when the lady looked at me with a mute appeal, that appeal was answered; on her rising and holding out her hand, I took it without hesitation, and allowed myself to be led up a fine set of stairs into a comfortable bedroom whose size and luxury proclaimed it that of the master or mistress of the house, and where a fire was ready burning (no doubt for the comfort of the lonely occupant, upon her retiring; but this now made the room all the more welcome for the purpose to which no doubt it was soon to be put).

It was once more no less my duty than my pleasure to allow my hostess to fix her lips to mine, while her hands slid down to my waist and even below it, the better to incline my body to her own. My own part in the proceedings was an obvious one: to loose those ties and buttons which confined the lady within the bounds of her clothing, and not only with her consent but her assistance, in a very few moments to strip her to that state most convenient for the consolation we both had in mind. In only a few additional moments I was myself bare as she – and the subject (as I could see from observing the glances from below the lady's eyelids) of some admiration, chiefly (from the direction of her gaze) for that object most germane to what was to come – *videlicet* my riding muscle, which, while not (I dare say) anything miraculous, has from time to time been commended as both sightly and sturdy.

The lady was no less the subject of my own complimentary gaze: she was of full figure, matronly without being overblown, her breasts large but firm, the pink nipples standing out from the darker aureole which surrounded them; below, a slim waist and flat belly were set upon sturdy thighs which my eyes told me were bereft of that flabbiness which is sometimes the attribute of ladies of a certain age, while surrounding that vessel where presently I trusted to step my mast was a cloud of charming yellow fronds just sufficiently voluminous to provide a garnish to, while not being sufficiently bushy entirely to hide, a pair of plump, pink lips.

Vinny – and since she presently invited me to call her by this diminutive (her name being Lavinia), I might as well use it in this narrative – now took once more a step towards me, and folding me in her arms whispered into my ear the enticing words, 'Are you ready to be loved?' – and without waiting for an answer began to kiss me all over my face: lips, chin, cheeks, nose, eyebrows and ears – into the whorls of which she inserted her sharp-pointed tongue in an irresistibly lascivious gesture.

But this was only the first intimation of that natural gift for making love which made me envy the late Mr Job everything but his death: for his widow now gradually slid down the length of my body, allowing me to do nothing but stand as she first nipped my shoulders, then raising my arms one by one licked at that space below them to which few women permit themselves to attend, but which are remarkably sensitive to such attention; then playing with her tongue about my nipples, which were elevated so briskly that they were almost painful; then all the time murmuring words so soft that I could not catch them (though their import was unmistakable) sank to her knees and kissed and licked my belly and the tops of my thighs, even taking some of the hairs which grew there between her lips and stretching them (as it were) so that at the roots there was the most delicious prickling sensation.

She ignored the chief signal of my appreciation, though it positively wept with frustration at her neglect – instead persuading me to raise one foot and place it upon a convenient stool in order that she might transfer her attention to my cods, and – stretching the cheeks of my arse apart with her fingers – at last to that aperture beloved of sodomites but unduly neglected by women. How glad was I that before setting out I had had an industrious bath! – for I was able to persuade myself that no odour could stand in the way of her giving herself enthusiastically to the titillation of the area in question, first touching with the most gentle motion the ring of muscle which surrounds the *anus*, then positively diving the tip of her tongue into it, an action productive of a sensation which brought tears of pleasure to my eyes, affording such a galvanic stimulation that I feared an involuntary collapse!

But it must surely now be my duty to afford the lady an equivalent degree of attention, and catching her by the shoulders and briefly kissing those admirable breasts – which were indeed as firm and elastic to the touch as I had supposed – inclined Vinny backwards until feeling the edge of the bed at her knees she collapsed backwards upon it, allowing me to part her thighs and kneel between them, thus commanding the field where I must suppose the chief source of delight must lie.

Taking my cue from her, I approached with an appreciative lethargy, finding the utmost sensual gratification in kissing and caressing with my tongue the skin of her thighs, which was soft as velvet, or like that of some delightful fruit. I mirrored her own action in avoiding those lips which now seemed to pout in welcome, and neglecting for the moment that little ornament which now peeped shyly at the upper junction of her pussy, which I knew to be as keen a receptor of stimulation as the crown of my own cock (which was now so distended by the force of blood as to be positively painful).

Instead, I hoisted her legs so that her ankles hung upon my shoulders, and, raising her back side with my hands, approached that usually secret part which in me she had found so rewarding to attend to.

My own attentiveness had a result quite equal to that she must have observed in me, as her sighs and wrigglings testified: but more – in a moment I felt her attempting to lift my head from its place, and consenting to this (believing her to wish me to transfer my attentions to the more common source of pleasure) was greeted by an appealing look which I failed to understand. Seeing my confusion, she took my prick between her fingers and to my astonishment pulled me towards her so that its tip stood against not its usual receptacle, but that other which I had recently stimulated. So thoroughly indeed had I attended to it that my saliva had acted as a lubrication sufficiently juicy to enable her – pulling me more spiritedly towards her – to begin to impale herself! – an act to the completion of which it was impossible for me (so roused was I) not to contribute.

I was not so innocent as to suppose that some ladies did not exist for whom this act was desirable, though as a matter of fact my only previous experience of a positive enthusiasm for it had been with a young gentleman friend of mine whose services had been so great that I was persuaded to allow him to perform the action upon myself (a description of which the reader must seek elsewhere in these works). I must confess that for myself the only attraction in the act was the play which preceded it; once penetration had been completed, as the subject I felt little sensation. However, it may be that for some reason I was unreceptive (other than in the physical sense); for Vinny was certainly not disappointed, gasping and almost screaming with pleasure as, steering me with her hands upon my hips, she persuaded me to complete that act in the performance of which I was a tyro, but chiefly through appreciation of my partner's pleasure overcame any scruples I might at first have possessed.

It now occurred to me (as my own enjoyment reached its apogee) that there was a further act I could perform which might add a frisson to Vinny's pleasure, and dampening my forefinger at my lips I found with it that knub of flesh of which I have previously spoken; upon my touching, my companion's whole body opened wide as though in the course of a fit, and with a wild shriek she kicked out with her heels, sending me sprawling while she collapsed upon the bed, wide as a starfish and as devoid (for some moments) of all movement!

Upon our recovering our senses, I realised that a full hour had passed while we had been engaged in our diversions, and that the darkness had entirely closed in; I therefore rose, and with apologies for a somewhat abrupt departure made my excuses – not neglecting however to compliment and thank my hostess upon her hospitality, the generosity of which had so far exceeded the bounds expected by a casual caller. Mrs Job was kind enough to suggest that any thanks were due to me, for my appreciation of her situation and my efforts to ameliorate it.

My ride into Fowey was a careful one, for the darkness made the roads somewhat treacherous to my horse's hooves. However, I safely reached the centre of the town with only one challenge from the watch, and, knocking on the door of a handsome Customs House at the end of Lostwithiel Street, was greeted by the officer, Mr Bright, or Jeremy as he swiftly invited me to call him. We sat late into the night over a few glasses of brandy only slightly less fine than Mrs Job's (I suspected it to have been drawn from some captured liquor barrel, but said nothing!) discussing the matter in question: which was that Jeremy had been approached by one of the members of the crew of the *Marie Victoire*, who in the hope of mercy at his forthcoming trial had informed upon his masters.

It appeared that the caption of the vessel, one Josiah Barnett, took his orders from a superior with whom he regularly met in a small cottage at Readymoney Cove, near a beach at the entrance of the port, and that the crewman had been able to divulge the date and time of the next meeting – which would be upon the following evening at ten of the clock.

With some doubts as to how I would receive the tidings, Jeremy admitted to me now that he had permitted Captain Barnett to escape the net which had gathered in the rest of the crew – for it had even then been suspected that he might lead the way to the commander of the gang, an expectation now about to be fulfilled, though at first there had been a fear of failure, for the captain had easily evaded the man set to watch him. Happily, that was now a matter of no importance, for we had only to secrete ourselves in the said cottage, contrive a way of overhearing the captain's consultation with his superior, and pounce upon the pair – when myself having power of arrest, and being a witness to the plotting, a conviction must follow.

I congratulated the steadfast officer upon his quickness of wit, and naturally fell in with his plans. Lest news of my presence should arouse suspicion, I spent the next day pent up in the Customs House, which despite some comforts I found somewhat boring, having for reading matter only the Customs Regulations Act and an ancient copy of *Tristram Shandy*, a book which I already knew backwards (and which read in such a way made little more sense than when perused in the conventional manner!).

However slowly hours may pass, eventually time winds to an end; and, at half past the hour of nine we left the Customs House and, our way lit only by a dark lantern, walked along the path above the harbour towards Readymoney, a cove which stands under one of the two blockhouses which King Henry VIII erected at the harbour entrance as a fortification against piratical attacks. Here, we found the cottage which had been named as the meeting place, dark and deserted; and had no difficulty in entering it through an insecure back window.

The place was little more than a shack. In the single downstairs room was nothing more than a ramshackle table, a couple of chairs and a truckle bed; while mounting the stairs (so rickety that the climb was a perilous one) we found ourselves in what had once no doubt been a bedroom but was now devoid of all furniture. The floor, happily, was in as bad a state of repair as the rest of the structure, and the chinks between the planks must afford a clear view of the room below when it was lit. Disposing ourselves as comfortably as we could, we settled down to wait – but only a few minutes passed before we heard the rattle of shingle on the nearby beach as a rowing boat was drawn upon it – then footsteps approaching. Lying upon the floor and applying our eyes to the chinks, we saw the door open and a dark figure enter.

The man set out candles upon the table and, striking a flint, lit them, then removing the dark cloak which (no doubt to aid his passing unnoticed through the town) revealed himself: glancing at Jeremy, I was assured through a nod that this was Captain Josiah Barnett. Somehow the name – in particular the Christian name – had the ring of age about it, and I had expected a grizzled ancient mariner. Instead, however, the figure that now stood below us was one which might have appeared upon any stage as exemplifying the hero of a romantic comedy: apart from the fact that his face was uncommonly handsome, a lick of jet black hair falling across his forehead to give just that touch of satanity to his visage, he was slim and athletic in build, as could be seen from his dress consisting only of a shirt and breeches (a light garb for what I had found a somewhat chilly evening for the time of the year). About his waist was a broad belt, where hung a pistol – a somewhat ominous sight, though Jeremy too was armed.

Sitting at the table, he removed a wallet of papers from his pocket and began to study them by the light of the candles. The minutes seemed long, for we must not move so much as a quarter inch for fear of disturbing him: indeed, on an itch making it imperative for me to move my right arm, he raised his head for a moment – but concluded I suppose that the cause was a rat, and returned to his study.

It seemed several hours, but was probably but a matter of minutes before he raised his head again, and at the same time I became conscious of a sound from outside the building. The captain's hand fell upon the butt of his pistol as the door opened: but he clearly recognised the figure which now entered – and to my astonishment rose to his feet, stepped forward, took the visitor in his arms and clapped a kiss upon his lips before he had so much as removed his hat!

Here was a strange event! – not only did it seem odd that the leaders of a smugglers' band should be revealed as gentlemen of the sodomitic persuasion, but the captain had not had (to me) the appearance of one such – though I reminded myself that there was no inevitable sign which invariably betrayed gentlemen of that sort.

However, in a moment the question was resolved: for on the newcomer raising his hands to his hat and sweeping it from his head a great cloud of blonde hair fell about her shoulders, and there was revealed none other than Mrs Lavinia Job!

My gasp would certainly have been heard below had not the couple been once more engaged in an embrace, while Jeremy laid his hand over my mouth and put his finger to his lip, then making a listening gesture with his hand at his ear – meaning that we must overhear some words germane to the matter of smuggling before we could afford to reveal ourselves.

It appeared to me that we might have something of a wait, however, for, when I returned my eye to the chink, Vinny (with that adeptness of which I had previously been the subject) had already removed Captain Barnett's shirt, while the latter had laid by his pistol and set it upon the table in order more freely to remove that clothing which had previously hidden a pistol of another (no less imposing) sort; and in less time than it takes to tell, the couple were rolling upon the pile of sacking directly below us, naked as the day on which they were born, and with no less enthusiasm than that which on the previous night one of them had similarly tumbled with me!

I was somewhat amused to note that the captain had been instructed in his duty by his employer, for after a brief preliminary skirmish he turned his back upon the lady and, kneeling upon all fours, lowered his head upon his folded arms and elevated his shapely back side, the two halves of which were only slightly dusted with black hairs, and to which she was happy to devote those attentions which I had myself enjoyed, the captain's expression making it clear that he was also delighted by them. Upon the caresses of her tongue, joined by the tickling of those fingers which at the same time were playing about his bollocks and prick, becoming too much for him (and I perfectly knew the feelings which he was experiencing) he suddenly jerked away, and turning fell upon her with a violence unexpected in an employee with his master/mistress, tumbling her backwards, lifting her calves over his shoulders, and without so much of a preliminary courtesy as to ensure that his prick was sufficiently lubricated, thrusting into her back passage.

I felt poor Jeremy (to whom all this was entirely unexpected) wince, and I myself feared that some damage might have been done; however the only reaction from the lady was a cry much more expressive of pleasure than pain, and the gasps with which she greeted the captain's lunging were such as must convince any listener of her enjoyment of the unusual process.

It was now Jeremy's turn to make a rash movement, forced upon him (as I guessed) by the enlargement of his own riding-muscle, a phenomenon which the scene below us must provoke in any red-blooded man (I myself had had to make certain adjustments in my position upon the floor). I was amused to see that the officer's eyes were now firmly closed, as though to watch further would be (as might be the truth) too unbearably arousing in its lubriciousness.

With a final leap of his buttocks, the captain concluded his business, and the lady seemed no whit dissatisfied by the conclusion; the pair picked themselves up, and no doubt heated by their activities failed to resume their clothing, immediately seating themselves at the table and beginning immediately discussing the importation of brandy from Holland.

When we had heard enough, Jeremy gave me a signal; and before the couple below could connect the noise we inevitably made with any immediate threat, we had dropped down the staircase and were confronting them – Jeremy's pistol so steadily pointing at the captain's head that, though the latter's own weapon was ready to hand, he dared not reach for it.

'If you would watch the lady,' said Jeremy, 'I will see to this villain.' And, placing the barrel of his gun against the captain's head, bade him dress himself.

Mrs Job meanwhile had recognised me, and, rising to her feet and displaying her body to me in all its remembered glory, gave a mute glance of appeal which she must have known that I (who am always susceptible to any appeal from the eyes of a beautiful female) could not resist! I gave a barely noticeable nod – at which she reached out for the Captain's pistol, and, stepping behind me, reached around and, with what I must confess was a gesture as uncomfortable as it was humorous, pointed it straight at that portion of my anatomy with which she had earlier been familiar. She then, in a voice as assured as it was gentle, called upon Mr Bright to be aware of the calamity that would disable his superior should he persist in arresting the captain.

Turning, Jeremy had no course but to drop his

pistol (though his look informed me with what scorn he regarded a magistrate who could so easily be used as a tool by a woman!).

In no time, the pair had us trussed like chicken, though with a hint of a wink Mrs Job ensured that my own bonds were sufficiently weak for me to escape at any time. They then dressed themselves and took their leave.

We lay for just such a time as I felt must ensure the couple's escape, when, after pretending for some time to struggle with the ropes which bound me, I contrived to seem to undo them, and releasing myself then untied my companion (who had been good enough to excuse my foolishness by remarking that he should himself have kept a stricter watch upon the lady).

Making our way ruefully back to the Customs House we took ourselves to bed. My own rue was, I must say, assumed: I could not regret having permitted Mrs Job to escape, and could only hope that she was at this moment making her way towards some other part of the country, no doubt accompanied by the captain. Jeremy Bright was certainly of that opinion, for it would be worthless (he said) to make a raid upon her farm, which would be found deserted – except perhaps for a small store of contraband liquor which might as well be collected the next day as that night. He had not been as surprised as he might have been at the identity of the smugglers' leader, for Mrs Job's late husband (he now revealed) had been a notorious participant in the illegal trade, and indeed had for some time run a bank in the nearby village of

Polpier, entirely supported by the income made by the villagers from the illegal importation of liquor!

He blamed himself for going alone, apart from my inexperienced self, upon the venture; but I cheered him by assuring him of the complimentary remarks which I would pass to his superiors. And for myself: I had always regarded smuggling as a venial sin, and had no regrets at allowing one of the most picturesque of offenders to escape!

Chapter Twelve

Sophie's Story

It was a matter of course that as acting chief magistrate for the area – a position to which Andy had been elevated, as a courtesy, during the few months we were spending in the county – he should take his place with the others at the quarterly Assize at Bodmin, and I was glad to accept his invitation to sit with him – not only because the cases to be tried, while no doubt melancholy in their implications for the accused, were likely to provide some interest for one deprived of the usual entertainments of Town, but because the presiding judge was to be His Honour Mr Justice Stele, a gentleman of whom much was being made since his somewhat unexpected elevation to the Bench a couple of months previously.

His Honour was continually described by the *cognoscenti* as the coming man; not only was he a brilliant lawyer, whose accomplishments in advocacy had been heard of in London while he was yet at work only in the courts of the more remote northern counties, but he was said to be that rare creature, a man implacable in his sense of justice, yet not without mercy, and incapable of being bribed – yet by no means devoid of an appetite for the pleasures of the society, though sparing in his enjoyment of them. And yet he was only thirty years of age!

I must confess I looked forward to seeing, and even meeting, this paragon, though my previous encounters with members of the judiciary had not persuaded me that he was likely to meet my criteria of pleasurable acquaintance, for they had almost invariably been plump and somnambulant (doubtless from years of sleeping on the bench), and often uncouth and inconsiderate (through those same years of having their own way, their every wish pandered to by obsequious colleagues and servants, being observed with terror by those who came before them and afforded the uncritical respect of members of the public – who for the most part were men who feared they might one day stand in the dock before him, and women who were terrified at the power he wielded).

At all events, it was with pleasurable anticipation that I accompanied Andy into Bodmin early on the day appointed for the opening of the Assize, where we presented ourselves to the Mayor (Mr Alderman Truscott) at his Parlour, in order to take sherry with His Honour, who had been due to arrive the previous night.

Here, however, we were informed that unfortunately, due to the sudden overturning of his carriage at Bideford (happily without injury to himself), His Honour had suffered considerable delay; there had been no sign of him on the previous night, when he had been expected at his lodgings, nor had he yet presented himself at the Mayor's Parlour. Indeed it seemed for some time that the opening of the Assize itself must be postponed – but half an hour before time a breathless servant galloped up to the town hall, and throwing himself from his horse (upon which he had preceded his master) advised the Mayor that he and his party should proceed to the Court, where His Honour would present himself immediately upon his arrival, which should be within minutes of the appointed time.

We all therefore made our way in procession from the Parlour through the streets to the Court, which stood in cold grey granite in a square to the south of the town; and took our places upon the lower bench – able to amuse ourselves by observing the gallery, which was packed with a rabble as eager to see the proceedings as myself.

Precisely upon the striking of ten, the door at the back of the bench behind us was thrown open, and turning we saw the tall figure of Mr Justice Stele take his place.

Immediately I was struck by his uncommon appearance and demeanour. The latter was just what one should always expect of a presiding judge: the man was dignified, carried himself with grace and greeted the court with condescending courtesy. His appearance, however, was much more extraordinary. He looked if possible even younger than he was. His figure was tall and slim, and his robes hung upon him as though carefully arranged by some artist determined to give the wearer an additional impression of authority.

His wig fell to his shoulders, framing a face which was a most interesting combination of youth and strength: his eyes were black as currants, and looked out from beneath dark brows with such keenness that it seemed that they could see the bones beneath one's skin. His lips were well shaped but somewhat thin, and compressed so that it seemed unlikely that they could ever part in a smile. Two lines which fell from his nostrils to the sides of his mouth gave him an additionally grave air; as for the rest of his face, it was as smooth as a schoolboy's, and as free of the slightest wrinkle or mark.

He bowed to left and to right, took his seat, and the first case was brought before him. It was that of a man arrested for strangling his wife, at Doublebois, and then proceeding to murder her brother in order to steal his watch and cash before attempting to flee the county. There was not the slightest excuse for a crime that was as despicable as it had been violent, and Mr Justice Stele heard it with a face which seemed to grow ever more grim as the facts were recited to him.

After the lawyer appearing for the defence had made what plea he could for the man (which consisted merely of the excuse that he had been in drink at the time of the offence), he directed the jury in the most economic terms that the villain must be guilty; and the twelve good men and true having returned such a verdict as must have been anticipated even by the murderer, placing the black cap upon his head the judge pronounced the death sentence in a voice remarkably deep and sonorous for so young a man, and in tones which struck a chill to the heart of the most innocent person in the court – and certainly into my own.

The next case was very different: it was that of a poor woman whose husband had been killed in a mining accident, who had been denied any compensation by the owners, and who, reduced to the utmost penury, had resorted to stealing a loaf of bread from the local baker in order to feed her starving children.

Mr Justice Stele listened to the facts with just such a face as he had heard the previous one. The passionate plea of the defence lawyer seemed to leave him unmoved; and his address to the jury made it clear that there was no other course open to them but to find the unfortunate woman guilty.

This done, he turned a face to her as stony and devoid of emotion as that with which he had condemned the previous prisoner. I feared a sentence of deportation, at the least.

Then, in the most measured tones, he assured the prisoner that he was unable to disassociate himself from the verdict of the jury – for she was undoubtedly guilty as charged. I could scarcely bear to listen to what followed – but then became conscious that Mr Justice Stele was condemning not the prisoner but the mining company which had ignored the years of service her husband had given them, and denied her succour; he even suggested that the baker, instead of laying a charge against the prisoner, might have consulted his heart – 'If,' His Honour said, 'he possesses such an organ' – and himself done something to succour the family.

'Finally, however,' he remarked, 'the fact remains that the prisoner at the bar has committed an act of theft, for which society must expect to be recompensed. I am minded to release her on the provision that she should for the course of one year do work which shall benefit that society – perhaps in connection with the administrative offices of this town; I am sure that His Worship the Mayor will be able to find her employment, and that the ratepayers will not repine at paying her some small weekly sum for the services which she may provide. If His Worship will kindly present himself in my chambers, I will confer with him upon the subject.'

He then nodded, and the poor woman was taken from the court. Meanwhile, the judge whispered to his clerk, who temporarily left the court and (I later discovered) gave her two shillings from His Honour's own purse with which to buy immediate food for her family; later, he persuaded the somewhat unwilling Mayor to give the woman cleaning work at the town hall, for which she was paid a decent if tiny wage; and in the meantime, pressure was put upon the mining company, which after two years of haggling reluctantly disbursed ten pounds, which helped to place the widow upon a satisfactory footing.

The rest of the day convinced me that Mr Justice Stele was a rare man indeed: strict with those whose cases demanded strictness, he was just but kindly to the guilty but piteous, and it was clear that the innocent had nothing to fear from him. The court was abuzz with praises for him when the sitting was adjourned, though one or two of the more wealthy citizens expressed the opinion that he was too kindly, and even Andy wondered what would become of the country if all judges were so merciful – and I think doubted my own view that England would be a better place for it.

A select few of us were to dine with the Judge at his lodging – a handsome house on the outskirts of the town – and it was with pleasure that I found myself placed upon his left hand side, where he treated me with great courtesy. He was in person just so astonishingly attractive a man as I had inferred from a more distant view, and, while even in the generally informal atmosphere of the dining room he remained somewhat aloof, I thought that I discerned beneath the carapace of dignity, which he maintained, an attitude almost of familiarity towards me which I certainly did not resent – though my best efforts were unable to fan it into so much as a flicker of more overt warmth.

The explanation for this came later: after we ladies had retired (and the local women had expressed their view on His Honour, which was that he was a cold fish – an attitude with which I did not argue, though my own feeling was that there were uncommonly warm fires damped down beneath that cool exterior), the gentlemen remained for a while over their wine, but remarkably soon rejoined us – His Honour being of the unfashionable opinion (as he remarked) that it was somewhat insulting to members of the female sex to regard them as incapable of serious conversation.

I was soon forced to the opinion that it was chiefly to myself that he referred, for having undergone for only a very few minutes the enquiries of the other ladies as to his impressions of the county (which must necessarily be slender, since he had been in it no more than a few hours, and those spent in travel) he took his place next me, and invited me to give my opinion upon the present state of justice in England – a subject which my various experiences enabled me to discuss with the appearance at least of intelligence.

The subject of punishment was, as a matter of course, included in our conversation. His Honour proved amenable even to my view – which I scarcely dared advance, since upon the rare occasions when I had ventured to express it in public I had been unanimously condemned for it – that hanging, while certainly a cure-all, was not a punishment I liked to see inflicted, for the very reason others commended it: certainly it deprived a culprit of the opportunity to repeat his crime, but it also deprived the innocent of the chance of a reprieve – for once hanged, no proof of his innocence, subsequently discovered, could recover him.

The judge, to my surprise, somewhat agreed; though the law, he said, must be enforced in its present state until such arguments as mine succeeded (which might take longer than even I supposed). And what of corporal punishment?

This, I averred, was perhaps a proper sanction especially against the violent criminal, but should it not be expressed moderately, care being taken to avoid its expression being fatal to the criminal?

Certainly, said His Honour, Her Majesty's armed forces were somewhat over-enthusiastic in their use of the cat – a private in the army in this very town, he had heard, had recently been sentenced to no fewer than five hundred lashes for desertion – and despite his three times' fainting during punishment he had three times been revived in order that the punishment might continue, being cut down however after two hundred and fifty lashes in such a state that it seemed unlikely he would live.

Such a practice must be repulsive to every right thinking man, I opined, and Stele agreed, stating though that some violence must be employed, for after all there were those to whom a flogging meant nothing, or was even in moderation a pleasant and enlivening experience (something, he believed, which arose from the correction given them at our public schools, and perhaps especially at Eton – where, he confessed with a somewhat wry smile, he had himself received his education).

After we had talked for some time, addressing me in a low voice, he hoped that I had not thought his behaviour at dinner towards me unnecessarily formal.

'The fact is,' he said, 'that apart from that formality which I must necessarily preserve as concomitant with my position, I at that time believed you to be Lady Archer, the wife of the gentleman whom I believe is merely your . . .'

'My friend and companion,' I supplied, with a smile.

'It was an understandable mistake, your honour. And as to your gravity, I have been long enough in the world not to mistake seriousness for solemnity, or reserve for pride.'

He bowed.

'Perhaps,' he said, 'you will do me the honour of taking a glass of wine with me when the other ladies and gentlemen have left us? I would much value the opportunity of a further conversation . . .'

Those black eyes were fixed upon my own with an almost hypnotic gaze, and, while grateful that I was not a prisoner about to be sentenced, the power of his look persuaded me that I was right in believing his temperament to be far more sanguine that my fellow guests had believed.

'Alas, your honour,' I said, 'Mr Archer and I must return to our house in the country this evening – and before it is too late; while this is not a place known for the extremities of criminal activity, it is still unwise to venture abroad too late after nightfall.'

He nodded thoughtfully, and then addressed Andy, who was seated halfway down the table.

'Sir Andrew,' he said, 'I wonder if I might trespass upon your kindness? There is a case tomorrow before me upon which I would greatly be assisted by hearing your prior opinion. Would you be so good as to give me an hour of your time, after our guests have taken their leave?'

Andy was as I believe no less flattered than honoured; but at the same time found it necessary to raise the same objection as myself.

'But there are, I believe, rooms here which could be put at your convenience and that of Mrs Nelham?' said His Honour, beckoning a servant. He was assured that indeed two chambers were aired, for just such an eventuality as this; whereupon Andy could do nothing but defer to the Judge's wishes – and indeed was happy to do so.

His Honour now turned his attention to the Mayoress, a plump and pleasant country person of sixty years or so, seated upon his right hand; and conversed with her until the party broke up – though not without favouring me from time to time with a look in which there seemed a certain humour and no little warmth.

When the others had taken their leave, His Honour kindly instructed his servant to show me to my chamber, while he had some words with Andy. The room proved a pleasant enough one, in which a fire had been lit to make it more agreeable (the house having been closed for some time, since the last Assize). Somewhat tired, I in next to no time was stripped and abed, and fell into a light doze. But it cannot have been more than a half hour when a light tap was heard upon my door.

I immediately sat up and, hearing a slight rustle, reached for the candle – to see a small square of paper slipping beneath the door. Rising and wrapping a sheet about me I fetched it. It bore the following message:

> 'Madam
> If I have read the signals aright, you will neither be astonished nor insulted by an invitation to a conversation more intimate than that which we have so far been able to enjoy. In the case of your consenting, be assured of my welcome, in the next apartment. Stele.'

It did not of course occur to me to hesitate, for I was (as the judge had anticipated) neither surprised at his invitation nor averse to accepting it. I therefore quietly opened the door, took the few steps to the next one along the passage, and without knocking opened it and slipped inside.

His Honour was standing before the fire in a handsome night-gown splendidly embroidered – yet of a lawn sufficiently thin to allow the firelight to shine through, outlining a frame which was slim and elegant, and promised well. Shutting the door, I advanced, and then, in order to signal my expectation of the proceedings, dropped the sheet to the floor and, standing before him dressed in the fashion of Mother Eve, presented him with a sight to which he was clearly not averse; indeed, stepping forward, he took my hand and placed a kiss upon its palm – yet then bent, picked up the sheet, and placed it about my shoulders, escorting me not to the handsome four-poster, but to a chair in which he invited me to sit.

'My dear Mrs Nelham,' he then said, 'I must first

make it clear that my invitation was made *imprimis* because of my admiration for a lady whose physical beauty – as you have just been kind enough to confirm to me – matches in every way that expectation which I had formed of it. I shall do my best to pay a proper compliment to that beauty. But my conversation with you persuades me that you may be prepared to accede to a request which, because of the necessity to preserve a reputation which must not be coloured by too unusual a hue, I dare not make to any lady but those upon whose sympathy and discretion I can completely rely.'

As a matter of course I assured him that he could rely upon my discretion – at the same time wondering what request he was about to make. Taking my hands, he raised me to my feet, and taking me now to the bed pulled the curtain which surrounded it – to reveal, laid upon the sheets, some ropes and – a cat o' nine tails.

I was of course not shocked by the revelation, nor can I say that I was entirely surprised (for if one had to suggest to what vice a member of the judiciary was most likely to be prey, it would perhaps be that of flagellation, or a delight in being whipped; while the turn of his conversation after dinner was now put in its proper perspective). I could not avoid an involuntary show of disappointment, however; for it seemed a shame that so promising a gentleman should be forced by a natural predilection to take his pleasure in a manner many ladies would be averse to.

His Honour must have discerned my hesitation, for he now kissed my hand again, and promised that I would not myself he neglected in what should follow – and on his divesting himself of his night-gown, I could believe it, for the machinery then revealed was handsome, and, even in only a state of half-preparation, promised to be entirely efficient in the performance of its natural task.

Following my instinct rather than any instruction, I now took the ropes and with them bound His Honour's wrists to the bar which stood at the top of the four-poster, and (his legs now spread as far apart as was convenient) his ankles to the legs. The bed was sufficiently high to require his standing a-tiptoe, thus stretching his body, and so disposing it that I must confess it made a charming sight, the muscles of calves and thighs tensed and standing out beneath the skin, the globes of his arse plump and jutting yet entirely devoid of superfluous flesh, the long line of his spine marking the centre of a perfectly balanced back, sloping out from a narrow waist to shoulders sufficiently broad to suggest a sportsman. Between his spread thighs, however, that apparatus which is the seat of active pleasure was no more attentive to my presence than formerly; something must be done to remedy this sad failing.

It seemed a thousand pities to mark so handsome and velvet-skinned a back by striking it with the instrument which I now held, to whose wooden handle was bound a leather thong which separated into nine separate strands, at the ends of each of which a hard knot was tied. Indeed, I could not resist approaching His Honour and running my hands over his back; but upon pressing my own body to his, his back side firm against my belly, and taking the liberty of testing whether his manhood was not aroused by the action, I found a mere limber and soft triplicity of flesh within my palms, prick scarcely distinguishable from balls except by the slight fur which covered the latter!

'I fear, ma'am, that you will continue disappointed unless . . .'

I stepped back, and, raising the cat, brought the thongs down across the gentleman's back. Rosy lines were left marking the white skin – but the blow had clearly been insufficiently enthusiastic to be inspiriting, for His Honour invited me to strike again, hard and often.

This was much contrary to my instincts, for I am a mild woman (except to those who rouse me); yet how could I fail to perform a service which had so politely been requested of me? Moreover, I must confess that it occurred to me that any enjoyment I might receive during the coming hours was entirely reliant upon my rousing the gentleman's interest; so what with one thing and what with another, I disregarded my personal proclivities, and laid on.

That my strokes were now more effective, I could not doubt from the low moans of pleasure that the Judge shortly began to give, and which were the perfect counterparts of those sounds which any woman versed in the arts of love knows how to evoke from a lover – though usually by other actions than striking his body with a whip! Quick to learn, I soon discovered how to make the most of the situation – so disposing my weapon as to lay no two stripes one upon the other, striking now at his arse, now at his shoulders, neither neglecting his thighs nor his sides, his upper arms nor even his ankles.

It became clear very soon that I was satisfying those instincts which were the springs of His Honour's lust, for his body was so disposed that I could scarcely fail to see (even had I wished to avert my eyes) certain changes which inferred an arousal of his carnal spirits – for his bollocks were now drawn up almost out of sight, while the third member of that libidinous group had entirely disappeared (though I suspected that had a mirror been available to reflect a front view of his person, it might have been shown not only to be in evidence, but flagrantly so!).

I must confess that the thought excited to me a degree at which I lost, for a moment, all control – and though His Honour did not show by any sign or sound that my actions were anything but enjoyed by him, struck so strongly at his lower back that the skin was cut open in two places, and beads of blood appeared.

At the sight I was reminded of my own disinclination for such violence, and throwing down the tawse could not resist the instinct to sink to my knees and kiss the flesh I had so damaged. One of the cuts was so deep that a trickle of blood oozed from it and ran down into the crack of his arse – and feeling the salt of it upon my tongue, I could not resist following it, over that white skin (as velvet to the touch as to the eye), until I must necessarily probe the interstices of that delightful crack – at which I felt a new shudder pass through His Honour's body, and, reassured that he was not averse to the usual gestures of love, did not now resist a continuation – and parting the globes of his arse made an excuse of his injury to pursue my natural course until I was able to nip gently at his cods.

In a moment, a somewhat shaky voice was heard to suggest that I should turn my attention to satisfying my own wishes, lest my actions if continued should make that difficult. Taking the hint, I inserted my head between his thighs, and was able to wriggle through his legs until lying upon the bed I could see above me a prick of the most handsome proportions, its length (which I calculated to be not much less than ten inches) in delightful proportion to a proper thickness – nothing is less charming to the eye than too thin a cock, however effective it may be in action – and with a bulb which, half exposed by the skin being drawn back over its head, was enlarged and empurpled by the rush of blood which so properly expanded it.

Placing my hands upon the front of His Honour's thighs, I drew myself up until I was able to place an admiring kiss upon the tip of that fine instrument, and drawing the skin completely back with my fingers, was able to encircle it with my lips, at the same time moving my tongue softly about its under side – an action which (if I am to judge from the contractions recognised by my fingers, now playing about his cods) gave him much additional pleasure.

By this time the warmth between my own

of pleasure, that I noticed that the door had opened, and Andy was standing looking over us. He had heard the crash, and being in the room on the other side from mine, had come to see whether any accident had occurred – and not being averse to such a sight (indeed, he has confessed to me that the appetite of a *voyeur* is by no means unknown to him) proved incapable of not watching us reach our culmination (though he then took the hint I expressed by a wink, and withdrew – for I was not sure how His Honour would react to the presence of a third party).

Judge Stele was extremely complimentary with regard to my understanding of the nature of his appetite, and his gratitude was almost touching – which I did my best to dispel by complimenting him on his own abilities, which were long standing: too many gentlemen with similar proclivities come off while the whipping is taking place, thus disappointing any other participant in the action (other than a paid wh*re). He insisted on giving me his card, no less in the hope (he was kind enough to say) of some future repetition of our encounter than in case I should ever require the services of one whose position in society might enable him to be of service to me.

I slept soundly in my own bed for the rest of the night, waking only when Andy came, quite early the following morning, to complain that he had been so affected by the scene he had witnessed that he had spent a sleepless night (his *amour propre* preventing him from taking the young man's way out, i.e. by the disposition of Mrs Palm and her five children). I could not but offer to be of assistance, and thus it was that His Honour, coming to pay his respects, found us in much the posture in which Andy had discovered him, not too many hours earlier.

We could not but laugh at this – though neither Andy nor I thought it proper to divulge the fact that the chief magistrate of the town had been aware of the nocturnal activities of the visiting Judge – who must now dress himself and proceed to the second day of Assize, where with the same stern visage he disposed of the list of criminals with the same natural justice and mercy.

I am not normally greatly attracted by those gentlemen who must be aroused by way of flogging, dressing in women's clothing, being trodden upon, or any other of those doubtless innocent and harmless but somewhat unusual activities. However, I must confess that His Honour Justice Stele seemed to me to be a perfect model of a man, and a standing example to society of the fact that it is unwise to judge any person by those private activities that he or she indulges in the bedchamber.

Chapter Thirteen

The Adventures of Andy

My attendance at various festivities in the county and my upholding of local customs had got me something of a reputation as a student of antiquities – and the fact that this had led, as in the case of the sturgeon, to personal adventures of an interesting nature did nothing, I believe, to make me unpopular with my people – for the Cornish to this day have the reputation of being exceptionally free in their social manners. And indeed I was interested in those relics of bygone ages which are preserved in that county as in no other – so it was without hesitation that I accepted an invitation to attend the ceremony of electing the Mock Mayor at St Ives.

This town on the north coast of the county, towards its extreme western end, is remarkable for the success of its fishing community, the refreshing quality of its air, and the sparkling brightness of its sunlight – especially in spring, when both are inexpressibly vivid, and in combination lift the senses and enliven the spirits. Since I had not visited the town for some years, it was with the greatest pleasure that I travelled there to stay with a Parliamentary acquaintance, Mr Richard Bodinnick, the Member for that constituency of the county.

This gentleman inhabited a Castle upon a hill above the town – nothing ancient, but a building constructed by himself in recent years from the monies which fell to him as owner of a number of profitable tin mines and through the sale of land over which the Great Western Railway had driven a line from St Erth to St Ives – one of the most delightful of all the beautiful branch lines in the county.

Though not in a taste which I shared – running to false battlements, massive walls which encouraged damp in winter and excluded heat in summer, and an atmosphere somewhat of a prison – the castle was fitted out comfortably enough, and Bodinnick's hospitality ran to satisfying food and excellent wines.

I should perhaps say a few words about the gentleman. He cut no sort of a figure in the House, being bluff and hearty but no speaker; indeed, had he not been a fellow Member from the West Country I doubt that I would exchanged so much as a word with him. On doing so, however, I found him to be a cheerful enough person, though without any intellectual pretensions. He was a man of some forty years, and had been married, I learned, but was deserted by his wife some five years before his election to the House for reasons which were to most people obscure (she had gone cheerfully back to her family home in Shropshire bearing with her a quantity of family jewellery and a generous annuity).

The reason for her departure was no clearer to me until, after a convivial dinner at the House, I was invited to take a glass with Bodinnick at his apartments in Knightsbridge. There, he let us in with his key, averring that his servants would be out, having been given the evening to themselves; but on entering the hallway we were greeted by a young gentleman who appeared upon the staircase clad only in a shirt (as was perfectly clear, since we were almost directly below him, and could therefore observe his lack of any other clothing) with the words: 'Dickie! – who's your handsome friend?'

The compliment to my own appearance apart, and although I have been in the world long enough to accept almost any aspect of human behaviour without surprise, I could not but raise an eyebrow at this. Bodinnick however had taken sufficient drink to give him sufficient assurance to laugh the matter off, waving the young man down and introducing him by the strange sobriquet of Towser (a name more suited to a dog than a human), and as a boy with the most accommodating bottom in London!

This amused rather than offended me, and since Bodinnick had done me the honour of regarding me as so much a friend as to be allowed this glimpse of his intimate predilections, I did not repine, but took a glass with him and his friend – who I fear took me at first for a gentleman of similar tastes to my host's, throwing himself upon a chair immediately opposite, and taking no care to gather his shirt about him, thus placing upon full view a set of private – or in this case public – parts which I am sure would have taken the eye of any lady (however disappointed she might have been upon requiring them to be put to practical use).

I believe that Mr Towser thought that I had been invited back by Bodinnick for some kind of roistering, for after a glass of claret he enquired (scratching his parts with a meaningful gesture) whether we might not repair to more comfortable surroundings; at which I made an excuse and left, Bodinnick allowing me to make my own way out, since he (as had been for some minutes obvious) was eager to accompany his friend upstairs, eyeing with some enthusiasm those buttocks which were flirtatiously revealed by (as I could not but notice) the boy surreptitiously holding up his shirt with his hands so that it was considerably shorter than the tailor had intended.

I relate this anecdote merely to explain why Bodinnick does not play a greater part in this chapter than might have been expected of a host. During the days immediately following his revelation (which on recovering from his wine, he may have regretted) he had at first treated me with some reserve – but was soon assured that I neither condemned nor repined at his interest in his own sex, while making it perfectly clear that I did not share it. While by no means being intimate friends, we had at Westminster exchanged such compliments as were civil, and I was happy to accept his hospitality at the Castle (where his constant companion was a certain Ned Keen, formerly a footman in the house, for whom he had conceived an admiration – nay, a love – so violent that it had been the cause of his marriage terminating: a circumstance which afforded him some relief, and gave his wife little pain, since they had married at an early age and at the behest of their families, without more affection than might be expected of strangers so forced together).

Bodinnick's domestic arrangements were no concern of mine; Keen was pleasant enough, quiet and respectful, and any familiarity he showed towards his friend and master was without those excesses which would have been intolerable to a stranger, and did not express itself (except no doubt in private) in any overt or offensive manner. I was, therefore, quite comfortable at the Castle.

But to my narrative.

The election of the Mock Mayor was an ancient ceremony retained by the people as a matter of simple amusement (indeed, it was impossible to suppose that it had ever had any more important motive). Every year, a boy or young man was chosen by the voters of the town, and for a day had absolute authority (though this was circumscribed: he might free all townspeople from taxes for a year – but only a symbolic reduction of a ha'penny in their payments was the actual result).

At all events, I was one of the crowd which waited on the quayside above the harbour at twelve in the morning to see the Mock Mayor's procession go by. It was a pleasant, warm day, without a cloud in the blue sky, and without that thighs had grown so insistent that it would soon be as necessary as it was desirable to quench the flames. I therefore rose, and was stretching to untie the Judge's wrists, when a different idea occurred to me: if he enjoyed being so bound, why should he not remain so until completely satisfied? Happily, my strength and the degree of bodily dexterity which I had always been careful to maintain enabled me to put my idea into action. I reached up, and, placing my hands about the bar of the bed-rail, lifted my feet from the bed and throwing my legs about His Honour's slim hips, by a wriggling which gave me no less pleasure than himself, managed (so lubricated was I by the interesting circumstances) to catch at least the tip of his prick within my lower lips.

The jerking motion which he made at this was as involuntary as it was satisfying, assisting him to achieve the most complete penetration of my person; but it persisted for only a few moments, when from the weight of our two bodies (it not being contrived for such a burden) with a loud *crack*! the rail gave way and we were deposited upon the bed where, so roused was the Judge by what had passed, that without more than the slightest hesitation (caused by his enquiring whether the fall had injured me), he threw my ankles over his shoulders and, with my thighs pressed against a fine and muscular chest, gave me such a swiving as would have contented a lady even more devoted to the game than myself.

Indeed so delighted was I by his vigour that it was not until we had both spent, with a mutual cry cold breeze which so often spoils such May days in the West Country. The press was great, shoulder set against shoulder, and the high spirits of the people made for a jostling and cheerful lack of formality which was highly enjoyable.

At last the procession came into view: first, a drum and fife band, considerably louder than it was skilful; then a man with a bell, which he rang continually and with an enthusiasm which suggested he was trying to drown out the band's music; then a group of 'officials' – former mock mayors – riding upon donkeys; and finally a car upon which stood this year's Mayor, a young man with an imbecilically pleased grin, clearly already well gone in liquor, with a cow's chain and a tin pendant hanging about his neck.

As he passed, he was pelted with garlands, balls of paper, and the occasional fish, while the crowd enthusiastically cheered, rocking to and fro in its pleasure so that it almost became a thing entire, each body but a limb scarcely separated from the whole. My chest was against the back of a brawny fellow with a basket of rotten fish the smell of which, when it reached me, was extremely strong; upon one side was a large lady, no doubt a fishwife, and on the other a young man who was no doubt from the epithets he hurled a friend of the Mayor. At my back was what seemed a somewhat softer body, no doubt of the gentle sex, though I could by no means turn to see whether she was plain or pleasant. Used to such crowds, I found the jostling and pleasantries no more than I expected. What I did not expect, however, was to feel a hand upon one buttock, moving over it with an insinuation which suggested that the touch was not accidental, and doing its best to pass between my legs, where indeed the tips of the fingers made themselves familiar with an area sufficiently sensitive to have a result which (had I not been careful to keep it within bounds by a strenuous exercise of will) might have given the wrong idea to the gentleman against whose back I was still forced to press.

I could by no means extricate myself from the position in which I was pent up; nor, I must confess, did I much regret the fact, for the fingers to which I allude were by no means unskilful – and now stole under my coat, about my waist, and (upon my sucking in my belly, which I freely admit to doing) inserted themselves below my belt and (as I felt the body behind me pressing even closer, so that I believed I could feel the highly suggestive closeness of a pair of female breasts) in a moment were able to close about the root of a prick too closely confined for comfort, which as those fingers stroked and tickled it became indeed so painful in its imprisonment that I was forced to take the wrist above and remove the hand – though retaining my hold upon it, when it closed without reluctance upon my own.

The procession having passed, the crowd began to disperse, chiefly in the direction of the Three Pilchards and other public houses in the vicinity; and I was soon able to turn and look into a pair of the most enchanting, dancing black eyes, set in a face pale yet more refined than I expected (having convinced myself that only a wh*re or common slut would have the confidence to act in so familiar a manner with a complete stranger).

No sooner had my eyes met those of the lovely stranger than she forcibly removed her hand from mine and began to move away – though at the same time retaining my eye in what seemed a positive invitation to follow her – nor as I did so did she show any of those signs with which the female can, if she wishes, wordlessly dissuade an admirer from an impertinence she does not wish to be the object of.

The young woman (who I believed could not have been more than twenty at most) walked along the quayside for fifty feet, then turned aside into a narrow street into which in due course I also walked. For a moment I thought she had vanished; but then saw an arm beckoning me from a doorway, up a set of stairs halfway along the street. Mounting them, I found myself in what must have been a common fisherman's cottage, for it consisted only of a single room, in the corner of which was a set of wooden stairs at the top of which a flounce of skirt was just vanishing. Need I say that I also mounted them?

Having done so, I found myself in what passed for a bedroom, but which was so small that it contained indeed only the bed. The walls were of rough plaster, roughly painted; the ceiling seemed at first to have fallen in – but then I realised that what I saw was a sort of platform or loft upon which fishing nets, lobster pots and other detritus was piled. But all this I took in only with half an eye, for upon the bed lay the young woman I had followed, who in the moment when she had been alone had whisked off her dress and was now spread like a starfish, bare of all covering save her skin, upon sheets which were remarkably white considering the poverty of the place.

She was an exceedingly handsome figure, her face bright, intelligent, and it seemed to me alive to the possibilities of the situation; her neck long and slim, her shoulders equally slim, and her breasts (though it is always difficult to judge when the female is in a recumbent position) full without being too bulky; below a narrow waist stretched long legs now invitingly parted – though in a pose which seemed rather informal than of too lascivious an intention. The result however was the same, for the bush of black hair which lay between her thighs did not entirely disguise the pair of full lips which seemed already to shine with an inviting slipperiness.

I suppose that the reader will not be surprised to learn that I was not slow in stripping myself as bare as she, or that very little more than half a minute passed before I had stretched my length along hers, feeling those breasts once more pressed against me, though this time without the intervention of impertinent clothing, so that I was instantly aware that her nipples were hard as thimbles, surely as clear a symbol of her state of mind as the fact that her hands now closed over the cheeks of my arse, pressing my rampant riding-muscle against her belly.

Pressing kisses first upon her lips, I lowered my head in order to pay the same courtesy to those beautiful bubbies – but at the same time she threw her legs apart by main force and thrust her loins upward so that I felt against my prick the fuzz which marked a goal into which I could not but direct myself; whereupon she began to buck like some untried colt, it being with the utmost difficulty that I retained my place.

It behoves every gentleman to learn the science of containing his lust until his mistress has been satisfied. But when such a remarkable appetite is so clearly expressed as in the case I describe, this becomes (at least for me) almost impossible. The squirming and leaping of her body, together with the little animal cries which she gave out, the work of her hands, and the way in which she folded her legs about me so that her heels pressed into the channel of my fundament so excited me that in a very few moments, with a desperate cry of my own, I gave up the ghost – at which her movements immediately stopped, and she lay still.

Conscious of my greater weight and her slender body, I lifted myself and turned upon my back – and was at once amazed and angered to see a man's face peering down at us from the loft above. As I rose to my feet, fearful of an attack, a young man vaulted down and landed in the little space available to him. He was dressed in a shirt and what seemed to be military trousers, and there seemed to be indeed something of the trooper about him, though he was unkempt and unshaven. He was also clearly advised of my identity.

'Sir Andrew Archer,' he said, and gave a curt bow.

I nodded, equally curtly, but with as much self-possession as could be observed by a naked gentleman aware that his recent amorous activities had been closely observed by another (something which, unless the result of an invitation, can never be anything but disturbing).

'I am surprised,' the young man continued, with the appearance of making a threat, 'that you should so eagerly have pursued one of your female constituents – and I doubt not that the voters of this place will be equally surprised and disturbed.'

I replied that I doubted it, for a number of reasons. The first was that those who knew me were perfectly aware that I was no eunuch; the second was that I was there by the perfect invitation of the young lady; and the third was that the people of St Ives for the most part did not know me from Adam (a singular observation, considering my present undress!), since I was not their representative, but was Member for another constituency altogether.

The young man looked abashed at this, and the young woman (who had now set a sheet about her shoulders) addressed him scornfully to the effect that she had warned him that his plan was a ridiculous one, and that he should have left the matter to her.

'Forgive us, sir,' she continued, addressing me. 'The fact of the matter is that Jack and I find ourselves in a particular difficulty, from which you could perhaps assist us to escape; he inadvisably considered that blackmail would be successful with you, and I reluctantly allowed myself to be persuaded . . .'

I could not force myself to treat her with that scorn which no doubt she deserved; apart from the fact that I had so recently enjoyed her, a matter which no feeling man could altogether be unaware of, she looked entrancing, kneeling now upon the bed, the sheet over her shoulders imperfectly concealing a bosom which was now heaving from apprehension rather than desire, and falling aside to reveal the long length of one naked thigh.

'Madam,' I said, 'though nothing could excuse the stupidity – indeed, the potential criminality, of your lover's attempt to influence me . . .'

'Oh, sir,' she said – interrupting what threatened to be an over-pompous speech – 'do not call him my lover! He is my brother!'

This made the situation somewhat easier, perhaps; the idea that a lover could consign his mistress to the arms of another for some reason of gain had already angered me. Now, I merely invited her to explain the situation more fully. Her brother opened his mouth – but I gestured him into silence, and as I resumed my clothing the girl explained.

He, a wayward young man formerly the despair of his father (a country squire), was a trooper in the eleventh Blankshires, stationed at Bodmin. Falling in love with a young lady of the town, it had been his habit to sneak from the barracks at night to visit her ('for', she said, 'the lady concerned was of an accommodating disposition'.) Alas for him, his sergeant had suspected as much, had laid a trap, and had caught him just outside the barrack walls in the early hours of the morning. Court-martialled, he had been condemned to four hundred lashes!

'He would never survive it!' she said. 'Why, only three weeks ago a man died after taking only three hundred, and was then three times recovered from insensibility in order that the punishment might continue!

'With the help of a bribed gaoler I was able to remove him from prison; but a search is still being made throughout the county, and he must make his way abroad at the earliest opportunity. An order signed by a Member of Parliament is, as you know, a prerequisite before one can at present enter the continent, and, while a boat will be available this evening at Marazion to take the high tide for France, the order must first be obtained, and . . .'

I now understood all. I failed to point out with what success the couple could have blackmailed my fellow Member (for the discovery of his relationship with his former footman would have resulted either in his having to flee the country, or in the heaviest punishment of the law!). But I was minded to assist them. No man, for whatever crime, should have to undergo the kind of punishment still being enforced by his Majesty's Army for offences which were merely venial. If I had been whipped every time I had sneaked into bed with some doxy, the number of lashes would have been inestimable! I therefore reached into my pocket where I kept my seal, asked for some paper and a pen – which were instantly produced – and was about to write when commotion in the street interrupted me: the sound of marching feet, shouted orders, a knocking upon doors . . .

The girl lifted aside a curtain which covered the single window, and started back!

'It is the search party!' she whispered, pale as the sheet – even as there was a knocking below.

The brother and sister stood as though struck to stone. Only I retained my senses, and, gesturing to the young man to return to the loft – which he immediately did – threw off my clothing once more (which fortunately consisted only of two items, viz. shirt and trousers, for I had not yet donned my coat or boots), threw myself upon the bed, and virtually tore the sheet from my companion as the door below was thrown open, boots clattered across the floor, and began to mount the staircase.

The girl, naturally quick-witted, took my intention immediately – and, wriggling from my grasp, bent, took my prick in one slim hand, and began to suck upon it with what (even in that extremity) was the most delightful attentiveness and skill.

She was of course right to do so. The sight of a man and woman in a state of nature and wrapped in an embrace might have somewhat embarrassed an interloper; but such an intimate scene as now presented itself should have been a complete deterrent to any stranger. I say 'should', for the two rough fellows who now burst into the room hesitated but for a moment.

'Here's a frump enjoying a chew, Jack!' said one. 'Come, my beauty, we've just time for a quick wallow!' – and began to loosen his belt.

I immediately got to my feet (my prick, which despite the danger of the situation had been somewhat aroused, flopping in a most undignified manner); but on taking one step towards the fellow was threatened by a fist the size of a cannon-ball, and apparently as adamant.

Well, there were two of them; violence was not to be considered. Instead, I bent to my coat, and from it produced that document which identified me as a member of the House of Commons.

This had no immediate effect upon the first fellow, who had clearly been thrown into the most energetic state of lust by the sight with which he had been presented. The other, however, who perhaps was better educated, was impressed first by the appearance of the document, with its heavy seals; and then, taking it, quickly motioned to his friend to withdraw.

'I beg your pardon, Sir Andrew,' he said, in a tone which showed he was of a somewhat superior intelligence, and muttered something in his friend's ear, which the latter took badly, but nevertheless comprehended; for with an ill grace the couple then descended the stairs, and we heard the door shut and, shortly after, knocking upon the neighbouring door.

Appearing once more from his hiding place, the young trooper now expressed his gratitude in a touching manner, convinced no doubt of his earlier mistaking my character, relieved at a new escape – and grateful for my present action in now writing out an order passing him into Europe upon my recognisances, together with a note of introduction to a friend of mine in Marseilles who kept a factory, and who at my behest would give him refuge and some kind of work. I also made him a present, in my foolishness, of five guineas, to help him on his way.

'Now,' I said, 'how do you reach Marazion this evening?' (for the place was some seven miles away). The girl explained that she had already arranged transport with a local man to whom the roads at night were entirely familiar (I enquired no further: any man familiar with night-time travel in this part of the country is more likely to be a smuggler than not).

'Until dark, you must be careful to remain completely hidden,' I said, addressing the trooper in particular. 'Do not show yourself at the window, and however boring the hours, make sure you are seen by no one.'

'How can we thank you?' said his sister. And then, in an action which I must confess was (perhaps through its unexpected nature) particularly inspiriting, took a step forward, and laid a cool hand upon my cock, sending a shiver of pleasure up into my very belly!

'Perhaps,' she said, 'you will allow me to demonstrate that our recent passage was so speedy only because of my uncertainty as to your kindness and courtesy?' – saying which she fell to her knees, and once more placed those delightful lips in juxtaposition with those parts which they were best capable of pleasing – at the same time waving violently with her hand in an attempt to persuade her brother to return to the loft.

This, somewhat without enthusiasm, he did; and, while I was never entirely confident that he was incapable of spying upon us (despite the fact that it was his sister who was occupied, not five feet below him, in an activity conventionally pursued in isolation), I must avow that in a very short time the idea of his presence was completely banished by the attentions the lady now lavished upon me.

I must now confess that I was never made aware either of her name or station. I did not enquire the former, for it seemed best for me to be unaware of it; and, as to the latter, it would have been impertinent to make conjecture – but at all events it was clear that in matters of the bedchamber she had either been exceptionally well educated by some attentive lover, or had a natural ability far beyond that of most girls of her age – for far from simply clamping her legs about my middle, as had formerly been the case, she now addressed herself to pleasing me so keenly that only by the most extraordinary willpower was I capable of maintaining sufficient self-possession to enable me to contain myself. This I was determined to do, for I would have considered it quite improper not to have returned her compliments in kind (though I do not believe that this was in the least a concern of hers, for she was giving herself as a thank-offering; however, it is ever my own concern, and is an obligation I try never to neglect).

But it was a close-run thing. For a start, her gentle sucking upon my prick instilled the most delightful sensation; nor did she neglect to lick with her tongue along its length, and to run it around the crown beneath the hood, which she carefully drew back for the purpose. This, she ceased just in time! – then giving her attention to complimenting as it seemed every inch of my body, rousing my tits to hard nodules of flesh, sucking every finger and every toe, nuzzling into the every cavity – even those at the backs of my knees – exploring the crack of my arse to the most secret part – and each gesture seeming more attentive and arousing than the last.

By now we were both in just that state of heat and perspiration which attends the most rampant of orgies, and all nicety and politeness went clean out of the window – to my delight and I believe to hers, for what can be more delightful than a complete abandonment to Eros, when neither participant feels barred from any expression of pleasure which comes to mind?

I will not bore the reader with further descriptions of our activities, for I understand entirely that those who have come with me this far will have done so from a curiosity as to the social climate and manners of a westernmost county in the first half of our century, and will not be in the least interested in animadversions upon the postures of a couple in lascivious conjunction. I will merely say that, at what seemed almost the latest moment for both of us, the lady freed herself from my grasp, turned, and lowering her head upon her folded hands presented me with the most delightful, small, round bum it had been my pleasure to see for many a year, the twin curves culminating at their inward juncture in a fig-shaped target, outlined by charmingly glistening hair, which with her fingers she parted in order to invite me to pierce it – which I did with the greatest joy, being however no more than for a moment sheathed when both I and the recipient of my attentions were blessed with an explosion of joy which happily culminated to our efforts.

If the interlude had been sprung by the young lady's gratitude for my assistance, I must believe (so frank and pleasing was her response) that by that final moment she was as entirely engrossed in pleasure as I myself; and neither I nor she need allude to her obligation to myself other than by her pressing my hand – after I had dressed and was ready to be gone – with a look which spoke volumes.

Of the trooper I have less to say. He showed little sense of gratitude, and indeed seemed thoroughly out of temper, only thrusting his head over the edge of the loft to mutter a farewell; it may be that he was in no mood to make such a communication, for after all for a young man to have been suspended for some time a matter of inches above a couple engaged in the most intimate caresses, without the possibility of participating, cannot but have been depressing to the spirits.

I trusted that he made good his escape to France – but as to that, for the moment I say nothing; it may be that I shall have cause to return to the subject in the concluding pages of this journal.

Chapter Fourteen

Sophie's Story

I sat through the rest of the Cornwall Quarter Sessions with interest, though not without pain – for even such a Judge as Stele, by no means devoid of humanity, was in the current state of things forced to impose penalties far exceeding in pain the inconvenience the unfortunate victims had given society.

To give but a few examples of this, a poor young man called James Olmud was sentenced to imprisonment for three months of hard labour for stealing a pair of worsted stockings which had been left to dry upon a hedge; John James to a whipping and seven years' transportation for stealing a watch; and Issacher Binney, a boy fifteen years of age, to fourteen years' transportation for stealing two pounds of candles from a box at Poldhu mine.

His Honour had perfect excuse for his severity, arguing that if the law failed to impose those punishments (however severe) prescribed for particular offences the entire fabric of society would crack; to which my response was that the sooner such a fabric cracked the better. But it was remarkable that his attitude to crimes against property was many times more severe than that he adopted in cases of public or private disorder.

I must confess to being disgusted by this attitude, and was somewhat relieved when the Sessions ended and the Judge disappeared towards his next engagement (not without, as I believe, some regret in bidding farewell to me; regret expressed at a final meeting in his rooms by embraces which as usual involved the use of the birch, but which also encompassed the gift of some jewellery which I had not the heart to refuse, since it was given as a recognisance of the unusual services which I had agreed to perform as conducive to His Honour's pleasure).

I now set out for the West of Cornwall to join Andy – for we were to witness the famous Helston Furry Dance, a ceremony which takes place every year, and which is celebrated as much for its vivacity as for its ancient lineage.

On the way towards Helston, I put up once more at the Red Lion in Truro, where I was welcomed by the servants as something of an old friend, and given not the room I had formerly occupied, but another which was towards the back of the inn, and thus removed from the noise of the High Street. I took some supper in the dining room, which was not especially crowded – and indeed was occupied, besides myself, only by an elderly merchant and a young woman of about my own years, who regarded me so attentively that I almost felt she must recognise me, and was about to approach her and ask whether we were acquainted when she rose from her place and left the room.

I retired early, and after reading a little in the *Don Juan* of Lord Byron – a poem whose erogenous quality is all the keener for the wit in which it is expressed – retired to my bed, drawing the curtains around it against the draught from the window, which I left somewhat open, the air being fresh but not cold. I had been abed but ten minutes or so, and was just at that point where sleep begins to cloud the apprehension, when a noise brought me back with a start to full wakefulness – for I realised it came from the direction of the window.

Quietly getting to my knees, I crawled to the foot of the bed and, drawing the curtains only sufficiently to be able to apply my eye to a crack in them, saw that indeed the window had been drawn up sufficiently to permit the entrance of a dark figure which I only saw in silhouette as it climbed into the room.

Whether the gentleman's approach signalled rape or merely burglary I did not stop to consider, but reached for the brass candlestick which stood within the curtains (and was still faintly warm from the flame by which I had been reading). Returning to the foot of the bed, I then waited until, in a moment, the curtain (which I had returned to its former position) stirred and was drawn back, when I almost felt (rather than saw, the room being so dark) a head inserted between them – whereupon I brought the candlestick down upon it with as much force as I could muster, and the gentleman fell to the floor with a thud!

Recovering the candle, which had fallen from its socket with the force of my blow, I replaced and lit it. The man whom I had felled lay face downward, and my next action was to remove a belt from my day-gown and secure his hands behind his back – for while I had no intention that he should recover and either attack me or escape, to strike him again upon the head might be dangerous to his life.

I now turned him upon his back, and for the first time observed him. He was a young man clad in a shirt which had once no doubt been white, but was now extremely dirty and tattered, and a pair of trousers which seemed somewhat to resemble those worn by the military. I was at once glad that I had secured his hands, for he was extremely well built, the shirt – which had several rents in it – disclosing something of a body which was certainly not deficient in masculine lineaments; his face was agreeable enough, though his hair was unkempt and he was unshaven. A little trickle of blood ran down his forehead from the injury I had done him – for which however I felt no compunction; for who knew what damage he might have done had I not prevented him? And while (I must confess) the thought of being ravished by him would have held few terrors for me, I had always preferred to be seduced than forced, and, moreover, it might be that he had merely intended theft of my goods, which was another matter, and one I could not approve.

Now he groaned slightly, and stirred. Fetching some water from my dressing table, I dipped a corner of a sheet in it and applied it to his forehead, at which after a while he opened his eyes and in time managed to focus them upon me, and attempted to rise – but, apart from dizziness, was prevented by the inconvenience of his hands being secured.

'Ma'am,' he said, after a few moments, 'please have no fear . . .'

I could not but smile at this, for it was himself rather than me who should feel fear, since the summons of a servant would immediately result in his arrest!

My smile seemed rather to console than to worry him, for he himself weakly acknowledged it by one of his own.

'I beg you to hear me, before you place me in the hands of the authorities,' he said; and when I made no reply continued:

'I am sorry indeed to have given you any moment's apprehension or inconvenience; had I thought that this room was occupied, I would of course not have entered it – but it was necessary for me to find a night's accommodation without informing an innkeeper of my presence, for . . .'

He looked for a moment around the room (as best he could without being capable of complete freedom of movement), then resumed:

'. . . for I am pursued.'

Once more, I remained silent.

'I am, ma'am, a trooper in the Eleventh Blankshires, at present stationed in the Barracks at Bodmin. Unfortunately, as the result of an unwise but perhaps excusable intrigue, I have found it necessary to remove myself from the barracks . . .'

I raised an eyebrow.

'The truth is, ma'am, that I was seduced by a

young woman – the daughter of an Alderman of the town – and by force of her persuasion came into the habit of climbing from barracks at night and going to her house – whereupon she afforded me entry to her bedroom, and (if you will excuse the indelicacy) we spent the night together in just that occupation which lovers usually enjoy.'

He lowered his eyes in an approximation of shame, though I am sure he did not feel it – neither would I have wished him to do so, since the situation he described was entirely excusable. Moreover, it may be that he was somewhat diffident in looking directly at me, for – as was invariably my custom – I had retired to bed in a state of complete undress, and had been too busy to cover myself with the night-gown I usually kept by me in case I should need to make use of its convenience.

'Unfortunately,' he went on, 'due to the jealousy of a fellow trooper my absence was one night discovered, I was arrested upon climbing back into barracks, court-marshalled, and sentenced to receive four hundred lashes. I am by no means in delicate health, neither is my constitution a weak one but, had you any knowledge of the terrible consequences of such a punishment . . .' He seemed to grow pale at the very thought; nor did I wonder at it.

'I hope, ma'am, that you will feel able to release me. There is a search party out – indeed, I believe I hear it at this moment . . .'

There was certainly a sound of footsteps outside the inn, and going to the window I was just in time to see two men in uniform, briefly lit in the doorway below, where a door was opened to their knocking.

My next action was to release the hands of my prisoner and silently to gesture him to the bed, upon which he immediately slid beneath the sheets. Having placed the lighted candle upon the bedside table, I took my place beside him, propping myself upon the pillows with Lord Bryon in my hands.

Almost immediately there was a knock upon my door, and on my inviting entry Janie, the maid who looked after my room, appeared to request me to secure my window – for, she said, two officers from the Blankshires had informed the innkeeper that an escaped prisoner from the military gaol at Bodmin was suspected of hiding somewhere in the town. At this, I distinctly felt a trembling hand fall upon my thigh, beneath the sheets, perhaps rather too close to the seat of my being to be positively innocent, yet seeming to implore me to keep silence; which of course I had no compunction in doing, for I had no intention of placing any young man in the hands of gentlemen inclined to whip him to death for merely paying his compliments to a female friend.

I immediately invited Janie to secure the window for me, which she did, then retreating – after which the noise of footsteps and of the opening and closing of other doors indicated that a search was being made of the empty rooms along the corridor.

Now, I threw back the sheets, and half stifled the refugee appeared, and in a moment had fixed a kiss firmly upon my lips, as if to thank me with a firm gratitude for my assistance.

'If there is any way in which I can ever repay you,' he said – at which I must confess I gave him a look which any young man of experience would immediately construe correctly. Danger always stimulates my blood, and, as I have already remarked, the young gentleman was of considerable physical charm. He immediately took my meaning and gave me another kiss, this time placing a hand upon my bosom, to the springy fullness of which he evidently had no objection, for he now transferred his lips to it, and shortly afterwards I felt the coarse roughness of his beard scrape upon my belly as he lowered his head to pay his compliments elsewhere.

It was convenient, since his body was now bent over mine, for me first to pull his shirt from his trousers and then to release the belt of his trousers, whereupon in a very few moments he had shrugged both from his body. This proved as well made as I had supposed: the exercise which had no doubt been forced upon him on the parade ground and elsewhere had cultivated an admirable firmness – his shoulders bulged with muscles, which lay also along his back, upon each side of a spinal column which was as flexible as it was well marked. At his waist there was no sign of plumpness, and, though his arse comprised two lusciously full globes of flesh, these (on my clutching at them) revealed themselves as equally firm and equally devoid of fat. Being moreover entirely hairless, and through his willingness to enjoy my touch being thrust upward and perfectly offered to my palms, these were so tempting that I could not but run my hands several times over their surface, which had the result not only of pleasing the gentleman (which I could tell from his involuntary movements and the additional eagerness with which he lapped at my own person) but of convincing him, I believe, that I wished to pay my compliments to him in full: so, lifting his head, he turned upon his back, placed his hands behind his head, and awaited my attentions!

Such an act – as though to say 'Here I am! – take me!' – would normally result in my neglecting to do so, for I cannot abide those men content to lie back and let a female pleasure them. But I must confess that in this case the body stretched before me was one which it would be impossible for any female not to admire, and difficult for her to refrain from exploring; and after all he had already shown that he was by no means disposed to neglect a female friend. I therefore now passed my hands over his shoulders and breast, which swelled in just such a proportion as spoke of strength without appearing in the least feminine: I mean that those convex, low hills which sprang from the platform of his chest were firm and well-muscled, and that upon my agitating them with my palms I was rewarded by a solidity not at all resembling the springiness of the female breast – while though the brown aureoles of his nipples, decorated only by slight sprigs of hair, could have been mistaken for those of a female, the little firm nipples which stood at their centres were, though only the size of match heads, hard as pebbles – and, on my taking one between my teeth and testing it, proved far less sensitive than ours (while no less capable of giving pleasure).

I now turned my attention lower, where a belly so hard that one could have bounced a coin upon it was marked by the deep dint of a navel as perfectly formed as that of a classical sculpture – those ladies whose experience is not confined to the sight of only two or three of these, will agree that (as with another item of masculine furniture) no two are alike, and that some (especially the 'knotted', the result no doubt of the unkind cut of an irresponsible midwife) can be positively ugly.

No less individual are of course those features which must be the chief concern of the eager female, to one of which it was now no less my duty than my pleasure to turn. This (and the organ to which I refer need not be named) was as sturdy as the rest of my new friend's body, and no doubt even in a state of flaccidity would have been imposing enough; encouraged now by the proximity of a willing female, by those actions I have described and by the fact that one of my hands now fell to its base in order to raise it somewhat from the belly against which it lay, it was puffed up to its full extent, which, I saw, was of considerable pomposity.

It was mounted above two spheroids which were of no more than average size, but which seemed smaller through being drawn up into the bifurcation of his thighs by reason that the adjacent skin was required to cover the greatly enlarged area of flesh which was the result of the raising of Eros's staff.

On closer examination, from a distance of but three inches or so, this proved as admirably shaped as the rest of my new friend's body: that is, it was of entirely proportionate shape and size, the barrel sturdy and to the touch both firm and flexible; along that side first presented to the gaze (that is, the under side) ran a thick vein along which my fingers could discern a slight throbbing of blood; smaller, purple veins elsewhere threaded their way along the ivory staff by way of such decoration as a vine might provide to a classical column, while at the tip a circle of skin was drawn back to reveal half of a fine, shiny purple dome at the centre of which was an aperture drawn slightly open, in the eye of which stood already a complimentary tear.

My attempt to draw back the skin still further, in order to expose the entire head (the sensitivity of which would thereby be greatly enhanced), drew from the gentleman a slight wince of discomfort; whereupon I took the precaution of first slipping the instrument between my lips, when the application of a plentiful supply of saliva so lubricated the whole instrument that in a moment it was quite possible for me to reveal that area which previously had been protected: the result of which – upon my tongue being delicately applied to it – was indeed what might be expected: i.e. a shudder of pleasure which ran through the whole of the gentleman's body, even the muscles of his thighs (upon one of which one of my hands was conveniently resting) shuddering like ground affected by some earthquake.

I cannot altogether account for the extent to which lust had now raised me – except by suggesting that the practices to which my most recent lover, the Judge, had been so strongly addicted were not entirely sympathetic to me, and, while he was by his own lights an attentive enough lover and did not leave me unsatisfied, I had not experienced with him that complete abandon which alone can be the supreme experience of ecstasy. In consequence my excitement was extreme – indeed I could wait no longer – but, lifting my head from my task, I lost no time in throwing a leg across the gentleman's reclining body, and without further ado lowering myself upon him so that I could direct his staff into that socket where it could do its best work.

That he was not entirely averse to this was evident from the satisfied smile which passed across his face as his prick was swallowed by my greedy second mouth (though immediately before his lips parted in that smile, I had I believe read some uncertainty in his expression, and from it presumed that it might be that he was not used to a female taking such command of his person – in which case the lesson that I was teaching him would be of value to those future mistresses to whom even so admirable a frame would be capable of giving less pleasure were he not aware of some variations in posture). His manliness was now no less displayed in his command of his emotions than in the sturdiness of his equipment, for we were able to gallop the road to delight for quite as long as enabled me to reach a satisfactory climacteric, whereupon seizing his nipples between my fingers, and twisting them with more or less of violence, I was able to signal my wish that he should come off, which in a moment or two a scalding emission indeed signalled.

We were by our exertions in what the uncouth might call a muck of sweat, and it was a mark of the trooper's uncommon courtesy that taking the sheet he wiped my body carefully before performing the same office upon himself, when with another kiss he remarked that he now had even more to thank me for – on which I assured him that I was not used to accepting such compliments except from those to whom I took a liking, and added that it would be a hundred pities should such a pleasant body be scarred by the ignoble and too fierce punishment which had been proposed.

I then rose, and going to my travelling case removed some paper and, naked as I was (the cool air of the room positively beneficial after my recent heat), wrote a letter to a friend of mine, a fisherman in Penzance, who would be prepared to help the trooper on his way to France; to which end I also added a note to Andy, asking him to provide an exit visa for that purpose (required at the time for all those travelling to the continent) and advised my friend to go first to St Ives, where Andy was staying with a Parliamentary colleague; there to obtain the visa, and then to make his way out of the country.

The young man's thanks were voluble; but

though I would not have been averse to his remaining until morning, if only to fulfil my curiosity as to the manner in which he would express his manly emotions on being left, as it were, to his own devices, he insisted on donning his clothes and leaving immediately – for it would be best to travel to St Ives by night (he said); and moreover he would not wish to put me to the inconvenience of longer concealing him. And so, with some regret, I saw disappearing into his trousers those firm thighs, that happily sturdy bum, that . . .

I sent him on his way with further good wishes and with eight guineas – all I had about me in ready money – which he accepted with the prettiest show of reluctance, but which I hoped would give him a new start on the continent. Closing the window behind him, I was not displeased with my night's work; not only did my body feel the better for the business, but my spirit was pleased to have rescued someone from the cruel consequences of an act of love.

It was only when I had retired to bed and snuffed out the candle that I realised that in the adventures of the night I had not even enquired the trooper's name!

Chapter Fifteen

The Adventures of Andy

I have been extremely remiss in omitting from this narrative all details of the reconstruction of Vycken, which had been proceeding apace during the weeks when the episodes which we have recounted took place. I am ready to believe that my readers would have been as interested in those details than in the somewhat libidinous adventures which have been the subject of our pens, and must apologise for the omission.

Every effort had been made to rebuild the house as it had formerly been, with the exception that a few of the latest and most convenient domestic improvements were now included. Fortunately the damage to the house had not comprised the complete destruction of those walls which had first been raised in the middle of the seventeenth century, while the gatehouse (which bears the date 1658) had remained entirely undamaged, and indeed was used by Treweers as his headquarters, from which the builders were directed by himself and the architect, a Mr Coad.

The reconstruction was largely achieved upon the old lines, and upon the completion of the work, when we removed ourselves thither from Penruddock Monachorum in order to oversee the furnishing of the house, it looked largely as it had always looked: three wings contained a courtyard, the main entrance being in the centre of the west wing, and the building otherwise completely symmetrical. The old gate house stood somewhat down from it upon the east, and a new carriageway twisted and turned through the estate, and thus provided a more picturesque approach than the earlier straight drive.

In the furnishing of the chief bedrooms I had taken some care, knowing that Frank's tastes would allow no restraint where comfort and convenience were concerned. A new feature was the provision next to each of the chief bedrooms of a separate bathroom. The gentleman who had owned Vycken before Frank inherited it had at least in his youth copied the Duke of Queensberry's habit of bathing every day in milk – a custom which had the disadvantage, at least in summer, of rendering him by late evening sufficiently miasmatic to persuade his near companions to withdraw to a distance sufficient to render the odour less immediately offensive. For the purpose he had used a wooden tub which also positively stank – and continued to do so even when water replaced milk as a supposed agent of cleanliness. Happily, the tub had been among those articles which had perished in the late fire, and now Mr Coad advised the use of a metal bath, which was light, easy to empty, and larger than was common – so that one no longer had to bath in a crouched, contracted position, or else to sit in the tub with part of one's legs outside and one's feet on a bath-mat.

Another convenience remarkable in the country – it would indeed have been remarkable in many other areas of the country – was the water closet which Mr Coad advised we should install next to the chief bedroom. Some decades previously Mr Alexander Cumming had patented his 'Water Closet upon a New Construction', the theory of which was, to quote Mr Cumming himself, that 'the pipe which carried off the soil and water is curved about twelve or eighteen inches below the pan or basin, so as constantly to retain a quantity of water to cut off all communication of smell from below.'

But Coad recommended that we should purchase a closet as redesigned by John Randall Mann, of East Cowes in the Isle of Wight, whose Mann's Syphonic Improvement is odour-free, self-emptying and self-cleansing. The necessary water was supplied by Mr Rogers Field's Syphon Automatic Flushing Tank, and the convenience itself had a comfortable wooden seat (a great improvement upon the seatless stoneware object to which we were more used), while the pan was of white porcelain opulently decorated with blue irises, which grew upward from the syphon.

I apologise if any female readers find my writing of these matters unnecessary or offensive, but they may be of some historical or even contemporary interest – they certainly were so at Vycken, for within six months poor Treweers had had to show the bathroom and water closet to close on one hundred eager visitors – some from as far afield as Plymouth – who had heard of the improvements and wished to view them.

In the bedrooms themselves I replaced the best of the furniture which had been rescued, but placed new mattresses upon the beds, and devised new hangings, while Sophie had much to do with the wallpaper and painting of the wood work. All in all, by the end of spring we were able to send a message to Alcovary that the refurbishing of the house was altogether complete and ready for the inspection of its owner.

We were somewhat discouraged, though not altogether surprised, to receive in return a message excusing Frank and Lady Franklin from travelling to Cornwall at that time. He hoped, he said, that they might make their way there in the summer (though even this I took leave to doubt, since they both cordially hate removing from Alcovary upon any excuse).

'I hope,' (Frank added, however) 'that you will act as I would were I at Vycken: that you will summon the county to an entertainment at which the doubtless intense curiosity about the house may be satisfied, and that you will regale your guests in the best fashion, being entirely unmindful of the expense, which of course I shall happily defray. In short, you and Sophie are to look upon the house as your own, to live there for as long as you wish, as the Member of Parliament for the constituency and his hostess, and to entertain in the manner you feel best suited to your dignity in that position.'

Shortly after we received this missive, cards went out to the whole county in the names of Sir Andrew Archer, M.P. and Mrs Sophia Nelham, advertising a reception at Vycken upon St Hydroc's Day, to begin at six *post meridian*, carriages to be at midnight.

I will not weary readers with a description of the bustle and fuss that were necessary preludes to the occasion: of the number of pigs and chicken slaughtered, the number of tuns of wine sent for, the baking and roasting and boiling and pastry-making . . . Every five minutes of the day Sophie would present herself to me in a new dress, inviting me to give my opinion upon it; while I grew decidedly impatient for the arrival from London of a new suit of clothes which I had ordered from Gieves's in Savile Row.

That all was ready in time goes without saying; and by half an hour after six o'clock on the ordained day there was a positive line of carriages waiting to set down the guests at our door. These held members of the best known and most considerable families in the county, all of whom without exception were astonished and delighted by our refurbishment, and the ladies in particular seemed extremely envious of those conveniences invented by Messrs Alexander Cumming and Rogers Field!

Among the throng were of course several particular friends, including the Hon. Jack Fortescue (with whom Sophie had somewhat resumed an acquaintance), Charlotte and Maurice le Semblant (happily reunited), and Mlle Femelle and M. Lebaissant.

The evening went with considerable *eclat*, to use the French term. There was dancing in the gallery, where a small band played, and what the French call a 'running buffet' in the hall – though the food upon the tables bore little resemblance to that served in any place more foreign than Cornwall: but perhaps that may seem foreign enough to my readers. At all events, the inroads upon it were so considerable that it was all the kitchen staff could do to keep the table groaning under the weight of pies and roast and boiled dishes, comprising among other matters of the famous Cornish pasty, green pork cooked in unleavened bread (otherwise known as 'hoggen'), roast pork and beef, pilchards poached in cream, large quantities of bream, hake, cod, skate and ray, salted ling, dogfish, crabs, lobsters and soused conger eel in a pie.

The evening passed with considerable rapidity, and a large number of people had left the house by a quarter of midnight, when Sophie came up to me and asked if I could spare ten minutes of my time.

'It concerns an adventure I had at Truro,' she said – and told me in brief the facts with which the attentive reader of the last chapter will already be acquainted, but with which she had not so far regaled me, due to our having been so busy with arrangements for the party.

It will be understood that I immediately smelt a rat: the circumstances which the renegade trooper had described to Sophie being too much similar to those set before me by the couple I had met at St Ives. I now mentioned these to my friend, who immediately took my meaning – and now told me that she had seen her trooper friend upon the staircase, and with a young lady she recalled noticing in the dining room of the Red Lion, and who bore a close resemblance (from my description) to the one who had applied to me for help for her brother, at St Ives!

We immediately mounted the main staircase, and began a search of the upper part of the house, and had no sooner approached the door of a room set aside for guests than we heard sounds within which suggested occupancy – and, being in charge of the place, had no hesitation in bursting through the door (which indeed was not locked, for, as the habit then was, locks had been omitted from any interior doors).

To our astonishment, we immediately saw the trooper and his sister, both naked as cuckoos, lying upon the bed in a consanguinity somewhat more familiar than was normally to be expected between siblings, and certainly not recommended to them by Scripture – that is, placed top to tail, the young man lapping at the lady's cunny while she held his prick in her hand and seemed to be about to introduce it into her mouth.

To give them credit, the pair were immediately startled into a sense of shame by the door's opening, and straight way pulled the counterpane over themselves – which presented a sight which in other circumstances might have been comic: that is, of a strange sort of monster with a head at both ends of its body!

I closed the door behind me, and Sophie and I merely stood together, saying nothing – for it was surely up to the couple before us to explain (for they could scarcely excuse) their conduct.

I will say for them that both seemed not only embarrassed but downright ashamed; and I will add that they immediately volunteered to tell us all, which they then did without hesitation.

It seems that they were not, as I at least had been led to believe, brother and sister, but the son and daughter respectively of two highly regarded squires whose homes were within thirty miles of where we stood – one of whom, the young lady's father, Dick Treleaven, had actually proposed me for the Parliamentary seat which I now held: so that I must certainly have seen her before, though she might well, four years ago at the age of fourteen or thereabouts, have been sufficiently childish to fall from my memory before making an impression.

It seems that her father had been holding forth to her and her friend, who now presented himself as Bob St Clare, about my virtues and astuteness; and on the couple discussing the topic later, Ellen (which was the young lady's name) had remarked how ridiculous it was that one man should be put up as having such a full complement of accomplishments as I; while (with a marvellous naiveté) young Bob had remarked that as a matter of course a Member of Parliament must be above the common frailties of man – a statement at which Ellen, sensibly, laughed.

After some discussion or argument, the matter ended with the young woman claiming that she could by hook or by crook not only persuade me between the sheets, but also relieve me of five pounds – just the sum which I had presented to the imitation trooper (for he was no more a soldier than I). Having gained the ascendancy over him, Ellen had then betted her friend that he could not perform a similar trick upon some fine lady or other – and to that end had dined at the Red Lion Inn in Truro, where she had set eyes upon Sophie, and believed her to have sufficient good sense to see through any such plot as Bob was likely to lay before her.

I must confess that both Sophie and I felt some initial irritation at the narrative, which after all presented us both as gulls taken in by a fangle so simple that any fool might have been expected to see through it; yet we could not in the end but smile at the assurance and bare-faced trickery of the young couple – who now sat, somewhat blushing, before us; a pretty enough sight, for both were well made – even the young man, now that he was shaven and dressed for such a social occasion as this evening's (to which his father, Squire St Clare, had brought him) was by no means a repulsive figure.

They must have sensed that we were about to relent, for young Ellen now turned her big eyes upon me and invited me to believe that the occurrence which followed upon my kindness, on our last meeting, had proved to be far from the merely automatic task which she must perform in order to win her bet; 'for' (she blushed again as she said it) 'the exchange of emotions between us was peculiarly delightful to a young person whose only teacher in matters of the heart had been as youthful and inexperienced as herself.'

Young Bob looked slightly downcast at this (as well he might), and in turn addressed Sophie, exclaiming that her kindness at Truro was something he was unlikely to forget – 'especially', he said, 'since it was accompanied by gestures of sympathy far beyond any which might have been expected from a stranger.'

'And, of course,' said Ellen, 'we shall be happy to refund the monies you were kind enough to present us with – though,' (she added somewhat wryly) 'this will leave us out of pocket, since we had to engage the services of two gentlemen to pretend to be the search party out to catch this rogue.' She tapped Bob upon the shoulder.)

Naturally, we declined the offer, now being inclined to forgive and forget the impertinent pair.

'Then,' said Bob, smiling at Sophie, 'I trust that at least you might be prepared to countenance another form of reparation, which I would be happy – and am ready – to make?' And with an effrontery which would be difficult to match among the boldest lads in town, he threw off the counterpane revealing himself indeed ready for congress – and a sight which I imagine no woman would find repulsive, for he was a fine figure of a boy, whose person lacked neither dimensions nor vigour.

I could see that my friend was tempted: I have known her long enough to recognise the signals – and on her glancing at me I was happy to encourage her; while on her stepping forward I was not disappointed to find that Miss Ellen was no more hesitant than her friend in offering to repeat those embraces with which she had formerly regaled myself.

I must ask the reader – specially should he or she be unfamiliar with our previous writings – to believe that it is not usual with Sophie and myself to indulge our carnalities in any other company than each other's! But on this occasion the freshness and enthusiasm of the offer made, the deliciousness of the fruit set before us, and the fact that we had spent several days now in tedious and hard work and were much in need of recreation led us to cast aside custom, and in a very few moments my friend and I were in just so pristine a state of nature as our companions, and were reclining with them upon a bed which – being designed to sleep only a couple in comfort – made it difficult to avoid a degree of familiarity which might under some circumstances be unwelcome, but now added a spice to the occasion.

I cannot recommend such a close approximation of two couples to any person of too tender a susceptibility in matters of privacy; for it was virtually impossible to make any gesture in the way of lechery which might not find some target other than that at which it was directed! Thus, while engaged in kissing Miss Ellen's scissure (an act which from her wriggling she found highly satisfactory) I at the same time reached out a hand to her back side, both in order to still her movements somewhat (for they made it a little difficult to be accurate in the directing of my tongue to her taste bud) and for the simple pleasure of embracing it, and I had been stroking and kneading the delightful spheres for some time before I realised from some slight growth of hair at the point of bifurcation of her buttocks that they in fact belonged to Mr Bob, who was half kneeling at our side while doing Sophie the same office as I was performing for Ellen!

It soon became clear that the chief intention of the young couple was to please us (perhaps in order to assure our silence, but also I do believe out of some pleasure in our company), and to that end exercised all their ingenuity and guile, positively inviting us to state a preference for any form of erotic pleasure, which they would then do their best to supply. This I always feel to be a mistake, and one only made by the amateur in the courts of love. The professional will always recognise those motions or attentions most desired by a client, through a careful observation of the movements of their limbs or eyes, even the incoherent exclamations which fall from their lips, Moreover, positively to invite a coarse statement, as (from a lady) 'kindly dip your head in my bush', or (from a gentleman) 'I wish you would kindly suck upon me', is often to embarrass one.

However, in not responding to the invitation, we nevertheless (and of course) offered no rebuke, for the young people meant well; and indeed their enthusiam made up for any lack of *finesse* in their performances; which were concluded in my paying Ellen the conventional compliment (with which she showed no sign of discontent) while Bob was making the same acknowledgement of Sophie's ever appreciative beauty.

It must be that any onlooker would have found the sight of the final stage of our symposiac a comic one: here were two sets of buttocks plunging in almost complete synchrony, two ladies squeaking with the pleasure of it in a rhythm which might have been part of the score of a symphony by Mr Haydn! However, there were no onlookers; the pleasure we took was innocently free, and upon our collapse (which took place almost simultaneously) the kisses which we exchanged were as innocent as they were enthusiastic.

We (Sophie and myself) would have been pleased to curl up with our young friends and fall asleep, as they immediately showed signs of doing; but we must in courtesy to our absent host rise and make sure that the house was secure – so donning not our complete finery but sufficient clothes to be decent we made our way downstairs, where we found that the final guest had gone some time before, and Treweers and the servants now clearing the last pieces of debris. Testing the locks, which were new and inclined to be stiff, we bade our staff goodnight, and returned upstairs. There I parted from Sophie, who sleepily closed the door of her room behind her, and I entered the main bedroom, so tired that it was as much as I could do to undress myself again, part the curtains which were drawn about the bed, and . . .

But no, I could scarcely throw myself upon it, for it was already occupied; at first I could not tell by whom, for both figures were upon all fours, and facing away from me; however, on the female turning in surprise, I found her to be none other than Mlle Femelle, while her lover proved to be M. Lebaissant. Though he showed sufficient embarrassment to withdraw from his position (thus displaying to me that feature which Sophie had remarked upon – that is, the utter nudity of his person), neither he nor M. Femelle showed any signs of withdrawing from my bed – and indeed, with a lascivious gesture which I will not particularise (but which came quite naturally from a Frenchwoman) even invited me to join them.

Alas, I was too exhausted (to say nothing of my recent milking by that minx Miss Treleaven) for even a spark of amorous interest to be struck either by the sight before me or the invitation; however, my exhaustion also prevented me from leaving – and so I merely laid myself down at their side, inviting them to continue (but if possible, I asked, with as little tumult as their senses would permit), and almost immediately fell asleep, somewhat comfortably rocked by the motion of the mattress resulting from the couple resorting instantly to a renewal of their swiving.

I awoke as the early dawn lit the room and, falling across the bed, gilded the bodies which lay at my side. They both lay upon their face, the lady's leg thrown over the Frenchman's bum and a breast leaning against his side. No doubt as the result of a lascivious dream (which upon waking I had instantly forgot) my prick was almost painfully at a stand – a phenomenon I have noticed seems the more probable on the morning after carnal enjoyment; and I could not resist placing my hand upon it. But, before I could instigate those comforting motions which almost automatically follow such a gesture, a charming female hand was extended and delightfully slim fingers took the place of my own.

The gesture was a kind one; but Mlle Femelle was too accomplished in the arts of love to suppose that it would suffice to satisfy me completely, and in a moment climbed over the body of her lover and, bending, took my prick between her lips and applied to it a caress of such liquid smoothness that for sheer delight surely only one other part of her body could exceed it.

Seeing that I had almost bitten my bottom lip through in an attempt to resist the inevitable end of pleasure (which at that hour of the morning too immediately attends such a caress as this) she now fell upon her back and opening her thighs welcomed me between them, my prick recognising with an excited thrill the smooth depilated aperture which characterised my partner.

For better or for worse, M. Lebaissant had by now awakened, and being a young gentleman of normally healthy appetite could not but be somewhat put out to find his female companion occupied with another lover. However (and this I believe to be characteristic of the generous nature of the French lover) he did not allow the fact that he had had only the most formal introduction to annoy him, but began to run his hands over both our bodies with a most attentive sensuality, even slipping one between us in order to play the lover with the lady's button (while at the same time involuntarily contacting my own prick, the additional friction to which did nothing to reduce my own pleasure, even though it was administered by the hand of another gentleman).

Elaine meanwhile played about his prick and cods with her fingers – the result of which was a stimulation past bearing, for now he placed his lips to her ear and whispered something. She looked, I thought, a little doubtful; but then seemed to assent, and with a greater strength than I would have believed she possessed persuaded us to roll across the bed so that she lay atop me. Meanwhile, M. Lebaissant spat onto the palm of his hand and, liberally anointing his cock with saliva, before I could imagine what he was about, had sheathed that weapon deep into Mlle Femelle's back side – an action which, if it gave her any pain, she showed no sign of resenting; and indeed it seemed to give her pleasure an additional impetus. At all events, the considerable jolting resulting from two bodies jigging atop me in a very few moments brought me off, she and her compatriot being only a few moments behind.

This was the last connection of an amorous kind I had with the inhabitants of the far western county. As to Sophie, I can only remark that on rising and making my way downstairs to break my fast I could not avoid seeing a figure slip from her room which bore a remarkable resemblance to that of the Hon. Jack Fortescue. No doubt in time she will apprise me whether indeed he had decided at last to satisfy her curiosity as to his nocturnal powers, and to what extent he managed to accomplish that aim: we have no secrets from each other – and indeed none from our readers, for it is our desire that those who peruse these lines perhaps a century hence, when no doubt manners will have changed, may know whether to envy or pity the manners of our times.

At all events, later that very day we set out for Exeter, and then for the far east of the country – leaving Vycken to be managed by its steward, and our friends, new and old, to those devices with which they satisfy their generous desires and emotions, and which they were neither slow nor reluctant to share with us.

More Erotic Fiction from Headline:

EROS IN THE FAR EAST

Anonymous

Recuperating from a dampening experience at the hands of one of London's most demanding ladies, the ever-dauntless Andy resolves to titil.ate his palate with foreign pleasures: namely a return passage to Siam. After a riotously libidinous ocean crossing, he finds himself in southern Africa, sampling a warm welcome from its delightfully unabashed natives.

Meanwhile, herself escaping an unsavoury encounter in the English lakes, his lovely cousin Sophia sets sail for Panama and thence to the intriguing islands of Hawaii – and a series of bizarrely erotic tribal initiations which challenge the limits of even her sensuous imagination!

After a string of energetically abandoned frolics, Andy and Sophia fetch up in the stately city of Singapore, a city which holds all the dangerously piquant pleasures of the mysterious East, and an adventure more outrageous than any our plucky pair have yet encountered. . .

Follow Andy and Sophia's other erotic exploits:
EROS IN THE COUNTRY EROS IN TOWN
EROS IN THE NEW WORLD EROS ON THE GRAND TOUR

FICTION/EROTICA 0 7472 3449 3

More Erotic Fiction from Headline:

EROS IN THE NEW WORLD

Anonymous

Provoked once more by their unquenchable appetites for delight, the exquisite Sophia and her beloved Andy set sail for pastures new and naughty: the Americas. With open minds and open arms they resolve to experience the land of the free, from the most salacious Southern gentleman to the sauciest slave girl.

And for Sophia another challenge beckons: the carnal sampling of a dozen young studs, each of a different astrological aspect – and of intriguingly diverse erotic inclinations. From New York to New Orleans, from Montreal to the Mississippi our enthusiastic duo reveal a lusty land, bursting with an amorous ingenuity and enterprise to inspire the most sated of Old World sensualists . . .

Don't miss the other amorous adventures of Andy and Sophia:
EROS IN THE COUNTRY
EROS IN TOWN
EROS ON THE GRAND TOUR

FICTION/EROTICA 0 7472 3310 1